ALSO BY RACHAEL LIPPINCOTT

The Lucky List

ALSO COAUTHORED BY RACHAEL LIPPINCOTT

Five Feet Apart
All This Time
She Gets the Girl

PRIDE and PREJUDICE and PITTSBURGH

PRIDE and PREJUDICE and PITTSBURGH

RACHAEL LIPPINCOTT

SIMON & SCHUSTER BFYR

NEW YORK LONDON TORONTO SYDNEY NEW DELHI

SIMON & SCHUSTER BFYR

An imprint of Simon & Schuster Children's Publishing Division

1230 Avenue of the Americas, New York, New York 10020

SIMON & SCHUSTER BOOKS FOR YOUNG READERS

and related marks are trademarks of Simon & Schuster, Inc.

For information about special discounts for bulk purchases, please contact Simon & Schuster Special Sales at 1-866-506-1949 or business@simonandschuster.com.

The Simon & Schuster Speakers Bureau can bring authors to your live event. For more information or to book an event, contact the Simon & Schuster Speakers Bureau at 1-866-248-3049 or visit our website at www.simonspeakers.com.

Interior design by Hilary Zarycky

The text for this book was set in Bell

Manufactured in the United States of America

First Edition

2 4 6 8 10 9 7 5 3 1

Library of Congress Cataloging-in-Publication Data

Names: Lippincott, Rachael, author.

Title: Pride and prejudice and Pittsburgh / by Rachael Lippincott.

Description: First edition. | New York : Simon & Schuster, 2023.

Identifiers: LCCN 2023007562 (print) | LCCN 2023007563 (ebook) |

ISBN 9781665937535 (hardcover) | ISBN 9781665937559 (ebook)

Subjects: CYAC: Time travel—Fiction. | Love—Fiction. | Lesbians—Fiction. | Great Britain—History—Regency, 1811-1820—Fiction. | LCGFT: Romance fiction. | Lesbian fiction. | Historical fiction. | Novels.

Classification: LCC PZ7.1.L568 Pr 2023 (print) | LCC PZ7.1.L568 (ebook) | DDC [Fic]—dc23

LC record available at https://lccn.loc.gov/2023007562

LC ebook record available at https://lccn.loc.gov/2023007563

For Alyson and Poppy

CHAPTER 1

AUDREY

April 15, 2023

"If you don't get down here right now, you're fired!" a booming voice calls up the steps outside our apartment. I roll my eyes as I shove my feet into my worn Converse and double-knot the laces.

"I'd like to see you try, old man!" I call back, throwing open the door to reveal my bald dad smirking up at me from the entryway, our dog Cooper at his feet, tail wagging. "Good luck finding someone else who'll work for free."

I jog down to meet him, and he taps his watch, raising a thick eyebrow. "Six oh one. You're late."

I pull my phone out of my back pocket and hold it up to him. "Six o'clock. Your watch is off."

"Fine, you can stay another day," he says, his graying mustache ticking up at the corner as he slides past me to head upstairs and sleep after working the overnight shift.

"Don't forget the drink delivery at noon," he calls over his shoulder.

"Roger that." I pat Cooper's head on my way through the side door that leads directly into Cameron's Corner Shop, my usual Saturday morning duties waiting for me.

As I make the coffee, I gaze out the window at Penn Avenue, at the new buildings, modern apartments, and hip restaurants that have moved in since I was a kid perched on my dad's shoulders while *he* made the coffee. This street, and so much of Pittsburgh, has changed over the past eighteen years.

But not Cameron's Corner Shop, with its scuffed floors, sagging shelves, and rusting sign. Our little slice of Pittsburgh has remained exactly the same, even if the customers have changed. Regulars come for the cheap coffee and scratch-offs. Students stumble in on Friday nights to get armfuls of snacks and mixers. Tourists pop their heads in to ask for directions and recommendations. And the bougie people from the overpriced apartments meander in as a last resort when they forget to buy their premium milk and ancient-grain bread, settling for 2 percent and cardboard white.

It isn't much, but it's my dad's pride and joy, his childhood dream of opening a shop on the street where he grew up brought to life after a CVS took the place of the one he used to visit. Something simple and homegrown and constant, for our community, the people that have always been here and always will be here. And that dream became my whole family's, in a way, his love for the place and the customers and the unusual hours infecting me and my mom.

Plus, it's easy to be coerced when you get free chips and soda for working the register or stocking the shelves. Can't say no to a bag of Cheetos and a Cherry Coke. At least not when you're a kid, before sleeping in and dreams of your own start to seep in. But I try not to think about that now.

Coffee made, I fall into the dull but steady rhythm of the morning, perching behind the counter on a squeaking barstool my dad got off Craigslist with Cooper curled up at my feet, reading a new cartoon-cover romance novel in between greeting the blur of familiar and unfamiliar faces that pass through the front door. Gary the bus driver stops in for his powdered donuts, telling me about an accident on 376 that has traffic backed up all the way to the airport. The cool artist girl who moved in over Vince's Pizza just down the street grabs a yellow pack of American Spirits, paying in crumpled dollar bills and quarters while I try and fail again to work up the courage to ask her about what she's working on. A guy I've never seen before sprints in to buy a pack of toilet paper, slamming a twenty on the counter and bolting before I even have time to ring him up.

Finally, at eight o'clock sharp, the bells on the front door jingle, and my favorite grumpy customer lumbers inside, bony fingers curled around a wooden cane.

"Hi, Mr. Montgomery," I call out, and he grunts his usual hello at me before shuffling off to collect his newspaper.

"You draw anything yet?" he asks over his shoulder, and my stomach falls.

"Uh . . ." I glance at the worn, now-dust-covered sketchbook I've kept on the shelf underneath the cash register for years. "Not yet."

"Doesn't RISD want everything by May first?" he asks, checking his analog wristwatch. "It's already—"

I cut him off. "Trust me. I know." I've been acutely aware of the date ever since I was wait-listed at my dream school a few months ago and told to submit a portfolio with five "new and different" pieces as my art "showed promise" but was "too passive, lacking confidence and a strong enough personal point of view."

Which, like, if they thought I was lacking confidence *before* that glowing review, imagine what little I had left after.

I reach down and pick up the sketchbook, flipping through the older pages. Faces and hands and bodies flash in front of my eyes, all belonging to customers who passed through our doors. In some way, it doesn't even feel like my art anymore, all done so long ago that I'm not even sure I remember what it felt like to put a pencil to the paper and have a furrowed brow or unruly hair or gnarled fingers appear.

I watch as slowly but surely filled pages give way to half-started sketches and empty spaces, and then . . .

Nothing. Blank page after blank page after blank page. The shitty, overwhelming, helpless feeling swims into my bones as I watch my inspiration, my passion, my *excitement* dry up and disappear completely.

I flip to one of the last marked-up pages, pausing when I see a tiny doodle from last summer, the style different from everything else around it, a cartoon Cooper with a thought bubble saying, "I love you!"

Charlie.

I grimace and slam the sketchbook shut.

How am I supposed to draw when I can't even *look* at my sketchbook without thinking of him?

Three years ago, when we met at a summer program at the Rhode Island School of Design that our high school shipped the best ninth- and tenth-grade artists off to, it felt like the best thing that could have happened to me. I hadn't even wanted to leave Pittsburgh, but when our paths crossed and I'd discovered how much possibility was out there, away from this worn barstool, I was so glad I had. He became my critique partner, then my late-night, slightly buzzed sketching buddy, and from that first warm summer night after a full day in the studio, lying on the grass under a darkening sky, I felt *seen*. He was a year older, a rising junior, but he just . . . got me. How much art meant to me. How much it was a part of me.

Or at least I thought he did.

After that we did everything together. We were supposed to go to RISD together, too, back to where it all started.

But then he got rejected last spring and gave up on art

altogether, encouraging me to do the same. To stop taking it so *seriously* and to focus on something more practical, like he'd never actually wanted it at all. It didn't help that all our friends agreed with him. Ben, Hannah, Claire all nodding away at our lunch table like they hadn't been begging me to sketch them just last week. Maybe because they'd been his friends first. Or maybe because they knew in their bones we'd drift apart after they graduated and I was left behind. And that was exactly what happened with them, but I still thought Charlie and I would make it. That he'd see me again, even if he didn't want to see that part of himself anymore.

So when he finally came home from Penn State just before Halloween, I wasn't expecting the breakup. Even though looking at it now, I should have been.

He claimed the distance was too hard. Deep down, I don't think he meant the miles.

So, taking the leap and applying after he dumped me felt like . . . a chance to prove him wrong. Sure, I was heartbroken, but if I got in, I could prove to the girl who stayed up late drawing underneath her blanket, the girl who would sneak off to the art museum every chance she got, the girl who kept drawing when he told her it was pointless, that it *had* all been worth it.

Which made it sting that much more when it turned out he was right.

I was wait-listed a mere month and a half after he dumped me. And, naturally, I spiraled into a deep, dark sadness that felt like I was literally dying and would never experience joy and happiness ever again.

Or something like that. I don't know.

He was my first love and my first heartbreak, so I'm allowed to be a little dramatic.

The worst part, maybe, is that while the heartbreak has mostly healed, I haven't been able to draw since. I've spent hours upon hours these last few months staring at blank pages, pencil frozen in midair, unable to bring myself to draw anything past a stick figure.

Even my old tricks haven't been able to work their magic. I've had my dad point to every random object in our apartment as a prompt, the plants crowding around the windowsill, our lumpy couch, even the ornate French music box on our living room shelf I've always loved, and I can't ever get past the first sweeping line. I'll draw it over and over and over, because it just doesn't *look* right. It just doesn't *feel* right.

I don't feel right. The spark I've always had when drawing is just . . . gone. Missing. I feel about as distant from the page in front of me as I do from Charlie at Penn State. Maybe more. So getting one new piece for RISD feels impossible. And here they are wanting *five*.

I let out a long sigh as I slide Mr. Montgomery his usual black coffee with three granules of sugar across the faded yellow counter. "Guess I'll just stay in Pittsburgh and annoy you for the rest of my life."

7

"You sure you want that?"

"I guess so." I shrug. I've pretty much resigned myself to it at this point.

I love the corner shop, and I love my parents, and I know I can always take classes at the community college and do something else. It wouldn't be terrible. But saying it, I realize there's no denying the heaviness that still tugs at my chest over the thought of never getting out from behind this cash register. Of giving up on my dream of being an artist, the one that started even before Charlie and that summer program. The feeling that even though it does scare me to leave this shop and this city, *here* would never quite be enough the way it is for my dad.

He snorts. "In my day we called that wimping out."

"Back in the 1800s?"

He grumbles something under his breath and shoots me a glower from underneath his wispy white eyebrows, but I can see the trace of a smile lingering around the edges of his mouth.

"Well, anyway." He takes a sip of his coffee before digging around in his pockets until his hand emerges brandishing a new pack of black Faber-Castell pens. *My favorite.* "Just in case you get the urge."

He chucks them on top of the sketchbook and grabs his newspaper off the counter while I bite the inside of my cheek, my eyes growing surprisingly misty.

"Thanks, Mr. Montgomery," I manage to croak out as he

toddles toward the door. At first he just waves his cane in reply, but then he turns back, his hand on the door handle.

"The Audrey Cameron I know wouldn't let some boy ruin her fancy art school dreams. You've been talking about that shit since before you got those braces off." The two of us exchange a small smile, because of course he's not wrong. "Don't give up, kid. If you won't get your spark back, I'm gonna have to find something to do about it!"

Before I can ask what that could possibly be, he's through the door, making his way back to the Lawrenceville town house he's lived in for a thousand or so years, watching me and this whole block grow up. My dad hasn't let him pay for his coffee or newspaper for as long as I can remember, and moments like these are why. He may be the neighborhood curmudgeon, but he's also the guy who brought dinner every night for a week when my uncle died. The guy who attends local kids' dance recitals and graduations. The guy who, as Mom and Dad tell it, helped them through a rough patch back when I was in elementary school. And now he's the one giving me a pack of my favorite pens when I've all but given up hope completely.

"Well, Coop," I say as I let out a long sigh. "Maybe these'll do the trick."

Cooper peers up at me adoringly, his big brown eyes like perfect little quarters, and I reach down to scratch the top of his fluffy black head until his tail wags happily.

Then I turn to a blank page and hope for a spark.

CHAPTER 2

LUCY

June 7, 1812

It is horrid for me to admit, but I might prefer it when my father is in London on business instead of home at Radcliffe.

The loneliness is something I've become accustomed to, the quiet of our house almost comfortable. Freeing. Reading novels he would disapprove of over breakfast. Writing my own songs on the pianoforte in the afternoon instead of whatever etude or nocturne the accomplished women in London are currently expected to play. Going on long walks of the grounds as the sun dips, with no glares of disgust at the dirty hem of my dress when I return.

When he is here, like now, the loneliness remains, but the silence is different. It's stifling—no, deafening, drowning out even the cutlery on the plates as we eat our dinner, scarcely a word said between us.

Things used to be different. The house felt . . . *alive*, years ago, before Mother passed. Infectious laughter during afternoon tea, furniture pushed noisily aside as she taught me new dances, and no hem was more valuable than an adventure on a sunny day.

My father never joined us. His arrogance and obvious disdain have been a constant since the day I was born. But he tolerated it, not out of love for her, I've come to realize, but because of the size of her dowry and her family's status. It kept us both of some value to a man who has no use or regard for love.

Now he can't wait to be rid of me, too, the only thing keeping me here the prospect of my own marriage and what it will do for him.

Our housekeeper, Martha, tries to fill the hole Mother left, but still—

My father clears his throat, and my head snaps up to look at his icy blue eyes narrowing from across the long dinner table.

"Mr. Hawkins will be holding his annual ball in one month's time," he says, breaking the loud silence as he dabs at the corners of his mouth. "Mr. Caldwell, despite your best efforts and his warranted hesitation, has invited you to accompany him, and I sincerely hope you use this opportunity to secure his proposal once and for all."

My stomach sinks at the thought of it. Being *married*. To Mr. Caldwell.

I try to imagine myself walking down the aisle to him, and

my stomach inevitably twists. Mr. Caldwell is a fool. Not to mention twice my age.

He's extraordinarily rich, though. The richest man in the county, in fact, my father a rather envious second. An alliance between our two families would be the crowning jewel for not only my father's social status but his business ventures, and all I can do, all I *should* do, is make sure it happens. And an event of the magnitude of the Hawkins ball, the finale to the season, would certainly be the place to do it.

Yet I've tried my best to subtly resist his advances the past two months, hoping he would lose interest. I've been a dull conversationalist, stopped dancing halfway through a set, complaining my feet were aching, and even fumbled a piano passage I know by heart when my father invited him over for tea. (That earned me a week of practicing nothing but the song under my father's watchful eye.) But with this invitation, it appears it was all for nothing.

Marriage. It feels, in this moment, at my father's words, well and truly inevitable. Made fully clear this time, instead of implied. And I have no choice but to comply.

For what purpose do I have but this? What purpose does *any* woman have but this?

All my life, especially these last few years, I have been pruned and prepared for this single, solitary objective.

To marry well. Not for love or for romance, like my mother always spoke of, hoping my fate would be vastly different from hers, but for repairing a tiny bit of the damage I had done by being born a woman.

So I nod, like I will when Mr. Caldwell asks me for my hand, and look down at my plate, my eyes fixating on the intricate blue flowers twisting around the edge. "Yes, Father. I shall."

"And since I cannot trust you to do it on your own charm, you'll go into town tomorrow to get a new gown. Martha will accompany you. Miss Burton will be expecting you at two o'clock sharp," he adds. Or rather, commands, but this request I don't mind. Miss Burton set up shop three years ago and has in a very short time become quite a reputable dressmaker. Her prices are reasonable, her staff extraordinarily kind, and her work exquisite. Not to mention, a trip there always means a few hours away from the solitude of Radcliffe or my father's wrath. "She will design something that will catch Caldwell's eye and hold it, since you seem to be having such a difficult time of doing so."

I watch as he stands and checks his pocket watch before heading for the door, ending our dinner without even asking if I am finished. "I haven't time to discuss it further. I leave in a week for London, but I shall return in time for the ball."

And with that, he is gone, disappearing to his study. I let out a breath I have been holding for what feels like the entirety of dinner. Martha gives my shoulder a squeeze as she motions to Abigail, one of the scullery maids, to clear away his plate.

"I wish he wouldn't come back at all," I whisper just loud enough for her to hear.

She gives me a sympathetic smile, the wrinkled corners of her mouth turning up. "Well, dear, I can't say you'd be alone in that sentiment." Abigail nods in agreement as she shuffles out of the room, silverware clattering noisily as she goes.

Martha would have left Radcliffe long ago and sought new employment if it weren't for me. I was sure she would leave after her husband, Samuel, our former steward, died.

But Martha is fiercely loyal to the people she cares about. To my mother and to me. So she stayed, which makes me feel all the more guilty because it means my existence forces someone as dear as her to be stuck here too.

Perhaps that's the one good thing about marrying Mr. Caldwell.

Martha will finally be free.

After reading Fordyce's dreadfully dull sermons in the drawing room as expected until night falls, I retire to bed early but find myself tossing and turning as unwelcome thoughts of Mr. Caldwell keep me awake. His sweat-lined brow, the nauseating, trapped feeling I had when we first danced together two months ago at a mutual acquaintance's ball in Langford. I'd thought I was just being polite, but my father's intentions were made obvious when I noticed the calculating glint in his eye as he watched the two of us from across the room, looking away only to converse with Mr. Caldwell's sister. My suspicions were confirmed when he invited Mr. Caldwell for tea the following week.

My fingers twist into my bedsheets, forming a fist. I feel it again now. The same tightening in my chest. The same discomfort.

Will I feel like this for the rest of my life? Do *all* young ladies whose marriages are entirely outside their control feel like this, forced to wed men they can hardly stand the sight of?

Did my mother?

While I've never *felt* that hint of love or *attraction* even for any of the men I've met, I can't help but feel a stab of pain over the fact that now I'll never know. Never experience what it would be like to fall in love with someone. To *want* someone.

Finally, I stop tossing and turning over these thoughts and slip out of bed. I light the candle on my nightstand, watching as the flame dances with every exhale, casting twisting shadows on the walls. I scoop it up, pull on my wrap, and tiptoe out into the moonlit corridor. The stillness of the house, save for the creaking floorboards underneath my feet, helps to ease my nerves as I wander down hallway after hallway.

I end up in the farthest wing, where a wall of portraits extends as far as the eye can see, past the glow of the flame. My father, and his father, and his father before him. All with the same hawk-like nose. The same proud squaring of their shoulders. The same cold blue eyes that feel like they are watching me even now.

I shudder and pull my wrap closer to my body, slipping through the door at the end of the hallway and into the library to see the only portrait in this house I care for.

My mother's.

I raise the candle, and her face is brought to life once more in the illumination: high cheekbones and golden hair. She wears a gold chain with a single teardrop pearl on it around her delicate neck, and the deep brown of her eyes is so different from my father's, so much warmer.

My fingers search my throat for the ghost of a necklace I've never been able to find as I study her features. People always said we looked alike, and she would smile at that, stroking my hair and nodding in agreement.

But I still see him. In my eyes. In the corners of my mouth. In the way I move.

Even when I leave this place, I will never be free of him.

The candle flickers in my hand before being extinguished completely as a draft blows in through the open door, leaving behind only a glowing ember and a swirling trail of smoke in the moonlight.

It feels almost delusional now that I'd believed her when she said I was destined to marry for love. Foolish to think, even if I found it, that love could possibly outweigh duty and expectation, when it certainly hadn't for her.

All I can think about now is how glad I am that she doesn't have to see how wrong she was.

CHAPTER 3

AUDREY

April 16, 2023

Pittsburgh weekends in the springtime have always been my favorite.

Biking around the city as the flowers begin to bloom, I see the streets hopping after a long winter, garage door windows pulled open at just about every restaurant, customers spilling out onto the sidewalks as summer looms hopefully on the horizon.

I zip around the corners, earbud dangling out of one ear, letting the playlist I put together this morning to kill time while I manned the cash register guide my pedals as I take in the sights from the bike lane.

This ride is important.

I'm searching, just like I used to before the shitshow of the last few months, trying to find *something* that will inspire me enough to fill the blank pages of my sketchbook for this application. Especially now that Mr. Montgomery gifted me those expensive pens.

I don't want to let myself down again, but something about letting him down too feels like the extra little bit of weight I might need to try again and not, as he said, *wimp out.*

As I take in all the colors and lines and shapes of every streetlight, every bustling bar, every couple arm in arm on the sidewalk, I feel the ghost of an itch in my fingertips. And when I catch sight of a blond girl in a bright floral dress, the sunlight seeming to perfectly outline her face and long flowing hair, my pointer finger actually twitches against my handlebars. I can *see* it, a blank page unfurling in front of me. The long strokes of each golden strand, the shading underneath her jaw, the oval shape of her—

Shit.

I slam on my brakes, trying to swerve out of the way as a blue car door flies open, but I smack right into it, face-planting on the glass as the bike tumbles out from underneath me. I hit the pavement and let out a long groan. When I roll onto my back, I find myself face-to-face with the cotton-candy pink and blue sky.

All things considered, it's a beautiful sunset.

Not a bad way to go out.

"Oh my gosh, I am so sorry," a voice says, and a head pops into my field of view. I zero in on the features of a worried-looking Asian girl. Cool nose ring. Bleached-blond hair. Arm full of tattoos. My stomach unexpectedly flutters in a way that feels both familiar and unfamiliar entirely. I sit up instead of thinking about why, pressing a hand to my stomach to quiet the feeling. "Are you okay? Do I need to call an ambulance or—"

I shake my head. I feel banged up and dazed but not *hospital*-level bad.

Looks like I'll live to see another sunset.

"No, I'm good. I'm cool, but . . ." I motion, my right hand reaching over to my left side, showing her how she *should* have opened the door. "You know the Dutch reach? You should start doing it. You could lose a car door, dude. Or a limb. Especially on this street. Some cars just fly . . ."

My voice trails off as a white guy gets out from the passenger seat, jogging around the front of the car to grab on to the hand of no-look-door-open girl.

Charlie.

"Jules, are you okay?" he asks her, like *she's* the one who left a visible face print on the driver's-side window.

I stumble to my feet, and his brown eyes widen when he sees me, the unflattering mustache he's grown since October twitching as his mouth falls open in surprise. As if I'm the one who isn't supposed to be here.

What is he even doing home?

I guess the distance was never really the issue.

"Audrey," he says as the two of us stare at each other for a long and totally not weird moment. "You're, uh, bleeding. . . ."

19

His voice trails off as he points at my forehead, just above my right eye.

I reach up, wincing as my fingers touch a cut. My hand comes away with enough blood to make me feel woozy.

But not as woozy as what I see in front of me.

My eyes flick down to their hands, fingers laced together, and I do that math.

Charlie is *dating* car-door girl. Like moved-on, visiting-his-hometown, going-out-to-dinner-on-a-Sunday-night, hitting-people-with-cars-for-funsies *dating*.

"Uh, how's it going?" I ask, quickly wiping my bloody hand on my pants before placing it oh so casually on my hip.

"Um," Charlie says, squinting at me. "Fine."

There's a long pause, broken by a drop of blood dripping right into my eyeball. I wipe it away with the back of my hand and take this as my cue to leave and find a first-aid kit and maybe a deep, cavernous hole to fall into and never come out of.

"I should, uh . . ." I stoop down and pick up my bike, which looks like it went through a trash compactor. "I should probably get home."

"Let me at least give you a ride," my replacement offers.

Jules.

Shit. Even her name is cool.

"No, no. I'll be fine," I say, but as I lean on my handlebars, the front tire of the bike slowly deflates, air hissing out for a good ten seconds as we all avoid eye contact.

"Audrey," Charlie says. "Let us drive you home."

Us.

Ew.

I open my mouth to protest again, but . . . my dented bike and aching body beat out my pride. I don't especially want to walk the mile and a half back like this.

Letting out a long sigh, I nod, and Jules helps me wrangle the bike into her trunk while Charlie returns with a fistful of napkins from Primanti's for my forehead.

I slide into the back seat, and Charlie's new girlfriend asks where to go.

"Just head straight down Penn," the two of us say at the same time, Charlie glancing back at me. I smack the pile of napkins to my forehead to stop the bleeding *and* the eye contact, then gaze out the window as we silently drive toward home.

"You two know each other from high school?" Jules asks cheerily. That question confirms that Charlie hasn't felt the need to tell her about me.

"Something like that," Charlie says, his tousled brown hair catching the breeze through his open window.

"We dated," I say, because I'm just the teensiest bit salty and maybe slightly concussed, and honestly, I lost my dignity about fifteen minutes ago when I flew over my handlebars, so what more do I have to lose by being honest?

"No way," she says, smiling as she shakes her head. "What are the odds."

"Not low enough," I murmur before leaning forward to point at the storefront we're thankfully approaching. She pulls the car into an open parking space out front.

We all get out, and I collect my bike. Then the three of us find ourselves awkwardly standing together on the sidewalk. *Why don't they just leave?* I almost walk straight into the street to get hit by another car and put myself out of my misery.

"I'll be sure to do the Dutch reach from now on," Jules says with a smile as Charlie slings an arm over her shoulder, giving the term a whole new meaning. "And if you go to the hospital or anything, definitely let me know so I can pay the bill."

"Uh, yeah. I'll be sure to text Charlie if I do." I laugh as I say it, hoping the joke can ease some of the tension, because he more than anyone knows I'm too stubborn to go to the hospital.

Instead, Charlie looks sheepishly down at his feet. "I don't have your number anymore," he says, and I resist the biggest eye roll known to man.

It's so Charlie. All or nothing. Art, art school, *me.*

Seeing him here now, ridiculous mustache and all, I feel like I'm finally seeing him clearly, without the glowing, malleable filter of memories.

And I feel . . . well . . .

Over him.

"Well, I'd be the one sending the hospital bill," I say,

unable to hide the slight edge to my voice. "Unless you two are just going to massacre your way around Pittsburgh tonight, in which case my last four digits are 2357."

Jules lets out an annoyingly cute giggle, while Charlie opens his mouth to say something, but after opening and closing it about a dozen times like he's a carnival goldfish, all that comes out is a long exhale of air.

"I'm gonna . . ." I motion toward Cameron's Corner Shop before turning on my heel, wanting to just get inside and away from this whole mess. "Bye."

I fumble my way through the door with my bike, bells jingling overhead as I clatter onto the black entry mat. I watch through the glass as Charlie and Jules smooch and melt into each other before getting into the car and driving off, me and my dented bike already an afterthought.

I'm so focused on watching them that I nearly have a heart attack when my mom lets out an overly dramatic scream and crashes over to me from behind the cash register.

"Oh, my baby! What happened?" she asks, squeezing my face between her hands, her brown eyes filled with worry.

"Charlie's new girlfriend hit me with her car."

"On purpose?"

"No," I admit, the ghost of a smile appearing on her lips. "And it was just her car door."

"*Jesus.* People really need to learn the Dutch reach around here. *Look at your head,*" she coos, studying the gash. "Do you think you have a concussion? We should probably take you to the hospital to see—"

"Mom. Stop. I'm fine." I wriggle out of her vise grip and cross my arms stubbornly over my chest.

"Well, let's at least get that cut fixed up, okay?" she says as she pats my cheek, turning her head to call upstairs. "Louis! Get your ass down here to man the register. I've got to perform emergency surgery!"

I roll my eyes, but I can't help but smile. When I was a kid, Mom was a nurse over at the children's hospital just down the street from here. She retired back when I was in elementary school to help my overworked dad and so that we could spend more time together as a family after years of their busy shifts misaligning. The arguments that used to carry through the walls of our tiny apartment stopped, and somehow, this little corner shop became her dream too. The only mending she does now is for the two of us, or the random neighborhood kid who will show up with a skinned knee or elbow, knowing Mrs. Cameron can help.

Sometimes I wonder if it became enough for my mom, here, the corner shop, if I could find a way to really, truly make it enough for me. Even though deep down, a tiny voice says it never will be.

"So," she says after we get up to our apartment, an alcohol pad stinging away at my cut. "Was she cute?"

"*Mom,*" I groan, swinging my calves against the bathroom cabinets from my perch on the counter, trying to distract myself from the pain. I know it isn't what she means, but I certainly don't want to have to unpack the unexpected butterflies I got over that fact, so I just keep it simple. "She was. Nose ring. Tattoos. Really cool."

When she pulls the alcohol pad away, I change the subject, shooting her a side-eye. "Charlie grew a mustache, though."

She lets out a horrified gasp. "Oh no. That boy does not have the face to pull off a mustache."

I laugh, and she moves to dig around in our mess of a first-aid kit but raises her eyebrows to give me a motherly look. "You okay, though? Seeing him again? Seeing him with someone else?"

I shrug, but now that the awkwardness is over, the realization I had as we were standing outside the shop is confirmed. That sting of pain from the end of our almost three years together feels like nothing more than a dull and distant ache. "You know, surprisingly . . . I think I am."

I think I *thought* I would be broken. I thought I *should* be. But after seeing who he is now instead of whatever fictionalized version I've held on to over the past few months, I feel like I got that last bit of closure.

"I'm sure the mustache helped," she says, chuckling to herself as she brandishes a Sesame Street Band-Aid whose crispiness leads me to believe it's been in there since I was still in diapers. "You ever think about getting back out there yourself? Meeting someone new? I mean, prom is *right* around the corner."

I groan. "Absolutely not."

"It could be fun!" she says as she peels off the disintegrating Band-Aid wrapper and sticks it to my forehead.

"Easy for you to say," I tease, deflecting. "You married your high school sweetheart."

But even with closure, something about running into Charlie tonight and the still stubbornly blank pages of my sketchbook make me feel more sure than ever that I don't want to take that leap into the unknown again anytime soon.

Not when it's clear now that wait lists and rejections and heartbreaks are all that's ever waited for me on the other side. Maybe getting hit with a car door was just the wake-up call I needed to realize that.

"Oh, honey. Your father was never a sweetheart," she says, squeezing my face between her hands again. "But you are. And Charlie missed out on a real gem."

She smooches my forehead before throwing out the bloody Primanti's napkins and washing her hands.

"Besides! Grandma always used to say the best way to get over someone is by getting un—"

"*Mom!*"

"I'm joking!" she says, flicking some water at me.

I wipe the droplets off my arm, and the two of us dissolve into laughter.

"Listen, you do whatever feels right, okay? Dating, drawing, getting out of Pittsburgh, staying here. The world is your oyster, baby, and you'll find someone cute to smooch and something worth filling your sketchbook up with when the time is right. I know you will."

My mouth pulls down into a grimace. "The deadline is *two weeks* away. And my little bike ride around town, hoping for some inspiration, ended with . . ." I motion to the crusty Band-Aid on my forehead. "It feels like a sign. Like I need to just . . . let RISD go."

"You'll figure it out, okay? Even if you miss the deadline, maybe you reapply after a term at the community college. Maybe you find a new dream. Maybe you go . . . I don't know . . . backpacking through Europe! Heck, if I can fall in love with that dingy little shop downstairs, you really never know what's possible."

I hop off the counter and give her a much-needed hug as she dries her hands. I don't feel like I have the guts to leave the safety of this house and little shop behind, let alone do any of that stuff right now. But having her believe that I can someday, having Mr. Montgomery believe I can someday, makes me feel a little better. Even if I don't believe it myself right now.

"But in the meantime," she says, patting my arm, "I think we should steal some ice cream sandwiches from the freezer and give Dad the debrief."

"I'm taking two," I say as we head downstairs. "I have a head injury to treat, after all."

CHAPTER 4

LUCY

June 8, 1812

I let out a long exhale of air as I make my way into town the very next day, grateful to be free from my father for a few brief moments, despite the fact that his looming presence continues to linger, never fully escapable. I know he's probably in his study at Radcliffe, clicking open his pocket watch to check the time, closely monitoring the length of my trip to ensure I don't go off anywhere else.

I glance over at Martha, sitting across from me, sent to chaperone and report back to him. He would be furious if he knew she often left me alone, to run errands while I enjoyed a few stolen moments to myself.

I peer out the glass window of the carriage at the stone buildings, teeth digging into my lower lip as I watch the people milling about on the dirt road outside. Their pace is lethargic due to the warm summer day, but their laughter and jovial voices fill the air despite the heat, sending a twinge of envy stabbing through my stomach.

I imagine what it would be like to be one of them out there, instead of *here*, trapped in a carriage taking me to select the dress destined to seal my fate as the future Mrs. Caldwell. To be able to mill about town, or travel to Paris, or study piano at a conservatory. For a brief moment I imagine that the carriage is taking me off to do just that, rolling through a city street so very different from this one, so far away from Radcliffe, where I can do as I please instead of what I am told I must.

I shake my head, the daydream fading into unavoidable reality as the carriage slows outside the shop.

"I'll meet you at the carriage after?" Martha asks, off to run her errands.

I nod and with a long sigh, I pull open my parasol to shield myself from the sun as I exit, quickly closing the short distance up the steps to the wooden door, where Miss Burton herself eagerly rushes to greet me the moment I open it.

"Miss Sinclair, what a pleasure it is to see you today. Are you quite well?" she says with a curtsy, which I return.

"Yes, indeed," I say, with more conviction than I feel at the moment. Then I notice the dark circles under her brown eyes. News of the ball later this month must have traveled fast, everyone buzzing over the biggest event this social season will have to offer. "Are you? I am sure you've been very busy as of late."

"Yes, yes," she says, hands twisting together as we move

farther inside. "But I always have time for you, Miss Sinclair. Always have time."

I sit on her familiar striped chaise lounge and am brought tea while she shows me an assortment of fashion sketches, gorgeous lines on worn paper. I have never been a remarkable artist, despite the extensive painting lessons Father had me take, but I have always loved art and greatly admire those who can fill a blank page with meaning the way Miss Burton can.

I'm first drawn to a slimmer, simpler silk dress, a design I recognize from three seasons past with *beautiful* floral embroidery along the hem that . . . will certainly not fulfill the task of impressing Mr. Caldwell.

So, instead, I am forced to reject it for one that will. Something new and expensive, something *eye-catching*, that will display not only my father's wealth but my knowledge of present trends.

I catch sight of one of her more recent drawings, showing a high waistline, with slightly puffed sleeves and a wide, V-shaped neckline. While it is certainly gorgeous and *very* fashionable, it's not . . . me.

But I'm not here for me, am I? And a dress like this would certainly meet Mr. Caldwell's expectations.

I flip back to the previous dress and trace my finger along the intricate embroidery. "Could we possibly add this?"

She nods. "Absolutely."

A small, subtle touch that feels like a part of myself can

still exist among the puffed sleeves and high waistline. A compromise of sorts that a gifted seamstress like Miss Burton is sure to make even more beautiful in person. I hold on to that.

"What color were you thinking? Perhaps a pastel?" Miss Burton waves her hand, and an assistant comes running with samples of cloth.

My eyes land almost instantly on a lilac, but Miss Burton scoops up a blue, holding it up to my face to compare it to my skin tone, nodding as she does it. "Oh, this one would be *beautiful*. And it would *certainly* bring out your eyes!"

I nod in agreement as the lilac fades from view, swallowing my opinion on the matter.

After selecting some lace trimmings and finalizing the design, we move on to getting my current measurements.

"I heard from an acquaintance that Mr. Caldwell was *very* eager for the upcoming ball, knowing you will be in attendance," she says as she measures my shoulders, giving me a small, knowing smile. Two of her assistants crane their necks in interest.

I look away, annoyed at the reminder, but when I meet my own icy gaze in the mirror, the sight is so remarkably similar to my father's that I soften almost instantly. "Is that so?" I comment politely but noncommittally.

I've never been much of a gossip, but Miss Burton is certainly guilty of it. It must be almost unintentional for her to gather news and information, as the comfortable atmosphere of her shop and her array of female patrons make loose conversation almost effortless.

But I certainly don't want to be its subject. Not about this.

"It is! Why, his cousin Mrs. Notley was in here just yesterday and told me herself how keen he was that you had accepted his invitation."

Well, I suppose that is a good thing, given the mission that sends me here.

Still, the inevitability of it all makes my stomach churn instead of leap.

Since I don't offer her any information about my own intentions, we finish with my measurements in silence, and the deeper I retreat into my thoughts, the more I . . . feel an unusual urge wash over me to commit some small act of rebellion. Something that, even for just a second, will make me feel like I have a granule of independence. Some small say in my own life, before it's too late.

My gaze drifts to the drawing of that first silk dress on the counter, tempting me to add it to the order, in that lilac I swallowed my desire for. I imagine my father's perplexed face when it shows up at our door unapproved by him.

"Interested in anything else, Miss Sinclair?" Miss Burton asks, catching me staring at the sketch.

Even though I will likely already be promised to Mr. Caldwell by then, even though my entire life, my entire future, will still be completely controlled and carefully constructed by my father, I could have this dress, tucked into the corner of my closet, a reminder of one small thing I chose for myself.

Before I can stop myself, I nod, my heart pounding with exhilaration. "This dress," I say, reaching out to tap it. "In that lilac you showed me earlier."

"Shall I include it in the tab to send to your father?"

"A separate tab, if possible," I say casually, trying to keep my voice level, my first genuine smile in what feels like weeks tugging at the corners of my mouth. "To be sent after the ball, perhaps?"

She nods and motions to one of her assistants to add it to the ledger before guiding me to the door. "Always a pleasure, Miss Sinclair," she says with a warm smile. "Your dress for the ball will be delivered within two weeks, plenty of time for alterations if you so desire."

"Thank you, Miss Burton. I shall be looking forward to it," I lie, curtsying before I exit the shop. I practically skip down the steps, so swept up in my spontaneous and unusual act of defiance that I almost run squarely into someone.

"Lucy!" a familiar voice says, and I look up to see my friend Grace Prewitt grabbing my shoulders to stop me from toppling over.

Or rather, my friend Grace *Harding* now. She married a clerk this past spring, a Mr. Simon Harding. As the youngest of her family, it was quite a respectable arrangement, made even more pleasant by the fact that she had actually fallen in love with the gentleman. In the time since, there have been so many things I have wanted to ask her about love, about marriage, but as my father has been home and openly discourages my acquaintance with her, I have not yet had an opportunity.

Despite the fact that her father is a well-respected merchant from whom my father has acquired many valuable art pieces, rare books, and priceless antiques, he still refuses to see the Prewitts as our equals. When Grace and I met over a decade ago, her father bringing her along with him to Radcliffe to drop off a pair of paintings, the two of us became fast friends, sneaking off the first chance we got to run through the fields and skip stones across the pond. That night my father made it enormously obvious to me his opinion of her, but this particular front has been my only other point of rebellion before today, and I have completely disregarded his wishes and gone behind his back to maintain and nurture this friendship.

"Grace," I say as the two of us clasp hands. "Have you been well?"

"Oh yes, remarkably so." She looks it. She is practically glowing, her dark hair pinned carefully up and her light eyes wide and bright. I watch her gaze travel past me to Miss Burton's shop. "Getting a dress for the upcoming ball?"

I nod in confirmation, grimacing. "My father tasked me with finding one to secure Mr. Caldwell's proposal there."

"You're kidding," she says, her face twisting with disgust. "So many eligible bachelors and he chooses *Mr. Caldwell*?"

"Ah," I say, raising an eyebrow. "But no eligible bachelor is as rich as he."

"Rich or not, I've never met a more unpleasant man."

I lean forward conspiratorially, glancing both ways as I lower my voice. "Actually, I think we both have."

Our smiles give way to laughter, and she squeezes my hand. "We must have you around for tea before that happens, then," she says, and I nod my agreement.

"My father leaves for London in a week. Perhaps after that?"

"Absolutely. A week from tomorrow it is." Her hand reaches up to tilt my parasol more directly above my head. "You better get back to Radcliffe before your father sends out a search party. I'll write to you soon!"

"It was lovely seeing you," I say, giving her hand another squeeze before my footman helps me into the carriage, Martha already waiting inside.

As we ride off, I watch through the glass and see Simon exit the milliner's shop. He joins Grace, and her arm slides comfortably into his as they make their way down the street, all smiles and adoring gazes.

I've never been in love, and now I know I never will be, but my goodness, Grace and Simon Harding make me want to be, even if for just a glimmering moment like this one.

CHAPTER 5

AUDREY

April 22, 2023

A week later my sketchbook is still blank.

Since face-planting on Charlie's girlfriend's car door, I've officially given up on the deadline but maybe not entirely on the art just yet. Turns out even taking the pressure off wasn't quite enough to tip the scales, though. Neither was a dent in my forehead and some good old-fashioned humiliation.

I have tried just about everything to flip the switch. YouTube videos, TikTok time lapses of other people drawing, even scrolling through online art collections like I'm doing now.

My leg bounces up and down as I man the cash register and swipe through a collection of portraits from Regency England. There was an exhibit back at Carnegie Museum of Art that I remember going to and being super inspired by when I was younger. The style of art has always spoken to me, with its realistic simplicity, telling the stories of the people depicted in a way I always wanted to use art to do. I used to draw and paint exclusively portraits before Charlie encouraged me to "branch out," to make my style more *unique* and modern and eye-catching, to try abstract and more of what's on trend, my submissions to RISD inspired by his years of suggestions. So maybe going back to my roots is worth a try.

The first portrait is an old guy in a navy-blue uniform with a red sash, the colors strong, the shadows dark, the hair . . . clearly a wig. Next. Two sisters painted against a tree, pastel dresses and heads pressed together, the shading on the skin so impressive, I zoom in to get a better look at it, letting out a low whistle. But I mean . . . if I can't even get started, no part of me thinks I could pull *that* off.

I take a quick sip of my coffee and swipe to the next image as the bells on the front door jingle, and I glance up for a fraction of a second to see Mr. Montgomery hobble inside.

"Morning, Mr. Montgomery," I say, which he returns with his usual grunt.

I move to get him his coffee, pulling out a cup and starting to pour, but my eyes forget to follow. They're fixed on my phone and a portrait of a woman with golden hair and warm brown eyes in a sage-green dress, something so inviting about her face, the colors so warm and—

"*Shit.*" I wince as the piping-hot coffee overflows the paper cup onto my skin, scalding me. I shake my hand, hissing through my teeth until the sting slowly subsides.

"What are you so busy with on that there phone?" Mr. Montgomery asks, his glassy green eyes narrowing as he peers at me over the cash register.

"Just . . ." My voice trails off and I shrug, flashing him my screen while I carefully slide his very full coffee across the counter. "Trying to find some inspiration."

"For your deadline?"

I shake my head. "No. I'm . . ." I hesitate. "I'm not going to apply. I think I just need to let that go."

"Mmm." He nods and frowns slightly but doesn't press any further. "How's that head of yours healing up?"

News of the incident did not take long to travel all around our little corner of Pittsburgh. Which is, you know, not super humiliating at all.

"Great! *Literally* running into Charlie was the perfect reminder that love is a total scam, and I should never put myself out there again." I roll my eyes. "It was nice discovering how over him I am, though."

"And they say romance isn't dead," he grumbles as he stoops down to pick up a newspaper.

"What do you know about romance, Mr. Montgomery?"

He snorts and puts an angry little hand on his hip. "Plenty," he says. "And I know plenty about you, too, Audrey. And what you're looking for? It's not here."

"And where am I going to find it?" I ask, forcing my eyes up.

He motions to the street, where a red Port Authority bus zooms by just outside the glass. "Out there. In the real world."

There's a long silence as I squint at the "real world."

"Mmm. No thanks." I turn my head to look at him, and he raises a bushy eyebrow at me. "Last time I met someone in the real world and got all swept up in a relationship, I had my heart pulverized. Not to mention, I got wait-listed at my dream school and my ability to do art flushed down the toilet."

He gives me a small shrug. "There's just as much heartbreak in *not* putting yourself out there, because it guarantees you're going to miss out. And I'm not just talking about love," he says.

I bite my lip and look out again at Pittsburgh, at my world that most days doesn't quite feel big enough. Once school is out, I'll be trapped in an endless routine of making coffee and restocking shelves and sitting behind the cash register, distracting myself with romance novels and making song playlists and scrolling on my phone.

"Just because you got hurt once by the wrong person doesn't mean it'll happen again if you find the right one. People always say that love comes knocking when you least expect it to, and that's true for a lot of things. True love, true inspiration, your next great art piece . . . It all might be waiting for you out there!"

I laugh at that, my gaze returning to his face, where

his eyes crinkle at the corners, but then they grow serious, thoughtful. "I can tell you one thing with absolute certainty, though. You won't find any of it if you hide from it here."

Who'd have thought *Mr. Montgomery* would be giving me free pens one week, and a therapy session about getting my shit together the next?

Thankfully, he doesn't wait for a response I don't have and continues on, face settling back into his curmudgeonly scowl. "Well, either way, I'm glad you're moving on from that Charlie fellow. Always thought you'd be with someone a little more . . . inspiring."

"You my matchmaker now?" I ask him.

"Something like that," he says. I watch as he glances down at my phone, where the portrait is still illuminated, a curious expression moving across his face as he rifles around in his pocket. "It's time to stop hiding, kid."

With a small smile and a wink, he surprises me by flicking a quarter in my direction, which is like $1.25 less than the coffee he never pays for costs, but, hey, at least the guy's trying.

I watch as it soars through the air almost in slow motion, turning head over tail, the metal reflecting in the fluorescent light hanging over the cash register.

I reach my hand out to grab it, but the second it touches my open palm . . . everything goes black.

CHAPTER 6

LUCY

June 15, 1812

I glance at the clock when my father looks away, this morning moving slower than I ever thought possible. My fingers anxiously tap out a piano melody on my upper thigh, music I'm excited to play once he finally takes his leave this afternoon, after he is finished pontificating about his expectations for me.

"I hope you will spend this time fully preparing yourself for what is to come. I expect Mr. Caldwell will invite you to his estate while I am gone, as I made such a suggestion to him, and I need every assurance that you will use such an opportunity to its fullest possible extent to impress him before the ball."

I watch as two footmen pass the door to the drawing room carrying his trunk, signaling freedom inching nearer.

"*Lucy*," he scolds, fingers wrapping tightly around my

forearm, halting the silent melody of my fidgeting hands. "Do you understand?"

"Yes, sir," I say with all the sincerity I can muster, but my nails dig into my palms as his cold eyes study my face.

"The carriage is ready for you, Mr. Caldwell," Martha says loudly from the doorway, and thankfully my father releases his grip on my arm as we stand. My gaze meets Martha's as I pass, and I note her eyebrows furrowing slightly with anger.

I follow him out to the carriage, but he gets inside without another word. Soon the wheels are crunching noisily against the gravel, dust billowing up after them, but I stay and watch as it sways slowly down the drive, farther and farther still, until it disappears completely. I squeeze my eyes shut and draw in a deep, long breath.

He's gone.

When I open them again, everything feels lighter. Brighter. The green of the grass, the blue of the sky, the sun shining on my skin.

Before I know it, I'm skipping, then *running* through the grounds, fingertips trailing in the tall grass, a laugh escaping my lips as I go. The hem of my dress is getting dirtier by the second, but *I do not care* how foolish I am being. For a few final luxurious weeks before he returns, before my fate with Mr. Caldwell is sealed, I am free. Totally and completely and utterly—

I skid to a stop, startled by a shape just ahead of me in the center of the field, a lump of black and white and gray.

With a horrifying jolt, I realize all at once that it is not an object.

It is a body.

A girl.

My heart leaps into my throat as I run to where she's lying and sink down next to her.

She's breathing.

"Thank heavens," I mutter, my hand reaching out to touch her shoulder. But when I do, I let out a soft gasp of surprise. The material under my fingertips is . . . unlike any I've ever felt before.

My eyes wander down, and I quickly realize it's more than just the material that's different.

I have *never* seen clothes like hers before.

Is she . . . in her undergarments?

I pull my hand away to clutch at my chest.

Underneath what appears to be a strange jacket of sorts is some kind of ill-fitting white chemise that leaves at least a few fingers' width of her *skin* showing.

And that's not all.

She's wearing men's *trousers*! The color is a faded black, with a small tear in the knee, and her strange white shoes, neither boots nor heels, are speckled with paint. Not to mention *the laces* . . . I don't know what to make of any of it.

She lets out a low groan, and my eyes snap back to her face. Her brown hair is strewn on the grass around her head, and her full lips part ever so slightly as her eyelids flutter, long eyelashes giving way to warm hazel eyes that wander around my face before locking onto my blue ones.

"Are you all right?" I ask as she sits up and rubs her head, squinting around at her surroundings.

"Where . . . ?" she mutters to herself.

"I think you must have fainted," I say, and she redirects her attention back to me, dark eyebrows pulling together in confusion. I notice a faint cut just above the right one, but it doesn't appear to be from whatever's just knocked her out. It's already begun to heal.

"I didn't faint. . . . I . . ." Her accent is not from around here. In fact, it sounds American, not unlike the Fields', the rather boisterous family from New York I met at Mr. Stanton's ball just a year ago. Instead of finishing her sentence, she lifts one of her hands, and her long fingers unfurl to reveal an unusual silver coin in the center of her palm.

"Am I dead?" she wonders aloud. "*How* did I get here?"

"No, you are not dead," I say, answering at least one of her questions, though I'm very curious about the answer to the other.

I watch as her eyes flick up from the coin, then dip down to take in my attire. My hand reaches out instinctively to smooth my skirt as the corner of her mouth turns up into a smile, revealing teeth that are remarkably white and even.

"What in the fresh reenactment hell is this?"

Hell. I wince at her swear, frowning. "I beg your pardon?"

"You know," she says as she pulls a small, bright pink package out of her pants pocket, thick white letters inexplicably spelling out TRIDENT along the side, and motions at me with it. "Your clothes."

"*My* clothes?" I ask. I watch as she unwraps a small metal sliver from the package to reveal a rectangular brick inside, which she pops into her mouth, chewing noisily. Noticing my curious expression, she holds the package out to me, sliding one of the metal slivers forward with her thumb.

Not wanting to be rude, I take one, frowning as I unwrap the small pink . . . candy? Cautiously, I put it in my mouth. The taste is remarkably sweet, but it's a consistency that's so unlike anything I've ever had before, the texture almost spongy.

When I swallow it, she frowns, and so do I, as it doesn't go down particularly easily.

"Did you just—" She shakes her head and stands, dusting herself off. "Well, that's the last time I share gum with you."

Gum?

I watch as she searches in the grass around where she was lying, looking for something. "Where am I?" she asks again.

"On my family's estate. Radcliffe."

An amused smile grows on her face, like I've just said something funny. "And what year is it on this 'estate'?"

"It's 1812."

She barks out a laugh as she finds what she's looking

for, a rectangular box that's now clutched in her hand. "It's 1812 . . . ," she repeats. "You're good. Really committed to this whole acting thing."

"What do you mean 'acting thing'?" I ask as I stand and we face each other for the first time. She is a head taller than me, and I crane my neck to meet her gaze, crossing my arms over my chest as I start to get annoyed. She's trespassing on *my* land, in this *scandalous* outfit, interrupting my first moments of sweet freedom, and she's making every indication that *I'm* the one who's strange?

She raises an eyebrow as she motions at me. "The costume, the accent, the 'Radcliffe, my family's estate' bit," she says, mimicking my voice.

"I don't understand your meaning. Nor do I appreciate you using that tone with—"

"Mm-hmm," she says, cutting me off as she lifts the rectangular box toward the sky and begins wandering around in circles.

Maybe she's . . . unwell? I mean, she's wearing *trousers* and a *chemise* in public.

I inspect her face as she paces around and around, muttering to herself. Then I see the box she's holding is almost . . . glowing. There's a painted picture on the front of a dog that looks *remarkably* realistic.

"No service," she says with a frustrated sigh, coming to a stop in front of me. "Do you have a phone at your house?"

I frown. "A phone?"

"You know"—she holds up the rectangular box, and the glow is bright enough to make me squint—"a phone?"

When I don't show any sign of recognition, she narrows her eyes at me. "Are you Amish?"

"Am I *what*?"

"I don't know! You don't know what a phone is, you swallowed my gum, you're dressed like *this*, and you think it's 1812."

"It *is* 1812," I say firmly, and she laughs again, but this time it doesn't quite meet her eyes. "Why is that so amusing to you?"

"Because it's not possible."

I roll my eyes and grab her arm, impatient to settle this and get back to my day. I pull her across the field in the direction of the house, glancing to the side to see her eyes widen as we crest the hill and Radcliffe comes into view. A few heads turn to look our way as we pass the staff, confusion painted on their features at the sight of this strange girl with me. Still, we continue on, crunching along the gravel drive and up the steps, until we come face-to-face with Martha, who opens the door for us.

"Hello, dear, are you quite—"

"Martha," I say, dropping the girl's arm. "What year is it?"

Martha looks as if she has seen a ghost, her blue eyes bulging out of her round face as she takes in the girl's attire.

"Martha?"

She shakes her head, coming back to herself. "It's 1812, of course."

"And do you know what a . . . ?" My head swivels around to look at the girl. "What was the word? Phone?"

The girl nods, but her confident smile slides fully off her face for the first time.

"Do you know what a phone is?"

"A . . ." Martha's voice trails off, a puzzled look clouding her gaze. "A *what?*"

"See?" I say, crossing my arms over my chest. The girl and I lock eyes as Martha begins to fuss over her.

"Are you lost, my dear? Unwell? Oh, *good heavens.* Walking around in trousers and your undergarments? I am quite sure we can find you something to—"

Just then Mr. Thompson, one of the footmen, strolls across the entryway in the direction of the kitchens. Martha quickly reaches out, pulling the girl's jacket together and attempting to shield her with her own body.

"Mr. Thompson!" I call out, and he turns, bowing quickly. "Miss?"

"What year is it?" I ask.

"It's . . ." Despite Martha's futile attempt at modesty, he notices the trousers and falls silent for five . . . ten . . . *fifteen* whole seconds. The gentleman is close to sixty, and I would not be surprised if this were enough to send him to an early grave.

Luckily, it does not. "Ah . . . it's 1812, Miss Sinclair," he replies finally.

I turn to face the girl and see her teeth gnawing nervously into her bottom lip as she processes what she's just heard.

But what could she possibly have expected?

Finally, she raises her hand to reveal the silver coin again. After a long moment of staring at it, her fist curls around it and she tilts her head back, squeezing her eyes shut.

"What the hell did he do?"

CHAPTER 7

AUDREY

June 15, 1812

My ears ring as I'm led past a marble staircase and down a hallway, searching for some small sign that this is just a terrible misunderstanding. A bad joke, even.

I search for a wall outlet, a light fixture, a power cord. But there's . . . nothing. Not even a pair of Adidas shoved into the corner or the hum of an air conditioner.

Everything seems to move in slow motion as I'm pushed back onto an ornate-looking striped couch. My eyes jump around this new room, taking in the fireplace, the gilded piano in the corner, the Regency-era paintings on the wall, too convincing to be replicas. Finally, they land on the girl from the field, her bright blue eyes sitting underneath furrowed eyebrows.

Her mouth is moving, but I can't make out what she's saying because my mind is stuck on what she's already said, playing it over and over again on a loop.

1812. 1812. 1812.

How is this possible? How did he—

The older woman shoves a tiny silver box under my nose, and I swear I see Jesus Christ himself as the pungent, almost chemical smell rips me back into reality, electrifying its way around my skull.

"What the . . . ?" I wiggle away from them both. *"What the hell was that?"*

"Smelling salts, dear," she says, like it's the most normal thing ever.

"Smelling salts?" A groan escapes my lips as I reach out to grab a book from the table next to the couch, flipping to the front to see the copyright date: *1807.*

Holy shit.

I slam it shut, my stomach queasy, and move to stand. I need to get home. To my mom and dad. To Cooper. To Pittsburgh. To 2023.

The field. That's where I arrived. It's the only place that makes sense to go.

I push past them both, feeling their hands grab for my arms as I bolt from the room and make my way down the hallway until I'm busting back out the front door. I hear the girl's voice calling after me, telling me to stop, but I can't.

I need to get the fuck out of here.

I retrace my steps, the long grass brushing against my ankles, as images flash in front of my eyes. My parents' smiling faces, the register I was *just* sitting at, the striped Target comforter on my bed.

Home.

I slow to a stop as I near the spot where an outline of my body is still imprinted in the grass. I lie down in it, chest heaving, and squeeze my eyes shut, thinking of the images of home again, but nothing happens.

"Come on . . . ," I gasp out, nails digging into my palms as my grip tightens around the quarter. *"Please."*

Still nothing.

I unfurl my hand to see George Washington's face.

"I think I've had enough of an adventure," I call out, remembering the conversation with Mr. Montgomery. "You've made your point! I mean, getting out of Pittsburgh and not hiding away in the corner store is one thing, but isn't this a little excessive?"

I toss it in the air, like he did, wishing over and over again to go back.

Nothing works.

I'm still here. *Stuck* here. Staring up at the cloudless blue sky, in a field, in *1812.*

"What is the matter with you?"

I turn my head to see the girl from earlier angrily trudging across the grass. Her cheeks are red, but her pinned-up golden hair is impressively without a single strand out of place.

All I can do is laugh and cry at the same time. Sitting up, I wipe the tears away with the back of my hand. "That's the problem. I have *no* idea."

She frowns at that. "You gave Martha quite a fright, bolting out of there like you did."

"Smelling-salt lady?" I think of the older woman and her tiny silver box of doom.

She nods, then hesitates slightly, before finally sitting down on the grass next to me, her back straighter than a ruler. "Let's start with something simpler, then. What is your name?"

"Audrey," I croak out. "You?"

"Lucy," she says, offering me an embroidered handkerchief for my snot-covered face, *L.S.* stitched into one of the corners. "Lucy Sinclair."

I blow my nose like my life depends on it, so it's no surprise that she motions for me to keep it after I try to give it back to her.

"Lucy," I say, squinting against the sun. "I'm not . . . I'm not *from* here. I'm . . ." But I trail off, because I have no idea how I can explain this to her.

"Well, I can help you return to where you are from. Maybe after some tea? I'll call for my footman, and he can—"

I snort at the absurdity of it all. "Your *footman*? Can he take me back to 2023?"

"I don't . . ."

"I'm from *the future*. More than two hundred years in the future. So, unless your footman knows how to zip through time and space itself, I'm not going home."

I swallow hard on the lump in my throat and watch as Lucy's blue eyes narrow, growing ever so slightly icy at the ridiculousness of what I just said.

"That's not possible."

"Yeah, that's what I thought until I woke up in your little field and you said it was 1812 and Martha smelling-salted me straight into this reality."

Her expression doesn't change, so I pull out my wallet and show her the driver's license my dad made me get in case I needed to run down to the Wholesale Depot on Thirty-Fifth Street to get more chips or soda for the store. (You can't lug four cases of soda back up the Lawrenceville hills with a bike—believe me, I've tried.)

I tap the plastic as she holds it weakly in her hands. "That's my birthday. December 11, *2005*."

Her pointer finger scratches at the plastic, eyes flicking between me and the unflattering DMV candid. "Is it a painting? It's so—"

"A photograph. It . . . How do I even explain . . . ? I guess it can capture any moment in time—you, me, this field, *anything*." I pull out my cell phone and tap through my photo album, showing her pictures of Cooper and my parents and a couple of sunsets. "See?"

Stopping on a time lapse I took from my bedroom window above the store, I shove the phone into her hands. She squints against the glare, but then . . .

Her face pales almost instantly, eyes widening as she watches the picture move and change. Penn Ave is brought to life in the palm of her hand, cars zipping in and out of frame, people flitting by, not to mention *electricity* everywhere.

The phone tumbles from her grip as her mouth falls agape. "What . . . ? How is it . . . ?"

I catch it before it hits the ground, holding it up to record her for a few seconds. "I guess it's kind of like a moving painting, but . . . different." A gasp escapes her lips as I spin it around and play it for her. "Like capturing a mirror. Or a memory."

Our eyes meet, and both of us stay silent for a long moment. "How are you—"

"Here?" I finish, shrugging as I pocket my phone with one hand and unfurl the fingers of the other to reveal Mr. Montgomery's quarter and the crescent-shaped marks lining my palm my nails digging into it. "I have *no* idea. One minute I was sitting behind the cash register at my parents' shop, talking to Mr. Montgomery. He tossed me this, and then . . ." I flip the coin up in the air. "*Poof.* You were there, dressed like *this*, waking me up."

Lucy takes the quarter from where it landed back in my hand, warm fingers brushing lightly against my own. I watch as she inspects it, thumbnail ticking along the grooves.

"So how will you return?"

"I . . ." I shake my head, an icy feeling clawing across my chest as I look out over the rolling fields of grass, my thoughts from earlier still ringing in my ears. "That's the problem, isn't it? I have no idea why I'm here in the first place, so I don't have any idea how to go back."

I know you, Audrey. And what you're looking for? It's not here, I hear his voice say.

Yeah, well, 1812 doesn't seem that promising either. I mean, how exactly does a prim-and-proper girl plucked from a Jane Austen novel and being *literal centuries in the past* have anything to do with what Mr. Montgomery was talking about for my future?

I bite at the inside of my cheek in an attempt to stop the frustrated tears from reappearing. "What if I *can't* get back? What if I'm stuck here *forever*? What about my parents? And Cooper? Where am I going to stay, and—"

Soft fingers wrap around my arm, stopping me from spiraling. *"Audrey."* I look over at her. "We will figure this out. We will figure out what exactly you are doing here. *And* how to get you home. I promise."

I nod my thanks, trying to get my shit together.

"In the meantime, I can answer one of your questions. You are more than welcome to stay with me at Radcliffe. We have plenty of space."

"Really?"

She nods and gives me a reassuring smile. I crane my neck back to watch as she stands and brushes at her skirt, all her movements so calculated and restrained. So precise. "Certainly."

She holds out her hand, and I take it, my fingertips sliding into her smooth palm. She pulls me to my feet, and then the two of us begin to walk slowly back the way we came, to the place I have to accept I will be stuck for the foreseeable future.

"Now, I would very much appreciate it if you tried to abstain from bolting from the drawing room the way you did earlier. I'm not sure Martha's heart can handle such excitement. We don't get a ton of it around here."

I smile at her. "Tell Martha as long as she keeps the smelling salts away from me, we've got a deal."

Lucy arches an eyebrow, but she surprises me the tiniest bit when I see her bite her lip like she's trying not to laugh.

CHAPTER 8

LUCY

June 15, 1812

I watch Audrey stare, aghast, at the chamber pot in what is now her bedroom, hazel eyes wide.

"Immediately no," she says.

"It's only if you need to relieve yourself in the night—"

She groans, pacing in tiny, fraught circles around the room.

"There's also the bourdaloue if you are—"

Audrey holds up her hand to stop me from speaking. "Lucy . . . I will run back out to the field, I swear to God."

I grab her arm and pull her toward the hallway before she has the chance. Martha and Abigail slide past us with fresh sheets and feather dusters to get the room ready for her stay. "Come on, let me at least show you the rest of the estate, then."

She stares at the portraits on the walls as we head down the corridor toward the library, her mouth agape. "It's the same guy in different fonts," she mutters before pointing finally to my father's sour face at the end. A chill climbs up my spine as I meet his gaze. "This one looks like he has a stick up his ass."

"That," I say as I open the door to the library, "is my father."

Audrey reddens almost instantly. "Oh my gosh, I am *so* sorry. I didn't—"

I wave my hand and usher her inside, shocked to discover she has *some* decorum. Although, admittedly, while I'm not certain what that phrase means, I'm guessing from her reaction that it is more than fitting. "I would perhaps say even worse," I reply. My fingers immediately rise to my mouth in surprise at what has just escaped.

She gives me a questioning look but quite thankfully doesn't press any further.

"This is the library," I say, quickly moving on from my unexpected slip. I motion to the walls of books and watch as Audrey reaches out to trail her fingers along the spines, her face curious.

She tilts her neck back, eyes traveling along the stacks, slowly taking everything in. "How many of these have you read?"

"All of them," I say, following her gaze through history, science, politics, geography, mathematics, poetry. Hundreds upon hundreds of books.

"All of them?"

I raise my shoulders, shrugging. "I'm alone here a lot." For many years, these books have acted as companions of sorts, since my father has not wished me to have any. Or at least not any besides those of his own design, for either status or business purposes. Except for stolen moments with Grace, dull teas and dinner parties with even duller companions are all I've been allowed, and books are vastly better company than that.

"What's your favorite thing to read?" she asks, gesturing to all the books. "Out of everything here?"

"Uh, I suppose books on etiquette. Or sermons," I lie, saying what my father would want to hear, the truth swallowed.

Audrey gives me a surprised look, hand frozen on the shelf. "That sounds . . . boring."

I bite my lip, knowing I can't agree with such a blunt and egregious statement again, however true it may be.

"I like romance myself," she says with a casual shrug.

I freeze over her admission, the answer I swallowed so easily said. Romance has *always* been my favorite. My mother loved such books and would read them to me often, but when she died, it was no surprise my father forbade them, claiming it wasn't proper for a well-brought-up lady to read such things, that the notions and foolishness of love are far below other subjects I should spend my time thinking about and studying. It was the first sign that my mother's hopes for my life would never come to be.

"What?" she asks, noticing my change in expression.

"Do you . . . ?" I hesitate, glancing past her to the closed door, excitement getting the better of me. "Do you want to see something?"

The affirmation has barely escaped her lips before I am leading her to the corner of the room, where I very carefully lift a loose floorboard. Underneath are about twenty books I have managed to sneak in from my trips into town, covers worn from reading them over and over again.

"*Cool,*" Audrey says as she pulls out a few, even though it's quite warm, not chilly in here at all. She blows the dust off to reveal the titles. "A little secret stash."

"My father would be livid if he knew these were here," I admit as I pick up my extremely worn copy of *Romeo and Juliet.* "But I . . . I love reading these books. Escaping into them. Pretending I'm someone else. Someone in a faraway, distant land who can be the heroine of her own story. It's . . ."

I trail off, my cheeks reddening at the words that have spilled out of my mouth, but it also feels good, sharing a real and genuine piece of myself without consequence. After all, Audrey will likely be gone very soon.

"It's comforting," Audrey says with a warm smile, flipping carefully through Frances Burney's second novel. "That's why I love them too."

I watch her for a brief moment, her words making me feel validated. Admittedly, I was wary and perhaps a bit annoyed when someone interrupted my final few weeks of freedom, but . . . maybe her being here isn't such a bad thing.

"Someone in a faraway, distant land," Audrey mutters, letting out a soft chuckle. "Sounds like me now."

I can't help but study her, eyes narrowing as I inspect her attire, the way she's sitting, the tilt of her head as she reads the first few lines of the book. She is . . . fascinating. The way she speaks, what she says, how she moves. I feel a million questions bubbling up about the future. What books are like there and why her clothes are like *that*. But . . . I don't want to be improper.

Speaking of questions to be avoided, at that moment I watch as her gaze starts to move past my head to my mother's portrait on the wall just behind me. Hastily, I grab the book from her grasp before she can ask about her. "We should head down for dinner," I say, far louder than I normally would.

Audrey's stomach growls in anticipation, so I don't think she notices my impolite change of subject. I tuck the book among the others and replace the floorboard, thinking about my father and how displeased he would be to know of their existence.

But he never will, because I hide these books on love and passion right here, directly underneath my mother's portrait, knowing it's the one place he will never stumble across them.

CHAPTER 9

AUDREY

June 15, 1812

That night, I toss and turn for the better part of an hour, until I finally decide to stay awake, peering at the barely decipherable shapes in the enormous guest room Lucy gave to me.

It's so *dark* here. And quiet.

And . . . well . . . *scary.*

Earlier, things almost started to seem like a bit of an adventure. I mean, I had *duck* for dinner. And it was *good*! I drank evening tea from a fancy little cup and poked around a few of the rooms, picking up ornate candlesticks and inspecting the paintings on the drawing room wall. Martha even let me see her little tin of smelling salts, though one peek under the lid did give me war flashbacks.

But now, in the quiet stillness of the night, in the scratchy nightgown I borrowed from Lucy, I feel this unavoidable fear again. This panic over the mind-blowing reality that I am somehow *here*. In 1812. With no way home.

I miss the muted sound of my parents' voices through the wall. I miss Coop snoring loudly and taking up too much of my twin bed. I miss my *room*, the art supplies, Polaroid pictures, books, and the pile of dirty laundry in the corner. I miss the glow of the streetlights on Penn Ave filtering through my blinds. The sound of cars driving past my bedroom window even in the dead of night, muffled sirens wailing somewhere in the distance.

Here it's just . . . an ear-ringing silence while I lie all alone in a giant but uncomfortable four-poster bed. I think I can hear my hair growing.

I mean, how did little Mr. Montgomery even do this? And *why*?

If this were a movie, I'd have been sent here for some special purpose. To learn some big lesson or to complete some kind of life-altering quest.

So . . . is that it? Am I here for some kind of great adventure that will show me the answer to getting me out of this rut I'm in, like the characters in those books under Lucy's library floorboard?

But I just don't see *how* I am going to figure that out in 1812. I mean, from the corset wearing to the hidden romance novels, I wouldn't say this seems like the time and place for a woman to really come into her own.

The more I think about it, the more I feel like I'm losing

my mind, and the urge to talk to the only person who knows this is really happening swims over me. Straitlaced, prim-and-proper *Lucy*. She's the one person I've got, since everyone I know and love won't even be born for another two centuries.

Letting out a long groan, I finally sit up, grab my pillows and a blanket, and tiptoe across the room to the door. It creaks noisily as I open it, revealing the empty hallway, a dark void without any electricity. I skitter two doors down to Lucy's room, then bite my lip as I knock lightly.

A few seconds later Lucy calls for me to come in.

"Audrey?" she asks as I slowly peek in, a match hissing to life as she lights the candle on her bedside table. "What's the matter?"

"Nothing, I just, uh . . ." I shrug and slip the rest of the way inside, then let the door click shut behind me. "Couldn't sleep, I guess. It's too . . . quiet."

She tilts her head slightly, blue eyes filling with curiosity. Her golden hair, which had been pulled back earlier, cascades around her face and onto her pillow, much longer than I was expecting.

"Is it not quiet where you are from?"

I pad across the room and sit on the floor next to her bed, burritoing myself in my blanket, already feeling a tiny bit better. "No," I say, forcing out a small smile. "I live in the city. In Pittsburgh, if you've heard of it."

She hums an affirmation, apparently knowing geography

better than most current American high schoolers.

"It is *far* from quiet, and not just because my dog snores ridiculously loud. Though, admittedly, that sounds like a damn plane taking off."

Lucy frowns with confusion, and I rephrase, realizing she has no idea what the heck a plane even is. "Louder than . . . a clap of thunder."

She nods, understanding.

"Can I . . . ?" I motion to the room. "Can I stay here for a bit? Just to have the sounds of another person instead of all the silence. It's, uh, kind of comforting."

"Yes," Lucy says after a long pause. "You can stay for as long as you like."

I lie back, and the two of us stare at each other, her soft features warm in the flicker of the candlelight.

"What is it like, in the future?" she finally asks.

"Well, we have cars, transportation that can get you places *much* faster than a horse and carriage. And planes, which cover longer distances even faster. They float in the sky, kind of like birds do."

"*In the sky?*" Lucy asks, incredulous, and I nod.

"There's the internet, where you can find information about just about anything, good or bad or . . . ugly." I think being horrified by something you've seen on Google is a rite of passage at this point. "And all kinds of technology. Cell phones, like I showed you, to contact anyone in the world.

Television, to watch, uh . . . shows and performances and news, all right in your home."

Her gaze is calculating as she tries to understand all that. I wonder if she'll ask more about television, my mind moving quickly to think of some shows she'd like—*The Great British Bake Off*, maybe? *The Crown*? *Downton Abbey*? Oh, *Bridgerton*! But instead she pivots to something more personal.

"What about you? What do you do in the future?"

The million-dollar question.

Maybe *the* question. What I'm here to figure out.

I think for a long moment before I answer, but I can't make the pieces fit together, so it comes out more of a ramble. "I don't know. For now I work at my parents' convenience store, and I have a dog named Cooper, and I go to school, and—"

"School? Like university?" Her eyes widen.

"Well, I'm still in high school, but, yeah, girls go to school in the future. College, university, all of that, as long as you're willing to take on a mountain of debt. You can be a doctor, or a scientist, or a teacher." I pause for a moment before adding, "Or an artist. Whatever you want, really."

She smiles so big at that, and I smile back at her. "*And* we can wear trousers," I say, repeating Martha's word from earlier.

Lucy laughs, and, for the first time since I got here, I feel myself relax the tiniest bit. It's like I'm not completely and totally alone, a feeling I've had more often than not, even in

2023, since Charlie and our—or rather *his*—friends graduated.

"And your parents?" Lucy asks. "They'd let you do all that?"

"Yeah," I say, feeling a pang of sadness return when I think of them. "They'd support me no matter what I wanted to do. I honestly think they'd be more upset if I *didn't* chase my dreams."

I hesitate, realizing how much truth those words have. I think of my mom in the bathroom, encouraging me to apply next year when I'd given up entirely. Not wanting me to throw everything away no matter how much I said I was ready to give up.

"I, uh . . ." I let out a long huff of air. "I think, of everything from the future, I miss my parents the most. They're probably the best thing about 2023."

Lucy shifts to get a better view of my face. "You're close with them."

I nod. "We've *always* been close. We live just above the convenience store in this small, worse-for-wear apartment, but it's . . . the best."

Early mornings behind the counter with my dad, learning family recipes from my mom in our tiny kitchen, and going to Pirates games even though they suck, because the tickets are cheap. Our worn but cozy couch, old windows cracked open on cool summer nights, laughing over some new Netflix show. They've always been there for me, but even more so after my breakup with Charlie and all my friends graduating last year. The constant when all else fails or leaves.

Why can't that be enough for forever? It should be. I *want* it to be, that safe little corner shop, my parents by my side, where I'd give anything to be now. Why can't I push the cracks away and let the dream that doesn't want to come true go? It doesn't sound like what Mr. Montgomery meant, but maybe that's what I'm going to learn here instead.

I chew on my cheek to stop the tears that sting at my eyes, and let out a half-hearted chuckle. "And to think I was worried about shipping off to college. Now I'm literally two whole centuries away from them."

Lucy watches me for a long moment. "That sounds nice," she says. "Being so close to them, I mean."

"Are you not close to your parents?"

She laughs. "To be quite honest, I think I'm the bane of my father's existence. I much prefer it when he's not here, like right now. It's the only time I am free to do as I please."

The words are barely out of her mouth before she presses her lips together, like she regrets what she said. I haven't been here for very long, but it seems like she does that a lot.

I think of that portrait in the hallway of the angry-looking man, most of the features so different from her own. "And your mother . . . ?"

"Dead," she says, her gaze hardening, a glimmer of resemblance finally revealing itself. "A fever seven winters ago."

"I'm so sorry."

"*We* . . . were close. Very close." Her voice trails off, and she stops talking completely.

Neither of us says anything for a long moment. Then Lucy finally breaks the silence, but not to continue the conversation.

"We should get to sleep," she says, nodding to the empty half of the bed beside her. "You don't have to sleep on the floor if you don't want to—"

The words are barely out of her mouth before I leap up next to her, burrowing into the covers with a contented sigh. My hips were already protesting from fifteen minutes on the hardwood.

She stifles a laugh, rolling over to blow the candle out, and the room grows dark around us.

I brace myself for the panic, the heaviness of the nineteenth-century silence, but this time I have the sound of her breathing for company, slowing and evening as she drifts off to sleep, and for just a moment, if I squeeze my eyes shut tightly, it's enough to pretend I'm home.

CHAPTER 10

LUCY

June 16, 1812

When I awake the next morning, the first thing I see is Audrey, curled up underneath the blanket, dark hair strewn across her pillow, lips slightly parted.

I feel a jolt of exhilaration at the sight of her.

Not only at the fact that she is indeed *real*, but that allowing her to stay here in my father's house when I know he certainly wouldn't is another enormous act of defiance. Bigger even than my dress rebellion.

There's no denying the fact I've done things in my tiny moments of freedom: secret trips to Grace's house, stretching errands about town a minute or two longer, reading books he would frown upon, dirtying my petticoats.

But *this*?

This is something different altogether. Like the last adventure I've been wanting before everything changes.

Perhaps it should be unsettling, having her here. A perfect stranger, not even of this time. But it isn't. I feel completely at ease, especially after our discussion last night, about Pittsburgh, and women going off to pursue their dreams, and all the future has to offer. Like it isn't so crazy or improper that I should want more than to be a dutiful daughter and a rich man's wife. It makes me feel . . . less alone.

Even if I can't have the opportunities or the family she has, at least these final few weeks of freedom with a kindred spirit are sure to be interesting, to say the least.

Provided she doesn't disappear just as quickly as she came.

I pull my eyes away from her face as she begins to stir and roll onto my back.

"Morning," she says, her voice gravelly.

"Good morning," I say, running a hand through my hair as I glance back in her direction. "We are to visit my friend Grace today. You'll need something to wear besides your trousers."

"I'm sure Grace is nice and all, but . . ." She props herself up on one arm. "Shouldn't I be trying to figure out a way back home?"

I shrug, trying to ignore the way my heart sinks a bit at her words. "Of course. But I assume there's some *point* to you being sent here, so perhaps the only way to figure it out is to, I suppose"—I motion to the room around us—"be here?"

She nods, considering that.

"And maybe then the answer will come to you."

"Fair point," she says as she gets out of bed and stretches, her long arms reaching toward the ceiling. "Do you, uh, have anything that will fit?"

I push the covers aside and follow suit, walking around the length of the bed to face her, my neck tilting ever so slightly back so I can meet her eyes.

Hmm, my things will definitely be too short.

"Here." I grab her hand, an idea taking shape. I lead her out of the room and down the hall to the very last door, just before the corridor to the library. A puff of dust greets us as I push inside.

Audrey coughs and pulls her hand out of my grasp, waving it in front of her face as we move toward the center of the room.

"What is all this stuff?"

"Old furniture, paintings, this and that." Out-of-season items, pictures my father has replaced with more expensive options from Mr. Prewitt, storage for sculptures and books and valuables.

And, most importantly, in a wardrobe by the window, my mother's old clothes.

I pull open the doors to reveal a sea of bright dresses and gowns, shoes and hats, capes and riding coats. Audrey catches up behind me, her shoulder brushing lightly against mine.

"These are—*were*," I correct myself, "my mother's. She was quite a bit taller than me, so they should fit you far better

73

than any of my dresses would. We may have to go into town this week for some slight alterations, if you don't suddenly jump back to the future. But one of these will certainly suffice for Grace's."

I remember my mother in all of these, floating across the dance floor in a beautiful lilac at a ball, the day-to-day florals she would wear when we roamed the grounds or sat in the drawing room, the thick pelisse she would tuck around me on chilly carriage rides home.

She was always so warm and vibrant and sure of herself. I don't know how, when my father was so horrendously the opposite. I know what glimmers of those traits I possessed in myself were impossible to maintain being stuck here alone with him.

I tug on the sleeves of a soft green gown, one of my favorites, lost in my memories.

"Are you sure you're okay with it? Me wearing . . . her clothes?" Audrey asks, hesitant.

I pull my eyes away from the dresses, trying my very best to move as far from the subject as possible. "They are not being worn by anyone else, are they?"

Not anymore.

The past is in the past. And the more I distance myself from it and her impossible hopes for an impossible life, the better.

Audrey remains quiet, while I attempt to pull off lighthearted. "I'll tell Martha to send someone in to help you dress while I do the same."

"To help me . . . ?" Her voice trails off as I pull a corset from the wardrobe.

"Ah," she says, understanding. "You know, I really don't think that will be necessary. I can probably just do it my—"

"Trust me. You're going to need help," I say, pressing it firmly into her hands before drifting from the room, leaving a trail of dust and unwanted reminiscence behind me, not wanting to live in the past or the future, but just . . . *here*. Now.

In this present adventure, where, for once, I'm in control.

CHAPTER 11

AUDREY

June 16, 1812

I've never seen so many layers in my life.

Not even during the polar vortex that hit Pittsburgh a few years ago.

I look back and forth between the massive pile of clothing and Abigail, the small, wiry girl who is putting a name to everything in front of me.

"All right, so we've got this nightgown-looking thing," I say as I start to point to each item.

"*Chemise.*"

"Rib crusher."

"*Corset.*"

"Gown for *over* the nightgown-looking thing."

"*Bodice petticoat.*"

"And, to top it all off, this little neck bib."

"*Chemisette.*"

And that's all *before* the dress, which is so heavy coming off the hanger I now understand why Lucy said I needed someone to help me put it on.

"Isn't this a bit . . . excessive?" I ask, and she shrugs, giving me a puzzled look.

"Do you not . . . ?" Her voice trails off, and she narrows her eyes at me. "Do you not wear any of this in America?"

"Uh, no, we *totally* do, just, you know . . . fewer layers, different names. Some of us don't wear corsets," I lie. Lucy and I decided earlier that it was probably best not to tell everyone exactly where I'm from.

Not that they'd believe it anyway.

As far as Abigail knows, I'm the daughter of one of Lucy's father's business acquaintances, doing a bit of traveling.

Somehow satisfied with my explanation, she smiles and says, "Wintertime here is even worse. Wool stockings and the like."

Well, thank God it's not wintertime.

I let out a long exhale of air and toss her the corset. "All right. Let's get this over with."

As it turns out, someone helping me get dressed is just as awkward as you'd expect. I make Abigail face the wall while I strip down to my birthday suit and wiggle into the chemise, thanking the Lord above for modern underwear and bras in a way I never have before.

As she helps tighten the corset, pulling on the intricately weaved ribbons, I pray to Jane Austen herself for strength.

"Maybe . . . a little . . . more breathing room," I gasp out.

"It is already *quite* loose," she says, but obliges, making it so my lungs are actually able to fully expand and contract, even though my boobs are still practically around my neck.

Maybe, if I'm lucky, I won't pass out today, which would be good because do they even *have* hospitals here? I shake my head, not wanting to think about the lack of modern medicine and, like . . . consumption.

"You know, these used to be *far* more constrictive," Abigail says as she moves on to the petticoat. "Made out of whalebones."

Well, considering the most constrictive thing I've worn prior to this was a major-lift push-up bra from Victoria's Secret to my ninth-grade winter formal, I'd hate to see what *that* was like.

"Oh really? We used, uh . . . *shark bones* in America," I say, because I'm apparently terrible at lying. And it's *barely* been twenty-four hours.

When we're done with the underclothes, I stare at myself in the mirror, wearing practically an entire clothes rack. "I feel like I've got more layers than an onion."

Abigail laughs at that, shaking her head and sending strands of fiery red hair falling in front of her face as she *finally* helps me into the soft green gown.

When she's done buttoning and tying the back so all the layers are now covered, I realize, all things considered . . . I look pretty good.

I turn right and left, inspecting my appearance in the dusty mirror, as the fabric smoothly and gracefully swishes against the wood floor.

Maybe Lucy is right. Maybe I have to try to embrace this whole 1812 thing. I mean, I'm here for a reason, right? And there's no denying I feel kind of unexpectedly cool right now. Like I'm Keira Knightley in a period drama, about to gaze forlornly out a window or cry a single tear in a bumpy carriage.

"All righty! Thanks, Abigail!" I say once I'm done being vain, spinning on my heel and heading toward the door. "Breakfast calls."

Abigail grabs my arm, motioning to the bird's nest of hair hanging around my shoulders. "Not just yet."

I groan as she leads me down the hallway back to my guest room, plunking me in front of a vanity. As if someone helping me get ready and waiting on me wasn't already uncomfy enough.

I try not to wince, but it turns out her hair-brushing skills are about as gentle as Mrs. Lowry's from down the block. My mom paid her to do my hair and makeup for junior prom last year, and my scalp was sore for about a week.

"Is this . . . ?" I say, trying to appear perfectly serene and not at all questioning how many strands of hair I'll have left on my head after this ordeal. "An *every day* kind of thing? Like the hair and the clothes and the . . . ?"

Abigail nods.

Good. Great. Awesome.

Well, if I don't make it back to Pittsburgh before the end of the week, I'm not going to have any hair left for Mrs. Lowry to torture for senior prom.

CHAPTER 12

LUCY

June 16, 1812

"Stop fidgeting," I say, putting a hand on Audrey's arm as the carriage bumps underneath us.

"Sorry, I'm not exactly used to being suffocated by my clothes," she says as she tugs at the sides of her dress, her cheeks red from what I can only assume is a combination of the afternoon heat and the clothing I have grown up accustomed to.

Even in the midst of her discomfort, she looks exceedingly pretty. She chose the soft green dress, and the color brings out the tiniest trace of it in her hazel eyes, while her high cheekbones and full lips are made all the more prominent with her hair pulled away from her face. If you didn't know, you would never guess she was from a different time.

I flick open my fan and wave it in her direction, until her face softens ever so slightly with relief.

"So, who are we hanging out with today?" she asks.

I frown. "Why would we be hanging out of anything?"

"No, I mean . . ." She lets out a disgruntled sigh. "Grace's, right? That's where we're going?"

"Yes. I shall be introducing you to one of my dear friends, Grace Harding." I peek out the window as the carriage slows, and a quaint brick house swims into view. "When you meet her, try not to use any of your . . . odd future phrases. Like 'hanging out.' After you curtsy, simply say you are pleased to make her acquaintance."

"*Curtsy?*" Audrey hisses.

My head whips around to face her, fan pausing in midair. "Do you not . . . ?"

"No!"

"Just . . ." My voice trails off as I rack my brain for a solution. "Just follow Grace's lead."

Audrey nods, shifting nervously in her seat as we come to a stop.

"And perhaps don't . . ."

"Say a lot?" she asks, and I nod. Grace is as lovely as they come, but I highly doubt she would believe or understand the concept of Audrey being from two hundred years in the future. I doubt I would have, had I not found her in the field and seen the proof with my own two eyes. And while I suppose we could show her too, there's no sense roping anyone else into this, when we have no idea why she's here or how long she'll remain.

82

A footman pulls open the door, and Audrey flashes me one more worried look before my hand slides into his grasp and I am whisked out of the carriage. She joins me much less gracefully a moment later, her shoulder bumping into mine.

"Be cool, Audrey," she mutters to herself as we head toward the house. "Be cool."

I smile to myself, reaching up to knock lightly on the door. A moment later Grace's housekeeper, Mrs. Dowding, appears to greet us. "Ah! Miss Sinclair! Come in, come in. Oh, I see you've brought a guest with you. I'll add another cup for tea."

"Yes. I hope it is no trouble."

"No trouble at all," Mrs. Dowding says, leading us to the parlor. Grace leaps up as we come inside.

"Lucy! You should have told me you were bringing a friend."

"I . . . yes. Forgive me. It's all very last minute, but this is Audrey Cameron. She is staying with me at Radcliffe for . . . a short while." My eyes flick to Audrey. "Her father is a business acquaintance of my father's."

"Audrey," Grace says with an enormous smile, dipping down into a curtsy. "I'm so pleased to make your acquaintance."

Despite myself, I find I am holding my breath.

"I am so pleased to make yours," Audrey parrots back, her curtsy rather stilted and clumsy but perfectly adequate.

"You are American!" Grace says as we all sit down, while Mrs. Dowding enters the parlor with a tray of tea.

"Yes, I am, uh . . ." She hesitates, fingers tapping on the arm of her chair. "Doing a bit of traveling at the moment."

"How exciting. And how are you liking it here?"

"It's been something. Feels like I was just dropped into another world."

Grace laughs, and I shoot a glare in Audrey's direction, which is returned with a rather mischievous smirk.

"Is it really so different?" Grace asks.

"Oh," Audrey says as she takes a long, slow sip from the cup of tea Mrs. Dowding handed her. "You have no idea."

I resist the urge to pour the entire pot of tea over her head.

"So, Grace, how is your father's business doing? I am sure the warmer weather has been quite good for all his traveling about," I interject in an attempt to change the topic of conversation.

Grace, thankfully, takes the bait, and Audrey quietly drinks her tea and peers around the room while we discuss Grace's father acquiring an ornate life-size horse statue for a duke living in London, then Simon planting a rose garden alongside their house, and finally my new dress for the upcoming ball, which should arrive soon.

"You will look lovely," Grace says, beaming at me.

"Yes, well, with any luck, it will secure the marriage proposal my father so desperately desires."

Grace's face falls, sympathy weighing heavy on all her features, but a loud cough from Audrey makes both of us look

over at her. "Sorry, I just . . . Something stuck in my throat."
Her eyes meet mine. "*Married?* Aren't you a little . . . young?"

"Hardly," I murmur into my cup of tea. "Grace was seventeen when she was married. I turned eighteen this past fall."

Do people marry later in the future? Heavens, why couldn't *I* have been sent *there?*

She bites her lip, perhaps to stop from saying anything else.

"But, Lucy," Grace says, exasperated as she is every time we have discussed this. "Is there really no other option? Can't you do *something* else? I thought surely after you intentionally fumbled that piano passage, he would be dissuaded. I mean, he's—"

"It's fine," I say curtly, completely resigned now to my fate, and Grace falters, surprised at the change from our previous discussions. But I'm not going to waste my time, or hurt myself further, by hoping for *something else* any longer. "It's not like a more suitable match will just appear in a few weeks' time."

Romantically *or* financially, for that matter. Not that my father would let me pursue the former even if it did.

Grace seems about to say something else when the sound of approaching footsteps echoes loudly in the hallway, murmured voices and laughter interrupting her as we all turn our attention toward the door.

The handle turns, and Simon enters, followed by a remarkably handsome gentleman, tall, with dark hair and sparkling blue eyes that his cravat fashionably matches. Grace and I stand, and Audrey thankfully follows suit.

"Lucy! So lovely to see you."

"Likewise, Simon," I say as he pushes his friend forward.

"We were just popping in to say goodbye to Grace before heading into town. This is an old classmate of mine from university, a Mr. Matthew Shepherd. He's just moved into Whitton Park."

He bows, I curtsy, and we exchange pleasantries while I study his features. A long, thin nose. Strong jaw. Dark, thick eyebrows. Suddenly I think I know what Grace was about to say.

For a brief moment, I imagine I'm meeting him in a world where Mr. Caldwell and my father don't exist. I search for a feeling, for *something*, like in all the books I've read, but, like always, it doesn't come.

And then I watch as his attention turns to Audrey.

"Might I introduce my good friend Audrey Cameron to you both," I say, remembering my manners.

My bottom teeth dig into my lip as I watch Audrey execute an absolutely abysmal curtsy this time, the lack of someone to imitate proving a problem. A faint blush climbs onto her cheeks as her gaze meets Mr. Shepherd's.

"Sorry, in America we don't really . . . curtsy."

"And what do you do?" he asks, not seeming to mind at all. "When you meet someone in America?"

"Just a handshake," Audrey says, and Mr. Shepherd takes a small step forward, gamely offering his right hand to her.

I watch as she reaches out and her fingertips slide into his grasp in a gesture reserved here for only our closest acquaintances.

And I can see why.

There's a palpable intimacy in the moment, neither of them wearing gloves, and Mr. Shepherd's mouth curves into a charming smile, which Audrey coyly returns.

"Well, Matthew, we had best be off," Simon says, clearing his throat. Audrey's hand slides out of Mr. Shepherd's, and I watch his fingers flex, open and then closed, as if trying to preserve the feeling of their touch, while Simon continues, "Miss Cameron, it was lovely to make your acquaintance."

"Yes," Mr. Shepherd says in agreement. "Lovely"—his eyes flick to mine out of courtesy—"to meet both of you."

They take their leave, and the door is barely shut before Grace gives me an excited smile, like she didn't just witness the same scene I did.

"He has an income of *five thousand* a year. *Quite* the eligible bachelor, if you ask me."

My dear friend. Still searching for a solution that doesn't exist.

"Oh, Grace," I say wistfully as I slide back into my chair. "Mr. Caldwell's is double that."

CHAPTER 13

AUDREY

June 16, 1812

Back at Radcliffe after tea, I lie in a heap on the striped sofa in the drawing room, which Lucy takes special care to inform me is "most unladylike."

I ignore her, because it feels like my corset is going to either chafe my underboob off or break a rib in any other position.

Or both, given the current state of my luck.

I'd be fine with both if it would send me back.

I *really* tried at Grace's to embrace the whole 1812 thing. Met a cute guy, learned Lucy is going to be *married*, drank some tea in a quaint little sitting room, but nothing felt like something I could grab on to. While they talked about horse statues and rose gardens, all I could think about was time travel movies and how *they* had made it home.

When we got back from Grace's, before I ended up in this

unladylike sprawl, I roped Lucy into tossing me the quarter like Mr. Montgomery had yesterday at the shop, but we just ended up playing a game of catch for ten minutes instead of sending me into the fabric of time and space itself.

Then I pulled an *About Time* and closed myself into a closet while a confused Lucy looked on, squeezing my eyes shut and picturing myself back in my bedroom, tucked into bed, like I used to do when I would have nightmares as a kid, but . . .

Clearly I'm still here.

I even asked Lucy if there were any giant stones on her property in an attempt to go full *Outlander*, but she just rolled her eyes at me.

Which means . . . Lucy must be right. I'm here for a *reason*. And apparently one day of diving into life here wasn't enough to get a sense of what that is yet.

I gaze up at the ornate chandelier in the center of the room, its golden arms extending outward, so different from the fluorescent lights of the corner shop. Even with all its splendor, I feel a pang of homesickness, and I pull my eyes away, watching as Lucy sits down at the piano in the corner, the late-afternoon sun illuminating her golden hair.

"Mr. Shepherd was quite handsome," she says casually as she begins to play, the melody soft and light but surprisingly intricate.

"Yeah, he was," I say. I would definitely swipe right on him. His eyes were *incredibly* blue. And his *jaw*? Sculpted by the gods. Not to mention he looked like he was *actually* 6'2" instead of 5'10" rounded up. "You into him?"

"I'm going to be married," she says with about as much enthusiasm as a middle school student finding out about a math test. "Besides, it was *quite* apparent he was far more interested in you."

I groan as I sit up, my head spinning slightly from the heat and the eighteen layers of chafing clothes I have on. I would kill for a crisp Brisk from the cooler and some good old-fashioned air-conditioning. "It would be pretty absurd for me to fall in love with someone from an entirely different time period," I deflect.

Wouldn't it? It's not like Mr. Montgomery didn't hint at love, but why would the "right person" be someone I can never actually be with in my real life?

I stand and cross the room before sliding onto the stool next to her. Lucy scooches over to make some room for me, and I watch her long, thin hands move smoothly across the keys, more than a little impressed at the music she produces.

"You're really good."

"I'm adequate," Lucy says, blue eyes flicking up to meet mine. Somehow they're even bluer than Mr. Shepherd's, more striking but also . . . piercing. Like she sees more of me than I want her to see. "Do you play?"

The music stops, and her hands slide off the piano, motioning like she's expecting *me* to have a little Beethoven moment.

"Eh, I guess I can tickle the ol' ivories," I say, and Lucy flashes me an already familiar look that screams, *WHAT ARE YOU EVEN TALKING ABOUT?*

I ignore it and make a big flourishing show of reaching up and putting my thumb on middle C, clearing my throat, and then . . .

I play the most clunky and grating rendition of "Chopsticks" known to mankind, loosely dredged up from my kindergarten piano recital. The keys clank noisily underneath my fingertips, made all the worse by a couple of clearly misplayed notes.

Lucy laughs and reaches out to put a hand over mine, putting a stop to it after only a few bars.

"I have never heard that song before, but it was . . ."

I grin. "Awful?"

"Yes."

We both laugh as she takes back over, the melody from before flowing out from underneath her fingertips.

"Do you like music?" I ask her, and she nods.

"I think it's my favorite thing. Even more so than reading. Where everything just . . ."

"Falls into place," we surprise ourselves by saying at the same time, and a smile of understanding passes between us. I feel the exact same way about my art. Drawing and painting.

Or at least I did.

I guess that's why the last few months have felt especially awful.

Not just because of Charlie and the breakup but because I lost the thing that always gave me a sense of peace, of completeness, with it.

And I don't know how to get it back.

"*Oh!* If you like music . . . ," I say as I jump up, hurrying over to the couch to get the small silk bag that Lucy gave me this morning before we left. I come back over, pulling my phone out to find the charge already under 30 percent.

Not that there's anyone alive to contact. There isn't exactly a "stuck two hundred years in the past" helpline. I tried calling my mom once, but making calls to the present apparently isn't included in our phone plan.

I try not to think about the fact that soon I won't even be able to look at pictures of home, the thought alone making me feel pretty sick to my stomach. The temporary comfort I get from seeing Cooper light up my home screen is something I've been clinging to, but I know if I was from 1812 and someone showed me Picasso or van Gogh or Frida Kahlo, it would've blown my mind in the best possible way, so I pull up Spotify, swipe to one of my downloaded playlists, *in your feels,* and scroll down to the bottom, where the modern classical shit I listen to while studying is. I have a feeling playing St. Vincent right off the bat would give her a heart attack; one sick guitar riff would have Martha rushing in here with her smelling salts. So I tap play on "River Flows in You" by Yiruma, figuring it'll be a gentle start, and watch as her blue eyes widen.

"*How?*"

She scooches closer to me, eager to get a look, and I hand her my phone.

"Any song in the world, right in your pocket. Or, uh, *reticule,*" I add, using the word she taught me earlier for that tiny silk bag.

"That's . . . incredible," she says as she holds it up to her ear, listening in awe to the rest of the song. I study her face in the afternoon sun as it changes with the music, the light reflecting off her long eyelashes, her delicate nose casting a shadow on her cheek.

And as the music makes her face come alive, I feel like I see her a little more clearly. Like as much as I'm dying to leave . . . it's cool that I can even be *here*, in this moment, face-to-face with a girl from two hundred years in the past. Cool that I can have so much in common with someone seemingly so different.

When it's over, her hands reach up and begin to play the melody on the piano in front of her as if it's an old favorite and she didn't just hear it for the first time five seconds ago.

We cycle through a few more. Some, she knows, like "Air on the G String" by Bach, which she saw performed once in London with her father, and some Mozart, which she plays along with. But then, slowly, I show her some stuff from the present. "Moon Song" by Phoebe Bridgers, which she surprisingly loves, and then "Los Ageless" by St. Vincent, which she will learn to love if we're going to be friends.

"What *is* that?" she asks.

"Electric guitar," I say, which she frowns at. "Like . . . guitar with lightning in it."

She nods, like that somehow makes sense, brow furrowing as she listens. She comments on the melodies, the harmonics, and the dissonance, playing a few notes on the piano and nodding along, her words going *way* over my head even though it's one of my favorite songs.

When the song fades out, she smiles at me. "It's so . . . *different*. But in a good way. It would be fascinating to study music like this. To *play* music like this. I—I think I'd like the future."

I nod, laughing as I scroll farther down the playlist. "I think you would too." Then I think about atomic bombs and health insurance and, like . . . climate change. "Well . . . most of it. I'd come watch you play."

When I find my favorite song, I tap to start it.

From the opening rhythmic beats of "I Wanna Dance with Somebody" by Whitney Houston, I'm on my feet, swaying around the drawing room like I'm back home with my mom, everything feeling a little brighter. This song is what she's always played to get me out of teary middle school funks, or on bright, sunny days when I was still in Pampers, or when the two of us are dissecting a rom-com we just watched over Friday-night pizza. It was her favorite ever since her dad took her to a concert back in 1987 at the Civic Arena, and it feels almost like she passed it down to me. A family heirloom of sorts, like, well . . .

Like the shop might be, I guess.

"I *love* this song," I say, spinning the complicated thoughts away. I turn and see Lucy staring at me from the piano bench, her eyes blinking in confusion.

I bop over to her and grab her hands, pulling her to her feet. "Come on," I say as she stands there, straight as a plank of wood, completely unmoving.

"I don't know the steps," she says, and I snort.

"There aren't any! You just . . ." I do a little shimmy while she crosses her arms over her chest, looking scandalized.

"It's un—"

"Ladylike," I finish, cutting her off with an eye roll. "Yeah, yeah. So *be* unladylike for a change. I've spent the entire day living in *your* world. It's your turn to experience some of mine. Your father's not here. Channel that part of you that hides romance novels under a loose plank in—"

Lucy's eyes widen, and she claps a hand over my mouth, shushing me. *"Audrey."*

I grin, peeling her hand away from my mouth and grabbing her other one, twirling her around until a laugh escapes her lips.

Slowly but surely, her shoulders begin to loosen, and a smile appears as we sway our hips and move our feet, twirling around the room in time with the beat.

And all at once, she isn't the prim-and-proper girl I pinned her to be, the image of the 1812 lady I've studied in history books or novels. Well . . . not *just* that. She's a girl who can play a melody a moment after she's heard it. She's a girl who hides romance books under floorboards. She's a girl who can dance to Whitney Houston when she stops feeling the weight of her father's expectations for half a freaking second. She's *real*.

She's so into it now, her eyes are closed, just feeling the music. I squeeze mine shut, and I'm here but suddenly I'm home in a way too. I'm dancing and giggling with Lucy, but I swear I can hear my mom's voice, *smell* her secret pizza sauce recipe, feel the rough living room carpet between my toes.

I guess, if I ever get back, if I ever find it in myself to leave home of my own accord instead of via a magical quarter, I'd have this to make me feel like Pittsburgh and my mom are never too far away, the safety of the corner shop and our little apartment found tucked within a song.

The music comes to an end, and Lucy and I collapse onto the sofa, breathless, grins plastered on our faces. I clutch my phone to my heart and glance over to see that her golden hair is once again shockingly still perfectly in place, while my entire face is coated with loose strands tumbling out of the updo Abigail wrangled together earlier today.

"Admit it," I say, nudging her in the side. "That was fun."

She smiles and shakes her head but then shoots me a side-eye. "Maybe a little."

Her eyes travel to an armchair in the corner, and almost immediately I watch her demeanor change, back straightening, hands smoothing her skirt, an invisible presence guiding her actions. "But it won't happen again."

I go to put my phone back in the bag, but as I do, I realize the screen is now completely dark, the battery fried.

"Shit," I mutter, sitting up and holding down the power button, a wave of anxiety washing over me, something about it making me feel well and truly stranded. "Yeah, it *definitely* won't."

No more cute background of Coop. No more Whitney Houston. No more old texts and voicemails. There's nothing to remember home with now except the memories in my head for however long I'm stuck here.

As I slide my now useless phone into the bag, my fingertips brush against the quarter sitting at the bottom, and I pull it out to gaze at it for what feels like the millionth time. But my brow furrows when I notice something unexpected. Something I somehow didn't notice in those million other gazes.

Underneath George Washington's head, there isn't a year. Instead it's two numbers: 24.

"Huh," I say aloud, holding it out to Lucy. "It should say the year here, but it doesn't."

"Twenty-four?" she asks, leaning forward to read it. "Does that number mean anything to you?"

I shake my head. "Not that I know of."

Frowning, I look down at the quarter, wondering what it could mean, wishing once again I could just pick up my now-dead phone and call the one person who could answer that.

CHAPTER 14

LUCY

June 16, 1812

That night, I lie on my back, my gaze following the flickering candlelight dancing on the ceiling of my bedchamber as Audrey begins to hum one of the songs from earlier, her eyes fixated on the quarter. Despite myself I hum along for a few bars. I can scarcely believe the events of the past two days, from finding Audrey in the field, to hearing about the future, to listening to music the rest of the world will not listen to for another *two centuries*.

It's wonderful, finally having a companion in this big, empty house. Someone to fill my final days of freedom.

Though, admittedly, after we danced together this afternoon, some part of me almost began to resent her presence here. Audrey seems to effortlessly pull me out of that neat little box I so carefully and dutifully tuck myself into, letting me just *be*. But every whisper of the future, every peculiar dance in the drawing room, every seemingly joyful minute she's here has an underlying sadness to it.

Because soon my father will return. Soon I will be married to Mr. Caldwell. Sooner still, maybe, Audrey may disappear without a trace. These are only fleeting tastes of a life I can never have, and I can't help but wonder if it will be worse knowing what might be possible in another place and time or never having experienced it at all.

I'm so lost in thought I don't realize she's stopped humming until I hear her voice. "Twenty-four hours in a day? Twenty-four things I have to do? Twenty-four . . . *what*?"

She lets out a frustrated sigh, hand hitting the mattress with a thud as she lowers the quarter. She's quiet for a long moment, eyes fixed on the ceiling before her head swings over to look at me like she's just remembered something. "Who's Mr. Caldwell? I can't believe you have a whole *fiancé* and didn't mention it!"

I grimace before I can stop myself. "I don't yet, but he's the gentleman my father wants me to marry. He owns a lavish estate not too far from here, in the next town over."

She laughs. "Okay, maybe you shouldn't *write* those romance novels you like so much if that's how you talk about the man you're going to marry. Do *you* like him? Is he hot?" Audrey asks as she rolls over, propping herself up on her arm, chin resting on her hand.

I look up, puzzled. "How should I know if he's warm?"

99

"No, I mean, like, *handsome*. Like Mr. Shepherd."

"Oh." I shake my head as Mr. Caldwell's bony stature and thin, pointed nose pop into my head. "Certainly not. In both appearance and personality, he is far from 'hot.' And he's quite a bit older than me."

"Ew. That's gross."

I silently agree with her, even though I know so many girls who've made similar matches.

"Why are you going to marry him if you don't even like him?"

I let out a huff of a laugh. "Because none of those things matter as much as duty, I suppose. Expectations. He is the richest man in the entire county, which means it will be an excellent alliance that will greatly improve my father's business prospects. It's just . . . how things are, Audrey. What we as women are expected to do. Marry well, try not to be a burden, bear sons who won't have to suffer the same reality. It's as simple as that."

I try to sound firm and resolute, not wanting to let on or admit how much I have struggled with accepting such things in the past.

"That's ridiculous," she says flatly. "In the future, where I'm from, most people marry for love. It doesn't always work out, and sometimes you get your heart pulverized, but *you* get to decide, not just a man."

Love.

It's like my mother's words are resurfacing just when I thought I had managed to bury them.

"Yes, well, I don't live in the future." I meet her dark eyes in the fading candlelight. "I live here. In 1812. Where things are *like this*. Besides, having my heart pulverized doesn't sound particularly tempting."

Audrey nods. "Yeah, well, you're right about that. Maybe that's a bit of a silver lining. In some weird way, you might be lucky you don't have to."

She lets out a long sigh, like she speaks from experience, and . . . despite what I said, it doesn't quite feel like a silver lining to me.

"Someone once told me that there's just as much of a downside in not putting yourself out there, because it guarantees you're going to miss out, but maybe there's a bit of a plus side to that if you get to miss out on the heartbreak." I watch as she frowns thoughtfully, considering what she's just said. Finally, she shakes her head, disagreeing. "But . . . not if you don't get to choose that for yourself. I mean, if you don't know what you're missing out on, you wouldn't even be able to know if the risk is worth it. Because sometimes, when you want something bad enough, the risk *is* worth it. You don't even care if you'll get hurt and it'll all crash and burn, because, well . . . maybe it won't. At least I used to believe that."

I wonder what that would be like.

To want something bad enough, love or otherwise, that you'd risk everything for it.

"Anyway," she says with a shrug, "I guess I just wish that . . . you didn't have to do this. That you could make that choice of what to risk or not risk for yourself."

I fall silent, because, deep down, past the accepted inevitability of it all, I suppose I wish I didn't either. I wonder what it would be like, what I would choose, if I *did* have a chance at love.

Would it be worth the risk?

Would I be brave enough if I can't even risk my father's ire over some books?

Truth be told, I don't know. And I never will.

We stare at each other for a long moment, neither of us speaking.

Finally, her eyes narrow thoughtfully. "I think . . . ," she starts. "I think one sip of a crisp McDonald's Sprite would kill you."

I sigh, having not the faintest idea as to what she is talking about. Still, it makes me feel . . . lighter. I suppress a laugh as the candle goes out with a barely audible hiss, and the room grows black around us.

CHAPTER 15

AUDREY

June 17, 1812

I wake up the next morning having, shockingly, slept straight through the night, and Lucy is the first thing I see when I finally peel my eyelids apart.

She's still fast asleep, face perfectly serene, close enough for me to notice the freckle just underneath her right eye through a few loose strands of her golden hair.

An unexpected urge to reach out and brush the strands away, to tuck them behind her ear, comes over me. My fingers curl out from my palm as I picture it.

Instead, I roll away from her and onto my back.

I'm getting way too weirdly comfortable in 1812.

Quietly slipping out of bed, I grab the bag Lucy gave me from off the floor, where it rests next to the heap of blankets I left behind that first night. I crawl back under the warm covers and pull out my phone, holding down the side button in the hopes that I will be graced by the heavens with a tiny spark of power. Just enough time to see one of my most recent photos and remind myself where I actually belong.

I picture my camera roll. Coop, sprawled out on his bed in the living room. My mom and dad laughing on the back deck when we went to get happy hour tacos at Round Corner Cantina just a few days ago. Even a screenshot about my upcoming portfolio deadline, LAST CHANCE TO SUBMIT in bold, black letters.

I mean, I've already given up hope on the RISD front, but it hits different that I literally *can't* submit a portfolio from 1812, even if I could magically make something new and fresh and *better* than what I've already submitted.

It's scary to think about how time is just ticking along, and pretty soon that deadline will pass right by, then prom, and graduation, and my birthday, and New Year's, and maybe even my entire life in the present. If I don't get back, there will be a gaping hole where I just . . . stopped existing.

Although, I guess, being here has made me realize that in a lot of ways I stopped existing after the breakup and the wait list. Working at the convenience store and going to school, the same thing over and over again. Sitting behind the cash register, watching my friends turn into acquaintances after they left for college, watching the drawings not come, watching life go on pretty much without me on the other side of the window.

If anything, this little trip has certainly yanked me pretty far out of that routine. And, in a lot of ways, it feels kind of nice. Making a new friend. Experiencing new people and perspectives and foods and clothes. I feel like I'm not on autopilot anymore.

But at least when I was bored I couldn't get hurt. Now I have no idea what will happen. A wave of nausea rolls over me as I think of my parents, too. How worried they must be, Dad asking every customer who comes into the shop, Mom making posters on that special-occasion pink printer paper she keeps in our hall closet.

I abandon my attempt to revive my phone and squeeze my eyes shut, trying not to spiral. Sliding my phone back into the bag, I grab the quarter from the nightstand, rolling it back and forth between my thumb and pointer finger, my eyes zeroing in on the number underneath George Washington's head.

Wait.

It doesn't say twenty-four anymore.

It says twenty-three.

It's almost like . . . *Oh my God.*

"A countdown!" I shout, throwing my pillow at Lucy. Her eyes fly open as she tumbles out of bed and onto the floor with a screech.

When her head pops up, her eyes are narrowed in a glare, one hand rubbing her elbow.

"Sorry," I say with a sheepish grin. She grumbles to herself as she slides back onto the bed, but her curiosity quickly gets the better of her.

"A countdown?" she echoes, and I hand her the quarter, showing her the number at the bottom.

"Yesterday it said twenty-four, right? But now . . ."

"Twenty-three," she says with a nod, rubbing her right eye sleepily, getting where I'm going. "So, what happens in twenty-three days? Surely it must mean that's when you'll go back home. Isn't that good news?"

"That, or it's how long I have to figure out why I was sent here. Maybe it means if I don't complete some task by then, I won't get to go back," I mutter. "But what would I have to do?"

I hesitate as I think back to two days ago for the hundredth time, the quarter falling into my palm, everything going black. The moments just before it and my conversation with Mr. Montgomery.

Giving up on my deadline, searching for artistic inspiration, "the real world," and Charlie, and . . .

Always thought you'd be with someone a little more . . . inspiring.

"Oh my God. Lucy." I grab ahold of her arm. "Remember that old guy I told you about? The one who comes into my parents' shop every morning? Mr. Montgomery? The day he sent me here, we were talking about taking risks and inspiration and *love*, just like we were talking about last night."

I pause as I take the quarter from her. "I think he thinks they're all connected. I think that's why he sent me here. To

106

get me out of my comfort zone. To force me to put myself out there again. He thinks if I do, I might find my true love, which will lead to finding my *true inspiration* again or something like that. So, for whatever reason, that person must be *here. Now.* In 1812."

Someone different from Charlie. To be fair, I don't think you can get much more different than *someone from 1812.*

"And you think maybe this countdown is how long you have to find him?" she asks.

"I . . . think so."

That's when I start to falter, remembering my thoughts from the other day. What happens when I do find them here? Do I just . . . get my heart broken all over again when I leave?

I let out a long sigh, realizing how all this must sound. "Does that, I don't know, seem ridiculous?"

She's quiet for a moment, processing.

"I suppose not. You were transported through time to the past, so 'ridiculous' is certainly not the first word that comes to mind for anything else regarding your situation," she says, and my eyes flick back down to the quarter.

"What do you think happens if I fail?" I whisper, thinking about Charlie, what exactly *finding love* looked like the first time. How it felt so much worse to lose it than how great it was to discover it.

"What if you succeed?" Lucy asks.

I look up at her to see the corner of her mouth ticking up,

a dimple appearing. "If anything, it sounds kind of . . . exciting. Like a romance book with the happy ending guaranteed." She scooches toward me on the bed. "You say this Mr. Montgomery cares for you. So he wouldn't want you to fail, would he? You trust him?"

I think about that curmudgeonly old man I've seen more mornings than I haven't. The one who's shown up for me so many times throughout my life. I've valued his opinion ever since I was a kid, and he's never steered me wrong yet.

I nod, slightly reassured. "Maybe not as much, since he sent me here without any warning. But yeah. I do trust him."

"Then it will all be fine. He must have sent you specifically two hundred years into the past because an opportunity for love is *here*. You get to take the leap, Audrey, but with all odds saying *you will succeed* even if we don't know how just yet. I mean, as someone set to marry Mr. Caldwell and *never* find love, I feel like you *have* to seize the storybook opportunity right in front of you! For both of us!"

When she phrases it like that . . . it kind of *does* feel exciting. I mean, he wouldn't have sent me here just to fall flat on my face.

I collapse back onto the bed, finally giggling with excitement. "I'm gonna have a little *Bridgerton* moment!"

Peeking over, I see that familiar frown of confusion.

"Don't ask."

• • •

After spending most of the morning getting dressed to not even leave the house, we head down to breakfast.

I will say one thing about 1812: the food has been pretty delicious.

My usual mug of Honey Nut Cheerios and a coffee from the store don't hold a candle to the tea, rolls, eggs, and *especially* the honey cake I've been greeted with the past two mornings.

Lucy's nose wrinkles as she looks up from her book and watches me practically inhale all of it. "If you are going to win the affections of a suitor, we are going to have to get you ready for society, instead of just hiding you away here. Etiquette, dancing, manners." She points a fork in my direction, her voice commanding. "Elbows off the table, back straight."

I do as she says, the corset helping pinch me into good posture. "You can be my teacher, right?" I say through a mouthful of food, and Lucy literally pales at the thought.

"Goodness. There is *so* much to learn. I mean, a dinner party alone!" Her eyes widen and gloss over as she thinks, placing the book down on the table. "The seating, the conversation, the use of utensils."

I laugh, and she raises her eyebrows at me. "Let's start with the laugh. *Softly.* Barely more than a smile. Just . . . polite and cheerful, inviting—"

"Okay, you can teach me which fork to use or how to dance or whatever, but *that* is ridiculous. I'm not going to be someone I'm not. Especially if I'm trying to find love."

She smiles into her teacup, shaking her head. "I guess I should not be surprised. Admittedly, I'm not sure the thought of *just being myself* has ever crossed my mind when it comes to being out in society." She lowers her voice as she slides the teacup back onto the saucer. "To be honest, I don't think anyone would even *want* me to be myself."

I open my mouth to say something, to tell her when she's the most open, the *most herself*, has been the Lucy I've liked the most, but she moves quickly on to what to do with a cloth napkin and cutlery basics, and the moment passes.

After breakfast we head to the drawing room, where Lucy teaches me the bottom-of-the-barrel basics. Who knew greeting people required a whole tutorial? There's no denying, though, that with an actual purpose and some direction for being here, learning how to curtsy for real instead of whatever the heck I did yesterday at Grace's is a little exciting.

"Feet in a V formation," she says, lifting her skirts gently so I can see and mirror her. "One leg out, then back, and then . . . dip."

She watches me, circling as I curtsy, again and again, my left quad getting *quite* the workout. "Make more of a sweeping motion as you move your leg back."

I sweep my leg back too fast and nearly knock Lucy's legs out from under her. Her hands quickly grab ahold of my waist to steady us both.

"*Slower. Gentler.* There is no need to race through it."

She stops in front of me as I dip, reaching out again so her fingertips glide along my cheek and her thumb gently tilts my head down. "Bow your head." She pulls her hand away as I do one more, head bowed, sweeping my leg slowly, butterflies filling my stomach over just *preparing* for this adventure.

"*Yes.* That was perfect, Audrey!"

I beam like the Steelers just won the Super Bowl.

Home and true love, here I come. I can practically taste that welcome-back bag of Doritos.

Lucy moves on to how to make a good first impression, the etiquette around greetings and expected propriety, but this topic is so mind-numbingly dull, I can see why movies turn this little moment into a montage. I wonder what song would be playing in the background of ours?

Martha pops her head in to check if we need anything as Lucy's in the midst of explaining what to say and *how* to say it.

"Martha," Lucy says. "What do you believe is sound advice for Audrey here on making a good first impression?"

"Well," she says with a snort, putting a hand on her hip. "I'd say not traipsing around in your undergarments and trousers is already an *excellent* start."

I laugh as Martha leans against the doorframe, listening while Lucy continues on.

"When you meet someone new, an introduction must occur. A gentleman should be introduced to a lady, and a person of lower rank should be introduced to a person of higher rank. The men who will court you may ask for an introduction through a mutual connection, and it is up to you to decide if you want to be introduced and make such an acquaintance."

"So I can, like . . . say no if I don't want to talk to him?"

"It may be considered impolite, especially if he is a man of circumstance, but yes. If you are not yet acquainted, you can say no to being introduced to him."

Martha chuckles from the doorway. "Say no all you want, dear," she says to me. "I know I certainly can think of a man I wish Lucy here wasn't acquainted with."

A knowing look passes between the two of them, and while I feel bad for Lucy, I feel at least slightly relieved that I won't be forced into a convo or a marriage with a Mr. Caldwell type. I can't help but wonder how many of them there are around here. That can't be what Mr. Montgomery wants for me.

Lucy glides over to the sofa, back to talking about how to properly take a seat and how to sit once seated, as leaning back and slouching are apparently punishable by death, and my eyes glaze over. My mind drifts as I think of the quarter, tucked into my bag upstairs.

"Audrey." Lucy's voice pulls me back to the drawing room, her brow furrowing as she looks up at me.

"Sorry, I was just . . ." I slide onto the sofa next to her, trying to mimic how her fingers curl into the fabric of her dress to keep it smooth. "Even if I can learn all this, what if I just . . . *can't* fall in love? What if I don't click with anyone? Or worse, what if I just . . . get it wrong?"

I keep the "again" to myself. I mean, I *thought* something was love before, and look where it got me.

She doesn't say anything for a long moment, her face thoughtful.

I like that about her, that she always takes her time, always seems to actually *think* about what you just said before responding.

"I don't know much on the subject, but it doesn't seem like something that can be forced."

"That's very true," Martha says, her gaze wistful. "All I can say is you'll know. You'll feel it, deep within you, without any doubts, because you'll feel so seen."

"Seen?" I ask, thinking of Charlie.

"No. That's not quite right." She shakes her head. *"Known."*

Known. A different word all at once changing everything.

She sniffs a little, a sad smile pulling at her lips. "Best go check on lunch," she says before toddling from the room.

Lucy turns back to me, blue eyes staring straight through me as she chews thoughtfully on her lip. "Maybe . . ." She hesitates. "Maybe you're right about being yourself a bit."

"Giving up teaching me already?"

"No, certainly not. I'm not saying I won't help prepare you, but I think for this to succeed, we need to find the person who cares more about *you* than the dances and the pleasantries."

"Is that even possible?" I snort.

"Certainly. There are plenty of eligible gentlemen who aren't terrible. You are already acquainted with one who didn't turn his nose up at a fumbled curtsy. Like you said, Mr. Shepherd was quite *hot.*"

I let out a loud laugh, the noise definitely bordering on impolite. "Sorry," I say, reaching a hand up to cover my mouth.

"Don't be. You have a lovely laugh." Lucy gives me a small smile, dimples appearing once more. "I suppose some rules are made to be broken."

CHAPTER 16

LUCY

June 18, 1812

I hide a smile in my cup of tea, watching as Miss Burton and her assistants finish up Audrey's measurements. We've brought a few of my mother's dresses to be altered, and seeing as Audrey is here to find love, it is only logical for her to get a gown for the upcoming ball at the Hawkins estate as well. Not only does it fall less than a week before the end of her countdown, but with the ball set to be the height of the social season, and my proposal, and likely many proposals, expected to follow it, it simply makes sense that it would be *the* night for Audrey to seal the deal.

It is overwhelmingly apparent, though, that she has *never* had this done before, and I watch her suppress a giggle as they measure from armpit to fingertip, her wide eyes locking with mine in the mirror. This task will quite possibly be a bit trickier than I thought.

"Will there be any issue with the gown being done in time?" I ask Miss Burton as she walks us out a few minutes later.

"Certainly not, Miss Sinclair. Certainly not. Although there will not be time for any alterations to be made."

"I am sure there will be no trouble at all," I say. I have never had an issue in all my time coming here. Every gown she has made me has always fit like a glove and turns out exactly as expected, if not exceedingly better.

"Your father's tab, I assume?" she asks, and I hesitate before nodding.

Audrey must notice because she whispers to me when Miss Burton turns her back, "This *is* okay, right?"

"By the end of the summer I'm going to marry a man who will make him infinitely richer than he already is, Audrey. I doubt he'll care about a couple of dresses and a ball gown."

I say it with more confidence than I feel. Especially with the future arrival of the lilac dress from my last trip to Miss Burton's.

But for once, I'm not sure I care.

And something about *saying it*, declaring it, gives me that missing confidence. I may not be able to find love, but I can help Audrey do it. And another small act of defiance against him, against everything, feels *incredible*.

As Audrey and I take our leave, the afternoon heat washes over our skin, and I feel an odd sense of deflation at the fact that we have to go back to Radcliffe now.

"Can we explore?" she asks as we head down the steps.

"You want to *explore*? Were you not just complaining about the lack of . . . ?"

"Air-conditioning," Audrey supplies.

". . . on the carriage ride here?"

She gives me a big smile, perhaps a few degrees warmer than the summer sun, and laces her arm through mine. *"Lucy."*

"I'm not supposed to wander in town," I admit, casting a quick glance down the cobblestone street. Especially when he is away, my father is very strict about me lingering. If someone were to report back to him, if we were to run into an acquaintance of his, run into *Mr. Caldwell* even, he would be very displeased. And despite how good it felt after the dresses, I don't know if I can push my luck any further.

His banker once told him in passing that he saw me in the circulating library when I was supposed to be two stores over, buying a new pair of silk gloves. After ransacking my room looking for what I had snuck back with, he locked me in our library during the daylight hours for an entire week as punishment, to read books of his careful curation and oversight.

"And I doubt you're supposed to buy a ball gown and get a closetful of dresses altered, but you just did," she says. "Come on. You said it yourself. You're getting married by the end of the summer. So, my time here is like . . . a monthlong bachelorette party."

"A . . . ?"

"Until I leave, you're going to *have fun*. Do everything you always wished you could that your father would *never* let you do. It's like you said, you're doing exactly what he wants for the rest of your life by marrying Mr. Caldwell, so he practically owes it to you to let you do exactly what *you* want while you still can!"

I stand there, frozen, on the cobblestone street, heart hammering noisily in my chest.

Can I do that? I think about years and years' worth of repercussions I've faced for wanting anything. Locked doors and my head shoved into etiquette books and my hands shaking from playing the same phrase on the piano for hours and hours on end.

But maybe now, since I'm giving him exactly what he wants, the marriage that he so deeply desires, the repercussions would be different. What is one small skirmish when he's won the entire war?

I meet Audrey's gaze, something in it stirring me forward. Telling me I *can*. That maybe more than him owing it to me, I owe it to myself. That these final few weeks, with her by my side, can perhaps be the most exciting of my entire life. All I have to do, like she said the other night, is be brave enough to take the risk.

"Well," I say, waving our carriage on to let the driver know we're not getting in right now. "I suppose we *should* try to socialize a bit. Give you some practice. Perhaps get an invitation to a dinner party or the like."

"*Yes,*" Audrey says, giving my arm a little squeeze. "That's what I'm talking about!"

We head off down the street, and I watch as she gazes in awe at everything, brought even more alive by the hustle and bustle of town. She seems almost . . . content, comfortable amid all the people. I'm reminded of the city she showed me on her device. Her home.

I wonder what it would be like to live somewhere like that. Tall buildings and busy streets and a sea of faces. What it would be like to have a *phone* of my own, and to sit in a car, and to watch things on the television.

It's completely impossible, yet, despite myself, I still feel a pang of desire to have such an experience, if only for an afternoon.

"What is a milliner's shop?" Audrey asks, bringing me back to the present.

"They sell an assortment of things. Mostly hats and bonnets. But also shawls, or fans, or gloves."

The questions continue from there as she stops to peek into the Blue Lion, a boisterous inn on the edge of town. I grab her hand to pull her away, since we *certainly* shouldn't be seen there. She studies every outfit and person that passes by. She points out the shop signs and how "cute" they are. And while she is doing that, I watch her and the people around her. Quite a few gentlemen pay her a great deal of attention, her enthusiasm and bright smile and rosy cheeks catching their eyes. I suspect her worries from earlier are entirely unfounded.

My heart falls at the conflicting thought that maybe she'll find someone *too* fast and be gone sooner than the countdown says.

As we pass the post office, Mr. Prewitt, Grace's father, comes hobbling out, an assortment of rather large packages cradled in his arms.

"Ahh! Miss Sinclair," he says, a smile appearing underneath his finely groomed mustache. "Such a pleasure to see you."

"Likewise, Mr. Prewitt," I say as I motion to Audrey and make the introduction of my new friend, secretly quite pleased my teaching has been effective when nothing she does indicates any impropriety.

"I know this will likely not be of interest to you, but I would love to see you both at the dance at the assembly room a week from today. Consider this your invitation, if you have not already been given one."

Audrey's grip tightens around my arm, an excited smile appearing on her face, while I think of all the dances I will have to teach her before then. Not to mention the fact that, as Mr. Prewitt implied, my father not only despises but looks down upon such dances. They're far less formal and more *public* than balls.

But it would be the perfect way for Audrey to dip her toe into the social scene and . . .

I want to go.

Which, for just these few weeks, counts for something.

"We would be *delighted* to attend, Mr. Prewitt."

"Excellent! I shall very much be looking forward to it," he says, one of his packages nearly tumbling from his arms.

"We won't take up any more of your time," I say as I pull out of Audrey's grip, giving him the space to clamber off toward his carriage, whatever valuables he is holding safely intact.

"Quite impossible, Miss Sinclair. It is always a pleasure!" he calls over his shoulder.

"How is your dancing?" I ask Audrey as we head off down the street, arms linking once again. Thinking of her rather exuberant but unflattering movements the other day in the drawing room, I add, "Your *formal dancing*, I mean."

"Uh . . ." She hesitates, which is rarely a good sign. "I do a *mean* 'Cotton Eye Joe' and 'Wobble' at the right wedding reception. *And* I started a conga line at my eighth-grade formal."

I cast a sideways glance at her sheepish smile, unsure what those dances are but quite positive they won't help us in this situation.

"As expected," I say, and she laughs. "This is going to be quite—"

"Is that Lucy Sinclair? Out and about in town?" a voice calls out. My heart stops with worry at who has caught me wandering. But when Audrey and I whirl around, I see—

"Alexander!"

My cousin scoops me up into a hug, spinning me around before my feet meet solid ground again. I reach up to brush some dust off his crisp red regimentals, fingertips grazing his wide, strong shoulders, pleased to see he is as handsome as ever. Only two years older than me, with rich black skin and warm umber eyes, he enchants everyone he meets with his lopsided, carefree smile. His aristocrat father married my mother's sister, and being the youngest of their sons, Alexander has *greatly* enjoyed the lack of responsibilities that comes with such a position. Joining the militia and exploring have suited him remarkably well. Yet despite how different our lives are, we have always kept a close correspondence through his many travels, so I am surprised I did not know he was in town.

"Miss Audrey Cameron, allow me to introduce you to my cousin, Colonel Alexander Finch."

He bows and flashes her his smile, long fingers reaching out to take her hand before bringing it to his lips, a kiss brushing gently across her knuckles. A faint blush climbs to her cheeks as he winks at her, adding, "A pleasure to make your acquaintance, Miss Cameron."

"Likewise," Audrey says, the smile she gives him making it abundantly clear she means it.

Ah, Alexander. Always the charmer.

"You should have written! Told me you were coming to town," I say.

"I was planning on calling on you first thing tomorrow. Thought it would be a bit of a surprise," he says.

I smirk at him skeptically, eyes narrowing, and he holds up his hands with a laugh. "I swear it!"

I swat at his hands, shaking my head. "Well, it certainly is good to see you." His face was the last one I would have expected to see today. "You are more than welcome to come stay at Radcliffe. We have plenty of space."

He snorts, motioning to the crowded streets around him. "Certainly not. I don't believe I can sleep without the hustle and bustle of town."

"I understand that," Audrey says.

"The busier the better," Alexander says, his attention turning back to her. "Are you from a city, Miss Cameron?"

"Yes. It's almost impossible to sleep out in the country. It's too—"

"Quiet," he finishes, while Audrey nods.

"Exactly."

"My ears start to ring!"

"Mine too! The whole night long."

I look between the two of them as they share a commiserating moment, tinged with, well, *possibility*. And, quite unexpectedly, I feel a small stab of jealousy.

Likely over the fact that I'll never have *that*. Never have a moment with someone else, charged with potential.

"Alexander, you must come to a dance at the assembly

room next week," I say, brushing the feeling quickly aside, and he nods.

"I would be honored to accompany you both," he says, as I expected he would. He's never one to turn down a dance.

"And Miss Cameron is staying with me up at Radcliffe," I say, since he also *never* turns down the opportunity to talk to a beautiful woman. "Feel free to come visit us whenever you please."

I watch as he smiles once more at Audrey, warm and lopsided and as charming as ever. "I *certainly* will."

The clawing, jealous feeling swims over me again, and I realize it may be harder than I first expected to watch Audrey have the chance to do the one thing, if I'm honest, I've always wanted to do.

Fall in love.

CHAPTER 17

AUDREY

June 19–21, 1812

I think I'm dying.

"Audrey. You already learned the cotillion. The Boulanger is the *easiest* one. It is a *circle* dance, for goodness'—"

I wave my arm from the floor where I'm lying to silence her, finally reaching a break point after the past three days of nonstop practicing. "Lucy. If I hear you hum another note, I am going to go to the dance at the assembly room in the clothes I got here in." I peek up at her to see her mouth slam shut, forming a thin line. "Sans jacket. Full shoulders and undergarments showing! *And* I'll ruin the plot of every good book published for the next fifty years. Jane Austen? Louisa May Alcott? The Brontë sisters? *Ruined.* You'll curse my name until the day you die! So you might as well join me."

Lucy lets out an aggravated sigh before awkwardly managing to sit down on the floor next to my sprawled-out body.

"Don't sit on the floor a lot?" I ask her.

"Uh, never," she says, her posture freakishly straight. "At least not until you arrived."

I tug on the back of her blue floral dress until she lies back on the ornate carpet next to me and both of us are looking up at the crystal chandelier and crown molding swirling along the perimeter of the ceiling.

"Not to seem impolite, but . . ." Lucy looks over at me, eyebrows rising. "You don't play the pianoforte. Your dancing is, well . . ."

"Also awful?"

We both grin, Lucy nodding affirmatively. "What do you *do* in the present? What are you good at?"

I let out a long sigh, turning my attention back to the chandelier, seeing the blank canvas of the white ceiling just behind it. "I love to draw. I always have, ever since I was a kid with a pack of Crayola crayons. It's my favorite thing. Well . . ." I pause as Charlie's hideous mustache pops onto the blank canvas in my head, the wait-list letter following just behind it. The two had been linked from the very beginning to the bitter end. "I guess it *used* to be."

I turn my head to meet her bright blue eyes, the already familiar lines of her delicate nose, arching eyebrows, golden strands of hair greeting me. "I really wanted to go to art school. Spend my days studying composition, color theory, and *history*. Try new styles and really figure out my own, instead of what

126

other people told me it should be. Fill sketchbooks and canvases, stay up late to finish passion projects. Just . . . well . . . *all of it.*"

"And you were set to go? Back home?"

"No, I . . ." I pause, my voice trailing off, but I force myself to admit the truth. "I was wait-listed. Which means . . . they deferred the decision about accepting me until I showed them more art pieces. Then they would reject or accept me based on those. But . . . I couldn't find the inspiration to draw anything else. Not anything at all."

"Music, art . . . it can be like that sometimes," she says, nodding. "It ebbs and flows. Sometimes I can't bring myself to sit at the piano, and other times I can't be pulled away."

I snort. "It's never ebbed like this before."

"That doesn't mean it won't flow again," she says. "So I guess the question is, what do you think is stopping you?"

"I guess I'm afraid of getting rejected again," I admit. "I need to do something better, more confident and *me* if they're going to take me off the wait list, but I don't know what that means, so I never know where to start. And at least if I don't submit, it's my choice, not theirs."

"But do you still want it?"

"I . . ." I hesitate, debating between what I've been telling myself and, well . . . the truth.

"Be honest," she says, a wry smile pulling at her lips, those blue eyes seeing more than they should.

"I still want it," I say, realizing how much I mean it. Deep down I know that however much I try to hide it, try to tell my mom I don't want it, I can't snuff the dream out just yet.

"We'll get you back," Lucy says, voice sincere.

The fabric of her dress crinkles against the carpet as she reaches out, soft fingertips lightly tapping the back of my hand.

"Hey," I say, twisting my wrist around so they fall into my palm. "We should do something fun. I mean, you've helped me so much since I crash-landed here, I just feel like we gotta do something for you. Some bachelorette month bucket-list item."

She gives me an amused look. "Dancing *is* meant to be fun."

"No, I mean like something else. Something *you* really want to do."

"Audrey." Her fingers tighten around mine. "The dance is in *four* days. You still have much to learn, and I am *far* from a legitimate dance instru—"

"*Lucy,*" I say as I sit up, pulling her with me. "Come on. It's a beautiful day out, and as helpful as this is, I don't want you just spending your last days of freedom helping me count the steps to a cotillion and teaching me how to hold a teacup, okay? We've been working on this since breakfast! I mean, what else do we usually do in the afternoons? You play the piano while I complain about being bored on the couch? The birds are chirping. The sun is shining. . . ."

"Okay, okay!" She lets out a long sigh and shoots me a side-eye. "You are a terrible influence."

"Maybe just a bit."

Her gaze travels past me to the window, to the blue sky on the other side, face thoughtful. "We could go to the stables? Horseback riding might be fun. Plus, it *is* a good skill for a young lady to have."

The words are barely out of her mouth before I am jumping up to my feet. "Oh, heck yes."

Being from the city, the only horse I've ever seen up close and personal was at my rich cousin Christopher's eleventh birthday party out in Sewickley. Although we did less horseback riding and more giggling over the fact that the horse had a boner.

Lucy fetches— *Fetches?* God, she's rubbing off on me. Lucy *gets* a fitted jacket and a matching hat from her room, because of course she does, but she also squishes a bonnet on my head before we head out the front door.

I peer up at it with a grimace. *"Really?"*

She gives me a look. "What? It will help keep the sun out of your eyes."

We head out of the courtyard and across the field toward the stables, the feeling of the afternoon breeze on my face *extremely* nice after being trapped in the stuffy indoors dancing since after breakfast.

I swat a gnat away as we enter, the smell of hay and leather and horses filling my nose immediately. I look around eagerly as we walk along the wooden stalls until Lucy stops at a white horse, her hand patting its strong side as it gives her a familiar whinny.

"This is Henry."

I reach out a tentative hand and stroke his side nervously. "Hi, Henry."

"Our stable boy, James, will probably suggest you ride—"

The words are barely out of her mouth before the door swings open, and a guy looking like Westley from *The Princess Bride* walks in with a saddle slung over his shoulder.

He tosses his golden hair out of his face, everything moving in slow motion as a choir of angels sings from the heavens, praising God for his impeccable handiwork.

"Jesus Christ," I murmur, and Lucy shoots me an amused look.

"Miss Sinclair," he says with a bow. "Need me to get Henry saddled for you?"

"Yes, thank you. And a horse for my acquaintance, Miss Cameron, if you please, James."

James smiles at me, and *cue the damn wedding bells*, what a smile it is, straight teeth below sparkling eyes. He walks past us to a black horse, covered in patches of white, standing in the very last stall.

I follow him and watch his gloved hands reach out to ruffle the horse's dark mane. "This is Moby."

Moby nips at my bonnet, ripping it off my head before spitting it onto the stable floor.

I narrow my eyes at him.

He narrows his eyes at me.

After a solid fifteen seconds, I look away and grin at James. "I love him."

"It's improper for a lady not to ride sidesaddle," Lucy hisses at me a few minutes later as we stand in the tall grass outside the stable. I wave her away, getting ready to somehow launch myself onto Moby.

"Lucy, you *just* said you've always wanted to ride astride."

"But that doesn't mean I *should*," she says, and I turn back to put my hands on her shoulders.

"Exactly! This whole month is about *not* doing what you should and instead doing what you *want*," I say. "Besides, it's not like we're going to be riding through town or doing donuts across Mr. Caldwell's front lawn. Who's going to see?"

Her eyes flick behind me to James, who shrugs, giving her a rueful grin as he finishes putting a regular saddle on Henry. "I won't tell if you won't."

She bites her lip before I spin her around, pushing her forward so James can help her onto her horse. She looks annoyed as she clutches the reins, but there's no denying that the glare she shoots me is *definitely* half-hearted.

With Lucy set, James offers me a gloved hand of assistance, and I try to play it cool, putting a foot in a stirrup and attempting to swing my way up on my own. After nearly face-planting on the second attempt, James leans in, hands hovering over my waist.

"May I?" he asks.

I nod, or maybe swoon, and he, in all his Greek god, muscled glory, *lifts* me onto the saddle like I'm as fragile and delicate as a Dorito chip.

"Thank you," I say, collecting myself.

He dips his head, eyes crinkling at the corners.

Lucy rides over, her shoulders slowly relaxing as she makes a graceful loop around me, one and then another, clearly suppressing a laugh as James heads back to the stables.

"Shall we go over the basics, or do you just want to ogle James for a few more moments?"

"Ogle," I say without hesitation.

She snorts and begins the lesson anyway. We go over how to hold the reins, how to be steady in the saddle, how to make Moby move, turn, and trot, until the two of us are moving in small circles.

"And how do you make him stop—"

The words are barely out of my mouth before Moby launches across the vast field of grass at a full gallop, the world blurring around me as I hold on to his neck and try not to die, screaming my head off.

"Moby! What the fuuuck!" I yell into the wind, while Moby is having the time of his damn life, his thick, strong legs practically a blur underneath me.

"The reins, Audrey!" Lucy calls from somewhere behind me. "Pull back on the reins!"

I squint down to see the leather reins flapping in the wind and tentatively take a hand from around Moby's neck to snatch hold of them and tug back hard.

Moby, thankfully, slows to a trot and then a stop, whinnying with displeasure while I catch my breath.

"Are you all right?" Lucy asks, visibly disheveled for maybe the first time since I arrived here, her hat tipping off her head, strands of hair blowing around her face.

I nod, heart hammering in my chest. "That was"—I let out a long exhale of air—"*incredible!* Oh my gosh, did you see how *fast* I was going? Moby, you crazy son of a bitch."

I reach down and pat his heaving side, Moby neighing in agreement.

Lucy shakes her head and fixes her hat, clearly done with both of us. But then, surprising me for the hundredth time since I arrived, she cracks a small smile. "I've never ridden that fast before. It was . . . kind of fun."

"Then maybe we should do it again," I say, urging Moby forward. Lucy laughs and surges ahead of me until the two of us are flying across the grounds of Radcliffe as the sun coats everything in a warm, buttery glow. I pull even with her as we finally slow down and enter into a small forest, just past a pond she says her father apparently enjoys fishing from. Together, we follow the overgrown, winding path through the trees, able to talk again.

"Do you ride often?" I ask.

"Not as much as I'd like," Lucy says as she glances over her shoulder, face framed in the sunlight trickling through the branches around us. "Sadly, it's more a sign of . . . 'genteel upbringing,' for ladies in company, not a leisure activity. There are a lot of things I was forced to take lessons in when I was young to be deemed an 'accomplished woman,' but I'm not supposed to use them to actually accomplish anything."

I nod, learning more and more how many things she does because she is expected to but also how much she's restricted from actually enjoying them.

"I always try to when my father is gone, though."

"What else do you usually do when he is gone?"

"Read. Visit Grace's. Go on long walks. Slouch when I sit," she says, giving me a teasing smile. "Nothing even remotely as interesting or exciting as what we've done the past few days."

"Well, we'll definitely have to add to that list, then."

With dinnertime quickly approaching, we exit the forest and ride back to the stable, the enormous house looming in the distance. As we go, I find myself wanting to know what other secret things she wants. Who Lucy is underneath, well . . .

All of this.

James helps me down off the horse, but my thoughts are too filled with Lucy's situation to fully enjoy his arm muscles this time. I let out a surprised gasp when I practically collapse onto the ground after he lets go, my legs feeling like jelly after riding Moby for an hour.

"Are you quite all right?" Lucy asks, offering me a supportive arm as we head back toward the house.

I make a dramatic show of clutching her arm. "No, I think I'm quite unwell. . . ."

Then I grab Lucy's hat from her head and start sprint-limping as fast as I can across the grassy field, giggling maniacally.

"Audrey!" She laughs as she runs after me.

Just as we enter the courtyard, I feel her fingers finally wrap around my arm. She pulls me to a stop, and I turn to face her. Our chests are heaving, but her eyes dance around my face, the color softer in the fading light. And for the first time since I've arrived, she's completely unguarded. Open. And it's . . . beautiful. The word takes me by surprise, and I feel the air catch in my lungs before Lucy swipes her hat back and looks away, brushing past me.

"Come along. Martha will be wondering where we are," she says, returning to duty and obligation mode, the walls sliding up as quickly as they came down.

Sure enough, the door swings open before we can even push inside, Martha's sweet, cheery face greeting us.

"Lucy," she says, holding up an envelope. "An invitation

for a dinner party tomorrow evening has arrived. From Mr. Shepherd. At his estate."

"See, I told you you'd have no trouble, Audrey," Lucy says. She takes the envelope and leans against the doorframe, flicking it open to read the message inside.

For a brief moment I'd somehow almost forgotten about my quest to get home. Now . . . *a dinner party*? Talk about fancy. With Charlie, the fanciest thing we did was a movie date, complete with swiped candy and chips from the store. Or, like, coffee and painting in Frick Park? Maybe a Pirates game in the nosebleed seats if we wanted to spice things up a bit.

"A dinner party?" I start. "Am I really ready for—"

"More than ready," she insists, with enough confidence for both of us. "Martha, please send a messenger confirming our attendance."

Lucy holds the letter out to me with an amused grin. "Wouldn't want to keep the handsome Mr. Shepherd waiting."

CHAPTER 18

LUCY

June 22, 1812

I watch Audrey gaze out the carriage window, face pressed up against the glass as she stares, mouth agape, at Mr. Shepherd's estate.

She lets out a low whistle and shakes her head, sitting back in her seat. "If this were an episode of *The Bachelor*, he would definitely be getting the first impression rose."

As always, I haven't the faintest idea what that means.

With far more decorum, I peer out the window myself as the carriage slows to a stop and take in the stone columns, wide windows, and beautiful ivy creeping up the sides of the house, all illuminated by glowing lanterns.

Whitton Park is *quite* beautiful, but it is nothing I have not seen before, a hundred times over. And will see a hundred times more than this.

I know that is a privilege, but I wonder what it would be

like to feel so . . . in *awe* of a place, like Audrey is. To travel far enough to be filled with wonder by what I behold.

We are helped out of the carriage and led inside to the drawing room. Audrey tilts her head back, gaping at the high ceiling of the entryway, intricate floral wallpaper giving way to finely crafted molding.

I tap her shoulder to bring her back down to earth as the housekeeper opens the drawing room door, allowing the sounds of voices and laughter to greet us.

"Miss Sinclair, Miss Cameron," Mr. Shepherd says, coming over to us, as impeccably dressed as he was the first time we met but this time in a handsome black jacket and a blue floral cravat. The shade is once again identical to his eyes, which are now focused on the young lady next to me. "So lovely to see you both once more."

"Thank you so much for the invitation, Mr. Shepherd," I say as we both curtsy. Audrey nods in agreement, and a pleased smile appears on his face.

"Of course, of course. It's my pleasure."

But that's the moment my pleasure ends. I look past him, and a chill goes up my body as I see none other than Mr. Caldwell lounging against the fireplace in his usual dreary black attire. He gives me a rather toothy, unpleasant grin, and I quickly pull my eyes away, finding Grace seated in an armchair with a sour expression on her face, Simon standing just behind her.

She mouths an apology before her lips turn back down at the corners, indicating she's also not thrilled by his presence. Like my father, Mr. Caldwell treats Simon and Grace like they are beneath him.

Audrey and I are introduced to the other guests. A Mr. and Mrs. Barnes, who I saw in passing at a dance or two last season, and a Mr. Jennings and a Mr. Swinton, two more friends of Mr. Shepherd's and Simon's from university, one tall with a shock of orange hair, the other stocky and already balding.

I am about to make a beeline for the safety of the chairs next to Grace and Simon, when Mr. Caldwell swoops in.

"So delightful to see you here, Miss Sinclair," he says with a sharp bow, his eyes appraising me almost improperly, as if I already belong to him. I sicken at the thought that perhaps, on some level, I do. "And in such a *lovely* dress. Though, I will admit, I believe that peach dress from our last meeting was far more flattering, don't you think?"

No, I want to say, despising the way it looks with my skin tone. *I prefer this sage green.*

I feel Audrey tense next to me as well, her eyes narrowing as she catches the thinly veiled judgment he has just bestowed upon me. I reach quickly out to grab ahold of her arm before she can offend him in return, as I can feel her wanting to, and breeze past the insult.

"Mr. Caldwell, allow me to introduce you to my good friend Miss Audrey Cameron."

Audrey curtsies, giving him a thin-lipped smile. "A pleasure, Mr. Caldwell. You seem to be just as charming as people say you are."

I suppress a laugh as Mr. Caldwell adjusts his jacket proudly, the comment going completely over his head, since he naturally considers himself to be worthy of it.

Thankfully, the dinner bell rings before he can bother to give it much more thought. He plasters a pompous grin on his face as we all stand and make our way to the dining room.

It's remarkable how much a large fortune can compensate for.

And how no amount of money can buy you common sense or decency.

The dinner is exceedingly decadent, from soups and jellies to meat and puddings, each course more delicious than the last and all served on beautiful blue-and-white-stamped plates. Mr. Shepherd has greatly outdone himself in an attempt to ingratiate himself to north England society.

I keep a watchful eye on Audrey for the first half but find myself most impressed at how much she has learned in a short time. When she doesn't know or is unsure about something, I see her hold back and observe. Which utensil to use when, how to eat certain dishes, even when and how to speak.

And, if anything, something about the timidity of this makes her seem more modest and polite than I've ever seen her.

It makes me feel . . . I don't know. I'm glad, of course, that she's doing so well, but it also seems wrong, almost sad to see such a muted version of the vibrant person I have come to know.

"Miss Cameron, am I to understand you are from America?" Mr. Jennings asks, dabbing at his mouth with a cloth napkin.

"Yes," Audrey says as she carefully sets her cutlery down. "Born and raised."

"What state?"

"Pennsylvania."

"Pennsylvania!" he says excitedly. "I spent some time in Philadelphia just last year."

Audrey glows slightly at his enthusiasm. "Did you ever make it as far west as Pittsburgh?"

"I did not! A real manufacturing city." His eyes flick to Mr. Shepherd. "My friend here has never been to the States, even though his family has done a great deal of business there. Can you believe it?"

"I cannot," Audrey says, sending a smile over the candlesticks to Mr. Shepherd, who returns it wholeheartedly.

"Eh, perhaps I'll be lured there after all, Jennings," he says.

I'm surprised to find here as well that while things are moving exactly as expected . . . I don't feel happy the way I expected to.

Maybe because I'm the only one who sees how stilted her smile is.

Mr. Caldwell, unable to smell even a hint of romance in the air over the scent of the venison, decides to change the subject to shipping delays in the North Atlantic and the tax hikes on imports, effectively shutting us ladies out of the conversation until we return to the drawing room for tea.

Still, spurred on by Audrey's efforts, I decide to try to . . . I don't know . . . *flirt* with Mr. Caldwell to see if maybe, shockingly, there can be some sort of connection between the two of us. Perhaps there is a side to him I have yet to see.

My hand slides into his offered arm as we walk down the hall, and I even offer a polite smile to him.

"Have you traveled to America, Mr. Caldwell?"

"Once." He snorts. "An egregious waste of time, I assure you. You certainly wouldn't warm to it."

"Right, surely I would not." Though I can't see how he could determine that, I press on. "Have you traveled anywhere you *were* fond of?"

"Not particularly. Paris was nice enough, but I much prefer London or here, in the country."

I try to push past the sinking feeling over the fact that I will never have a chance to travel and see the world, something I had considered a possible source of solace, and continue on. "And would you—"

"So many questions," he remarks. "I thought you to be more modest."

I color at his words and clamp my mouth shut as we enter

the drawing room. I slide my hand out of his arm, words I can never say filling my head as I try to collect myself. Audrey, Grace, and I sit down on the sofa, and Audrey shoots a questioning glance in my direction, which I promptly ignore.

I feel almost foolish for having even tried to find a connection with such a terrible man.

Grace brings up the dance at the assembly room this upcoming weekend, sending the whole room buzzing while my fingers curl into my skirt.

"I'm really looking forward to it," Audrey says.

"Well, *we* would never be found in attendance, would we, Miss Sinclair?" Mr. Caldwell snorts loudly from the armchair by the fire in an attempt to draw a distinction between the two of us and Grace and Simon, his eyes flicking to Mr. Shepherd for an unspoken agreement, which is not returned in the slightest. "A country dance? *Quite* beneath us."

We.

Us.

Like we are already wed. My stomach churns at the thought.

"I'm going to have to disagree with you," Mr. Shepherd says, saving me from responding when I'm at a complete loss for words. He squares his shoulders proudly, chin high. "They can be quite enjoyable. I know I certainly have every intention of going. Happily so, as such delightful company has just confirmed their attendance."

He smiles at Audrey, but I'm more focused on the floundering look on Mr. Caldwell's bony face, feeling a certain kind of justice as I sip my tea. His blue eyes are rounder than a full moon, bushy eyebrows for once not casting a shadow over them.

Simon hastily suggests a game of cards, and everyone but Mr. Caldwell seems eager to play a few rounds of loo.

As we slide into seats around a table, I move immediately to explain the rules to Audrey, to tell her how three cards will be dealt to her, how the trump card will be turned up, what the winning combinations are, how it is almost entirely a game of luck, but . . . I see Mr. Shepherd has already taken my spot. Their heads are pressed closely together as he gestures toward the table.

I look away as the cards are dealt, the winning hand in front of me helping to push aside the return of the clawing feeling of jealousy I first experienced in town.

"Flush," I say, laying down my cards before the hand is even played, a technicality that allows me to win automatically, the entire pile of chips in the center of the table mine and mine alone.

"Well done, Lucy!" Grace says, and Mr. Shepherd nods heartily in agreement. As he leans closer to Audrey to explain what just happened, the feeling swims right back into my stomach.

The game continues on, round after round, and the room

comes alive, voices growing louder, cravats loosened. With a little bit of sherry, even the feeling dulls.

"Harding, do you remember that time at school when a third-year rode a horse through the dining hall?" Mr. Swinton asks Simon, before delving into an uproarious story about a disgruntled duke who wanted to spend his fortune traveling and doing as he pleased, so he saddled up in an attempt to get expelled and be given the freedom to do so.

"Can't say I entirely blame him," Mr. Jennings says, and a few of us laugh in agreement.

Can't say I blame him, indeed.

We don't leave until late into the night, after Audrey manages to beat us all with an impressive display of beginner's luck. When we finally stand to go, Mr. Shepherd walks us to the door, his gaze lingering yet again on Audrey as we climb slowly down the steps. It is beyond apparent he is *quite* smitten already.

I find myself stifling a yawn as we make our way toward the carriage, but my drowsy haze is broken when Mr. Caldwell clears his throat from behind us.

"Miss Sinclair," he squeaks out. I take a deep breath, collecting myself before turning to face him. "I would like to extend an invitation to you for dinner at my estate sometime in the coming week. I'll have to check my *rather* busy schedule, but I will let you know when you are expected."

My father had told me to anticipate something like this in his long list of expectations the morning of his departure. I thought invitations came with a choice, but apparently not.

I offer him a forced smile and a curtsy. "It would be my pleasure."

My father would be ecstatic with this performance.

"For just . . . *you*," he makes clear, turning his nose up and making no effort to hide his distaste for Audrey, though she has mostly behaved perfectly the entire night, except for one moment where she let an expletive slip out on a losing hand, everyone but him finding it amusing.

I bite my cheek to stop from saying something, afraid of what threatens to spill from between my lips. What an influence Audrey has had on me in just a few short days. These impulses, while I would never *act* on them, are certainly new and unusual.

"Good night, Mr. Caldwell," I manage to get out, remaining perfectly cordial as he helps me into the carriage, where Audrey is already waiting.

I slide onto the seat next to her carefully, looking over to see her roll her eyes, arms crossed over her chest. We are barely down the drive before she makes her opinion known.

"Well, he's a total asshat."

All at once, the Audrey I've grown so fond of returns. No more stilted smiles and cautious movements.

I laugh and shake my head, not knowing exactly what

"asshat" means, but able to surmise she is not wrong.

"He is . . ." I lower my voice before I complete my thought. "Exceedingly unpleasant."

It's exhilarating. Saying how I feel, admitting it out loud, instead of letting it eat slowly away at me.

Audrey snorts. "That's putting it mildly." She turns her head to look at me, eyes dark as the moonlight casts shadows across her face. "And while *I* didn't see your peach dress, I happen to think this one looks incredible on you."

My cheeks warm unexpectedly, and I look away, smoothing out my dress with my hands. "Thank you."

We fall silent, save for the sound of the horses' hooves on the gravel outside the carriage, the rolling crunch of the wheels.

"So," I say finally, "Mr. Shepherd seems to be *quite* taken with you."

"Does he?" she asks, her face thoughtful as she considers this. "He's nice, and *such* a gentleman, nothing like the frat boys 2023 has to offer. And his house is just . . ." Her voice trails off, and she shakes her head, eyes wide with admiration over Whitton Park. "But . . . I don't know."

"What don't you know?"

"I feel like . . ." She lets out a long exhale of air. "I feel like I'm just waiting for that *spark*, you know what I mean?"

I frown at her and shake my head. "I don't."

She reaches out and takes my hand, leaning toward me. "Like that *feeling*, Lucy. Chemistry. Magic. *Attraction*."

Ah. Like in the books tucked under the floorboards in the library, an experience I've read about but never felt.

I look into her eyes, long eyelashes casting a shadow on her rosy cheeks as she says, "I don't know. . . . You just know when you feel it."

It must be simply the power of suggestion, but at her words it's like I *do* feel it. From the tips of her fingers in my palm, a sparkling, warm, *fiery* feeling slowly burns its way up the length of my arm until my entire body is ablaze. My eyes flick down to her lips, so close to mine, and a pull I have never experienced before consumes my every thought, my every fiber until—

I rip my hand out of hers, laughing as I clutch it to my chest, heart hammering unsteadily beneath my palm. I turn my gaze out the window and shake my head. "You're ridiculous. A spark, Audrey? How impractical."

"Must be a future thing." Audrey laughs, completely unfazed, while I feel entirely off-kilter, certain it is not just a future thing.

My ears ring as the carriage falls silent once again. One minute. Two minutes.

Still, my heart hardly slows. I can *feel* her just next to me.

"It's more than just the spark problem, Lucy. I can't shake wondering even if I *do* actually fall in love with Mr. Shepherd or someone else if . . . if I'll be stuck here, rather than getting to go home," Audrey says, her voice soft, quiet.

Selfishly, there's a part of me that hopes she will be. That hopes she won't leave.

"If they love you," I say instead. "If they knew of the opportunities you could have in the future, the freedom you could have in the future that you can't have here . . . Maybe somehow they could go to the future with you. Your Mr. Montgomery must have a plan for that."

For the first, terrifying time, no matter how entirely impossible, I wonder what it would be like if that person, the person that Audrey loved, was . . . *me*.

But I push the thought from my head as quickly as it came.

CHAPTER 19

AUDREY

June 23, 1812

I lie on my back on the drawing room sofa after lunch, rolling the quarter around my pointer finger and my thumb.

Seventeen days left.

I've already been here over a week. The ball is ticking closer and closer and . . .

I don't know if I'm any closer to finding love or even farther from it.

Or if I even *want* to fall in love if there's the tiniest risk it means staying here without my family.

I mean, there's no shortage of eligible bachelors in 1812. Compared to the dudes at my high school, it's a pretty stark improvement.

There's Mr. Shepherd: rich, probably buys you flowers "just because," eyes the color of a cloudless sky on a perfect spring morning.

Alexander: adventurous, a city boy, well traveled, could charm the habit off a nun.

James: arms to die for, face that could start wars . . . Did I mention his arms already?

All of them are so different. Prince Charming, the swoony adventurer, the rugged outdoorsman.

But . . . no spark. With Charlie, it was just *there*, practically all at once.

I remember the day we met at the art program at RISD. I had been so excited for class that I'd forgotten my pencils back at my room, and he was the lanky brown-haired boy next to me noticing me digging around in my bag when the teacher told us to take them out.

"Forget yours?" he'd asked with a shy smile before sliding over an extra pack. "I accidentally bought two." His cheeks turned bright red when I beamed back at him.

After we were done for the day, I tried to just return them, but he asked me if I wanted to hang out instead. We sat down on a patch of grass, sketching and talking until the sun set. He'd tell me to add more texture to my old man, while I told him to add more shading to his tree, a steady rhythm forming until our drawings were done, made all the better together.

"I've always wanted to go here," I told him. "To art school."

He nodded, holding out an earbud, my favorite Phoebe Bridgers song playing. "Me too."

It was so normal, such an ordinary moment, but I swear you heard the air crackle when I took it from him, our fingers brushing together.

But how can someone in 1812 see me enough to create a spark like that when I have to pretend to be practically someone else entirely? Someone from this time. Someone hidden behind pleasantries and formalities. I know Lucy said I should try to be myself a bit, but it feels almost impossible. I feel like with each day that passes, I'm left with more questions and uncertainties than answers.

The door creaks open, interrupting my late-afternoon spiraling, and Lucy comes in, wearing a simple off-white dress, an arm hidden behind her back.

"I have a gift for you," she says.

"A one-way ticket back to Pittsburgh? A batch of Martha's finest smelling salts?" I ask, grinning and sitting up with a loud groan as she crosses the room and sits down on the sofa next to me.

"No." She laughs, and before I can make another ridiculous guess, she reveals a large sketchbook and some pencils with twine wrapped around them in a little bow.

My heart somehow leaps and sinks at the same time.

"You got me art supplies?" I say as I take them from her, touched.

"I thought . . . I don't know . . ." The usually so composed Lucy turns a deep crimson, more flustered than I've ever seen her. "You are *always* complaining about being bored, and I just thought that perhaps maybe—"

"Lucy," I say, putting a hand on her arm to stop her nervous babbling. "Thank you. If my face fell, it wasn't because of you or the art supplies. It's just . . . like I told you, I haven't been able to draw for months. It's like I'm blocked, and I can't get unblocked. I don't want you to waste them on me."

She smiles in relief, her whole face lighting up, eyes crinkling at the corners and dimples appearing. "If you can go to a dinner party and tea at Grace's and *travel back in time*, I can assure you that you've overcome worse than a blank page. A lot has happened since you last picked up a pencil. Maybe don't put so much pressure on yourself to draw for what you don't have and focus on what you do. I know there have been plenty of times I've secretly dreamed of going to a conservatory, of being a real musician, however impossible it may be. But what I do have is *this*." She motions to the piano. "Being able to play and create for myself, that's what matters most. So just do it for yourself, Audrey. And don't be critical about what you put on the page. Do it because you love art, just like I play because I love music. That's enough."

That's enough.

And, well . . . it feels like it could be.

"All right." I shrug, letting out a long exhale of air. "Here goes nothing."

I open the sketchbook as she crosses the room to the piano, sliding onto the bench. I pull out a graphite pencil, pressing

153

the tip onto the paper, expecting to still see that blank page in my head and . . .

I don't know.

Sitting in a drawing room in 1812, two hundred years in the past, drawing should feel more impossible than ever, but when I look at Lucy, the afternoon light is already painting her like a picture. I watch her at the piano, and it feels like the past few days—no, the past few *months*—of searching and waiting, fingertips twitching in my palm but leaving only blank pages devoid of inspiration, have all led to this. Like, with her words, the weight of the expectations and stakes have lifted, making it just . . . *this*. What it's always been.

Me, with a pencil in my hand.

I draw one line. And then, without thinking, I draw another. Slowly my lines turn into shapes, as everything around me stills and quiets.

I draw about a dozen figures, not stopping to critique a single stroke, until the page in front of me is *covered* in sketches.

Arched eyebrows.

Wisps of golden hair.

Sharp collarbones.

The same heart-shaped face, the same curved lips, the same long, elegant neck.

Lucy.

Over and over and over.

And looking at them, I feel it again.

Inspiration? I frown, shaking my head. *More than that.*

Like I'm able to finally give a part of myself, able to open myself up and pour it out onto the page in front of me, allowing it to become an extension of my thoughts, my feelings, my wants, my desires.

Passion. That's what was missing. Maybe for even longer than I realized. Maybe that's where my portfolio fell short. Because I was just doing the art I thought I should be doing, the art Charlie insisted was more important, abstract and modern and empty, instead of the art I wanted to be doing. Capturing real people, showing the parts of them they don't think anyone sees.

I hardly realize when the piano stops or that Lucy is talking to me until I finally notice that the lips I'm trying to draw are moving.

I shake my head, coming back to the drawing room.

"What?"

"I asked you how it is going." She motions to the page in front of me but politely doesn't crane her neck to peek. I lift my hand, the side splotched gray with graphite.

I cross the room and slide onto the bench next to her, hesitating nervously before presenting her the sketchbook.

I feel a wave of relief, and I'm a little too pleased with myself when her eyes widen in surprise.

"Well," she says, a grin dancing onto her lips. "It seems you *are* good at something."

We both laugh, and she shakes her head. "No. Not good. *Great.* This is really quite remarkable, Audrey." She studies the page in front of her. "There's a portrait of me that my father had painted a few years back and . . . they made my eyes look so much like his. Here, though . . ."

I take the sketchbook back. "They're not like his," I say adamantly. Although admittedly, I've only seen his portrait. "The same color, maybe, but they're . . . softer. Still striking, but they have a warmth his don't."

She seems moved by my words, but I look away, turning to a fresh page. Now that I'm finally going again, I don't want to stop. "So. What do you want me to draw?"

I missed this game. I used to play it with my dad when I was a kid, toddling after him while he stocked shelves or ran the cash register.

"A bag of chips," he'd say, pointing to some Barbecue Lay's.

"Prettiest gal in Pittsburgh," he'd say with a wink at my mom as she rolled her eyes and gave him a kiss.

"Uh, Mr. Johnson's Camry," as he pointed out the window to our neighbor's bumper-sticker-covered lemon.

And I would. It was how I learned to draw. One chip bag, one portrait, one parked car at a time.

It didn't work to get me out of my rut before, but now I'm itching to build on my momentum.

Lucy frowns, thinking, eyes jumping around the room before landing on me. "Draw yourself," she says finally, the frown lifting.

"So I have something to remember you by when you're gone."

I grin at her, bumping her shoulder with my own. "You'll *want* to remember me? Abysmal manners and all?"

I expect her to laugh, but her expression shrinks and her voice gets quiet enough that I have to lean forward to hear her. "I never want to forget."

Suddenly I feel the same feeling I get when I'm drawing. Like . . . I'm completely open. Seeing but also completely seen. It's deep in the pit of my stomach, warm and electrifying, as Lucy and I gaze at each other, and the only word for it is . . .

Well . . . a spark.

I feel it ignite and pull me toward her, toward . . .

I look away quickly, my cheeks growing hot as I stand abruptly.

"I, uh . . ." I look down at the sketchbook, and suddenly I see it all differently, an answer to a question I've been too afraid to ask myself.

I've never *been* with a girl before. I've had crushes, sure, and a deep, bordering-on-romantic, send-each-other-Taylor-Swift-songs, stay-up-late-talking, almost-kiss-on-my-thirteenth-birthday relationship with my childhood best friend, Leah, that ended in what felt like something pretty close to a breakup when she moved away. But I've never let myself even fully think about it for real.

And then I was with Charlie, and I could almost . . . avoid it entirely if I wanted to. Tuck it away into a neat little box, convincing myself it wasn't a part of myself I really needed to explore. Even the flutter I felt seeing Jules, I just convinced myself meant something else.

But now the box is flung open at the worst possible moment, because here it's a question I *can't* think of asking, even if maybe for the first time . . . some part of me wants to.

I mean, it's *1812*, for Pete's sake. Lucy can't even choose her own husband, let alone . . .

But . . . I . . . *this* . . .

"I'm going to go for a walk," I say as I slam the sketchbook closed and slide it onto the drawing room table.

I'm gone before she even has a chance to reply or join me. I jog down the front steps and across the courtyard, my head spinning. I storm through the grass, not even knowing where I'm going until I am pushing through the door of the stables, the familiar smell of hay and leather and horses greeting me.

I let out a long breath and run my fingers through my hair, forearms leaning on Moby's wooden stall.

"Moby, I think I've got a problem."

He gives me an unamused look, chewing noisily on some hay, mouth smacking open and closed.

I push off the stall door and start to pace around and around in circles, as if that will convince him how serious I am. "A big problem. No, a *huge* problem."

He spits out the hay and lets out a low neigh, almost like a scoff.

"You're right. You're right! I'm overthinking it," I say, with a hysterical laugh like I'm auditioning for the Wicked Witch of the West. "I mean, of course I'm being ridiculous. All of this"—I motion wildly with my arms, at the world I *literally* should not be walking around in for another two hundred years—"*is* ridiculous! Of course I'm just—"

"Easy to talk to someone when they don't talk back, eh?"

I whirl around to see James leaning on the stable door, wiping his hands on a worn cloth, an amused look on his face.

My cheeks burn, and I . . . would give anything for the ground to just suck me straight in. *Poof.* "How much did you . . . ?"

"Enough," he says, pocketing the rag and hopping up onto a wooden table, thick eyebrows rising in curiosity as he studies my face. "You're not from around here, are you, Miss Cameron?"

"Well, I mean, I'm clearly from America. . . ."

"No." He shakes his head. "Like, *here*. This kind of enormous estate, with the fancy dinner parties and the 'a pleasure to make your acquaintance, good sir,'" he says, his voice tipping higher, mimicking a posh voice we both know all too well, nice arms crossing against his chest. "I reckon you're more like me than you are like Miss Sinclair."

I smile, because, well . . . he's not wrong. My dad owns a convenience store, and we live in a small apartment just above it. Even if I get into RISD, I'll need a massive pile of financial aid and scholarships to go. I've worn the same beat-up Converse since my freshman year. Even with nineteenth-century social graces and formalities aside, I'd still definitely be a fish out of water here.

"I reckon you're probably right," I say, resting my back against the stall door. I study his face, skin tan from working outside, lines forming around his eyes when he smiles. He looks to be close to my age. A year or so younger, maybe. "How long have you worked here? At Radcliffe?"

"My whole life, really. My father was the stable master before me, my mother, a scullery maid up at the house. I've worked alongside him since I was a boy. Shoveling hay, caring for the horses, learning the ropes. I took over the job from him two years ago, when they moved south."

"Same," I say. "Well, sort of. There was a little less hay involved. My family owns a shop of sorts in America. I've worked there . . ."

"Since you were born?" he asks, and I nod.

"Maybe even *before* I was born," I say, smiling when I think of the picture on our refrigerator, my mom working the register at eight months pregnant. "I think I learned how to stock shelves before I learned how to walk."

He laughs at that, the sound rich and deep, blue eyes sparkling as he looks at me.

"I like you, Miss Cameron," he says, and I can't help but feel the same way about him. It's nice to talk to someone other than Lucy without feeling like I'm putting on airs or being graded on my performance or pretending to be someone else, like I did all last night at Mr. Shepherd's dinner party.

I see all the pieces align, so I wait for it, a glimmer of what I felt earlier in the drawing room, but . . . there's nothing. Sure, he's handsome as anything, and I'm enjoying myself, but there isn't the same undeniable spark I felt sitting on that piano bench with Lucy.

Even so, it's nice to feel like . . .

"Audrey," I correct him. "Call me Audrey."

"Audrey," he echoes, nodding. After a long moment, he motions through the wooden doors toward the house, hopping off the table. "Let me walk you back."

He doesn't pry. Doesn't force me to say what's bothering me. Doesn't even flirt further.

And I like him all the more for it.

We head slowly across the grass, James telling me about Moby, who he raised from a tiny, rambunctious foal. "Don't know where he gets his personality from. His mother was as sweet as anything."

I laugh. "Father?"

"A valid point," he says with a wry grin, faint stubble on his chin and sharp jawline. "Wildest stallion I know. Cost Mr. Sinclair a fortune and nearly bucked him off on his first ride."

"From what I've heard, can't say I blame him."

My eyes dance up the stone masonry of Radcliffe as we

continue chatting, landing on an upstairs window, where a flash of an off-white dress and golden hair disappears from view. My stomach flutters at just a glimpse, the spark rekindling whether I want it to or not.

But falling for Lucy would be futile. If nothing could ever happen between us, how would I make it home? Besides, just because I felt a spark with her doesn't mean I can't feel it with someone else. It could even still come with James or any of the others. It doesn't have to happen right away.

And with the dance at the assembly room in two days' time, I might as well put my best foot forward and see what, or *who*, comes my way.

CHAPTER 20

LUCY

June 24, 1812

"You think I'M ready for toMorrow?" Audrey asks as we trot on horseback side by side through the grassy fields of Radcliffe, her bonnet already a lost cause. It hangs limply from the messily tied strings around her neck.

Despite this, I answer, "I truly think you are ready," rather surprised to find that I mean it.

We spent most of the morning practicing the steps likely to be on the repertoire for the assembly room dance, Audrey taking it far more seriously than anything we've practiced thus far. Eyebrows furrowed, full lips counting out each step, she hardly even looked at me until late this afternoon, when *I* was the one who suggested we take a break to do something fun.

Still, she looks concerned, teeth digging into her lip. I wonder if that's why she stormed out of the drawing room yesterday. Now that she can draw again, she must be more anxious than ever to find her match and return home.

"*Audrey*," I say insistently, and her head swings over to look at me, hazel eyes almost liquid gold in the afternoon sun. "I am shocked to discover I'm telling *you* this, but dances are supposed to be fun. Entertaining! Not only will you get some practice for the upcoming ball, but even if you don't fall desperately in love, you get to make new acquaintances, drink some delightful punch, and twirl around until your feet hurt."

"Yeah, but if I make a total fool of myself and forget a step, or fall flat on my face in front of everyone, I won't just be embarrassing myself. I'll be embarrassing *you*," she says, and my heart unexpectedly and unwelcomely flutters.

"Since when do you care about embarrassing me?" I joke, but I tighten my grip on Henry's reins. I cast a sideways glance at her to see that her jaw is set despite my attempt at reassuring her.

I let out a long sigh and nudge Henry forward until I pull just in front of Moby, causing him to skid to a stop and paw angrily at the ground.

"Audrey," I say, my voice serious now. "You will not embarrass either of us, all right? People from *now* make mistakes all the time. And if you are so ashamed of it, I'll claim the dance is done differently in America. Or I'll have Alexander make the same mistake, and I'm sure he'll charm everyone there into doing it the new way. Or, who knows, maybe *I'll* be the embarrassing one! I'll drink far too much wine and make such an enormous spectacle of myself that I'll be the talk of the town for the rest of the summer, if not the entirety of my life."

Finally, slowly, the corner of her mouth ticks up. "A spectacle, huh?"

"A spectacle they'll still be talking about when you get back to the future."

Breathless from my impassioned speech, I find myself rather enjoying imagining making a spectacle.

Even *imagining* it has not been something I've allowed myself to do.

At least not before Audrey came.

"All right," she says, the heaviness gone as she rides around me, her leg grazing mine as she passes by. The feeling from the carriage and nearly every moment since roars awake.

I force objectivity and reason into it. It's just because of how free she makes me feel. It's something temporary. She will fall in love. She will leave. I will marry Mr. Caldwell.

I push it—no, force it—down as we start riding again, slowly making our way back toward the stables. Whether I like it or not, I've become accustomed to suppressing feelings I'm not allowed to have, and this will be no different.

So why does this feel harder to lock away?

"Do you want to hear something *truly* unpleasant? Worse than even your piano playing?" I ask to distract myself.

"Always."

"Mr. Caldwell sent over a messenger this morning. I'm to dine with him this Saturday at his estate."

She screws up her face. "Pretend you fell ill after the lowly assembly room dance."

I laugh and shake my head. "I wish I could," I admit, but that is one line I can't cross.

James comes out of the stables to greet us as we approach, then helps me down off Henry in one smooth, fluid motion before moving to assist Audrey.

"Moby was as sweet as pie today," Audrey says, and the two of them share a small, secretive smile. "I guess he takes after his mother after all."

Moby nips at Audrey's bonnet, refusing to be given such high praise, and they dissolve into laughter. "I reckon you spoke too soon," James says, eyes mischievous.

My fingers twist once more into the fabric of my dress as I watch them, so close to each other, so well acquainted, though I've no idea how that could be. Audrey's head tilts back to meet his gaze, her cheeks flushed from riding, and a familiar heavy feeling sits in the pit of my stomach as a word suddenly rings loudly in my head.

Jealousy.

Only this time I know its source isn't over Audrey's ability to fall in love.

It's over the fact that Audrey isn't falling in love with *me*.

I tear my eyes away and turn to look out over the field, ripping my gloves and my hat off. My fingers tug desperately at the bonnet strings around my neck, which now feel tight, *too tight.*

I hardly know what's come over me. This feeling is so confusing, so strange and illogical, the way it gnaws at my insides, finding a home in every corner of my chest.

Have some decorum, Lucy, I scold myself, forcing my breathing to steady, making my face impassive as I turn back to face the two of them.

Yet hidden inside, I broil.

This is what I should *want* to happen. For Audrey to find her spark. And James? He seems like a good match. Honest, hardworking, handsome. Clearly, they have a connection.

But when James's gaze lands on mine, I realize I must not be as impassive as I think, because his entire demeanor changes. He straightens his back, clearing his throat. "Anything else you need, Miss Sinclair? Are there any plans to ride later this week?"

"Not as of now. Thank you, James."

Audrey cracks a smile, leaning toward him to whisper, *"So formal."* James shushes her with a smirk.

And I can't hold it in another second. I turn and head back toward Radcliffe, stomach churning as I briskly cross the grass, squinting against the late afternoon sun.

I hear Audrey behind me, calling out my name, but I ignore it until we're in the courtyard and her hand wraps around my arm.

"Lucy, are you all right?" she asks, out of breath from jogging after me. "I was just joking—"

"Me? I'm fine," I say, trying to remember myself and my composure. "I got a bit warm. That's all." I laugh, trying to appear entirely unfazed, but this time I find I'm the one unable to meet her gaze, unable to even look at her.

It isn't until that night in bed, when Audrey's breathing has slowed, that I close the book I was pretending to read and roll over to take in her face in the flickering candlelight.

I don't know how to put words to what I'm feeling.

Or maybe I do, but I can't make sense of them.

The moment in the carriage. The jealousy at the stables. How I feel right now just looking at her, just being close to her.

Wanting to be closer.

I roll over quickly and blow out the candle, so I'm staring into the darkness, hardly able to make out much past the nose on my face.

Yet I find myself still acutely aware of Audrey next to me, the shape of her body in the bedsheets, barely a finger's width away from me. I feel her in the way my heart is thrumming with a question against the fabric of my nightgown.

I squeeze my eyes shut tightly, knowing I should stop searching for the answer.

My future with Mr. Caldwell ticks ever closer. My father's return even closer than that.

Soon she will be gone.

Soon she will love someone else.

Maybe she already does.

And that needs to be, *will* be, answer enough.

CHAPTER 21

AUDREY

June 25, 1812

I'M once again pressing my face up against the glass, peering out at the people exiting their carriages as they head inside. They're a flurry of laughter and beautiful dresses and general frivolity, but a fresh wave of nerves washes over me.

What is even happening? What the hell am I doing?

I feel like I ask myself that a thousand times a day now. Maybe more. Sometimes with a few more expletives thrown in. Really, just a perpetual state of confusion.

"Are you nervous?"

I turn my head to see Lucy elbow her cousin in the side at his question for me. A warm laugh bubbles out from between his lips as he rubs at his ribs. Then he shoots her a playful glare.

"No," I lie, raising my eyebrows at him. "Are you?"

"To dance with beautiful women? Certainly not."

He winks at me before swinging open the carriage door and hopping out onto the gravel. His white-gloved hand reaches in to help Lucy out, and she gives me a small encouraging smile that sends my stomach flip-flopping. My eyes linger on her until her cream-colored dress slips slowly out the door. Maybe some part of me wishes *I* was also going to be dancing with beautiful women.

Or, one in particular.

As if things aren't confusing enough.

Alexander pops his head in, arm extending to me. I let out a long exhale before my fingers slide into his palm and he pulls me out of the carriage. As I gape up at the simple stone building, columns illuminated by golden candlelight, I feel him lean closer to me until his mouth brushes against my ear, sending a trail of goose bumps cascading down the length of my body.

"Save a dance for me?" he whispers for only me to hear.

I look back at him, his handsome face so close to mine, his eyes dark and maybe even wanting in the dim light, reminding me of my mission.

Smirking, I pull my gaze away coyly, attempting to flirt. "I'll consider it."

But even though this is practically right out of a swoony rom-com, the "why doesn't this happen in real life moment" right here in front of me, it feels different. Fake. Paling to the butterflies I got from just Lucy's smile as she exited the carriage.

Still, I lean into it. Getting home has to stay my first priority. And I've only got fifteen more days left, after all.

He chuckles to himself and offers me an arm as we rejoin Lucy and head up the stone steps and inside together.

The moment we push through the doors, it's a *total* sensory overload.

The room is a sea of bright-colored dresses, blues and greens and pinks and yellows, blurring with elegant white gloves giving way to glowing, flushed faces. A live quartet plays above the talking and laughter, and people sway and dance along, illuminated by glittering crystal chandeliers that span the length of the room.

And, shockingly, after I take it all in, it puts me at ease. Because, on some level, it feels almost . . . familiar. Like junior prom last year in the gymnasium. True, our planning committee used up too much of the budget on snacks and drinks, so they had to use toilet paper as streamers instead of fancy chandeliers like these (which was totally the right call, in my opinion), but there's a glimmer of that night here, two hundred years in the past. The dresses may be nicer, the decorations fancier, the music a little different, but the *energy* is the same. There's still the groups of friends gossiping, the couple showing an awkward amount of PDA in the corner, the girl who took thirteen years of dance classes showing off her skills like her life depends on it.

It all combines to make me feel almost close to home, even

though I'm miles and miles—years and years—away from it. And as we cross the room, Alexander and Lucy nodding hello to their acquaintances, I feel all my nerves finally wash away.

Just as I chill out, I make eye contact with a familiar pair of bright blue eyes.

Mr. Shepherd.

He glides across the room to greet us, swerving around groups of people talking, all of them turning their heads with interest as he passes.

"Miss Sinclair, Miss Cameron," he says, bowing.

"How many blue cravats do you have?" I ask, and he laughs.

"Hundreds."

I watch Mr. Shepherd's blue eyes return to my face over and over again as Lucy introduces Alexander, who subtly puts his hand over mine.

Well, I've never had two guys interested in me like *this* before.

And even if it doesn't feel quite like I thought it would, I'd be lying if I said I didn't kind of like it. It makes me feel hopeful. Like maybe by the end of the night, I'll have a clearer head about what to do. About who to choose.

"Miss Cameron," Mr. Shepherd says, always so formal, "might I have the next dance?"

My arm slides out of Alexander's and into his. "Absolutely."

My voice is surprisingly level as I shoot a worried look back at Lucy, some nerves returning at the thought of dancing, but she gives me a reassuring smile, mouthing, "You will be fine."

I see her lips turn down slightly, indicating she is probably lying the tiniest bit. I mean, my dance moves certainly warrant that, but still, I appreciate the support. Alexander, on the other hand, raises an intrigued eyebrow, which I ignore.

We join the other dancers, girls on one side, boys on the other. They bow, we curtsy, and my heart rate quadruples as I try to remember everything I've crammed into my brain this past week.

I hold my breath, waiting, hoping—

Oh, thank God.

I almost start crying when the familiar notes of a cotillion Lucy taught me start to play. I step forward, take Mr. Shepherd's hand, and turn, toes pointed. The nerves are still there, but it's almost like through the violin and the flute and the cello, I can hear her. Humming the song, counting out the beats, telling me when to turn, where to go, what to do with my feet.

It's almost like . . . well.

Like I'm dancing with her.

Until . . .

"Are dances quite different in America?" Mr. Shepherd asks, breaking my concentration and making me completely forget the next step.

I stand, immobilized for a few seconds, before catching sight of the girls next to me, half a step ahead, their graceful turns jogging my memory.

He swoops in quickly to help me, hand wrapping around mine to pull me to the correct beat, a small smile on his face. "I will take that as a yes."

"I'm sorry, I . . . ," I say, cheeks turning red. "I can't dance and talk at the same time. It's like wearing a corset and going for a jog. It will not end well."

He laughs, shockingly charmed by that, while I remind myself yet again that I have to push all thoughts of Lucy out of my head and focus on throwing myself into the actually eligible and possible dating pool. Maybe if I can't talk, I can manage some sultry eye contact? A flirtatious smile or two?

Mr. Shepherd, all things considered, is a pretty good dancer, clearly *far* past the point of obsessing over every step. He must have been professionally taught like Lucy was, instead of taking a one-week crash course in a drawing room. Every time I fumble or miss a step, he guides me to the right one, a trust and understanding forming between us even though we aren't speaking. He even manages to make me giggle a few times when he comedically ducks out of the way of an enormous gold feather in the lady's hair next to us.

By the second song, I've managed to relax enough to actually enjoy myself. Especially when I catch sight of a girl on the opposite end forgetting the final turn. At least it's not just me.

We're about to start the next dance, a Scottish reel, when Alexander swoops in to steal me away. Mr. Shepherd looks disappointed but, ever the gentleman, allows the interruption and steps off the dance floor.

"Colonel Finch," I say, addressing him by his fancy title. I laugh as he twirls me around, completely off script for the dance, the corner of his mouth ticking up as my hand finds his strong shoulder.

"*Alexander*," he says as he leans in, making our cheeks graze lightly against each other. "Call me Alexander."

"Only if you call me Audrey."

We form a circle with the other couples and dance around and around, until my head is spinning, even more so maybe when I'm pulled back into his arms. Or, at least, that's what I try to convince myself.

Alexander improvises another turn, making me feel like it's okay to mess up. Maybe more than okay.

So I let go, and the two of us laugh as we twirl around the other dancers in time with the music but creating steps of our own. I glance around, and not a single person seems to mind, and suddenly I don't care if they do, Lucy's words of encouragement yesterday coming back to me. I'm here to risk it all anyway. To find love. I'm not going to even *be* here in fifteen days, so I might as well throw myself totally into it while I have the chance.

"To be honest, Audrey," Alexander says, chest steadily

rising and falling underneath my hands as the song ends. "I pinned you for someone who would like a little more adventure than a person like Mr. Shepherd would offer."

"Maybe you pinned me wrong," I say, raising my eyebrows challengingly.

His umber eyes narrow. "I'm not so sure about that."

I bite my lip to stop from smiling, because he's obviously right. Mr. Shepherd may be perfectly nice and ridiculously hot, but I'd be lying if I didn't have my doubts about how well we might actually click. I mean, I don't know if I'll even be here long enough to get past his formalities.

And even if I did, I feel like he just wouldn't . . . get me. Not in the same way that Alexander and James have, the two of them already making me feel comfortable.

And certainly not in the way Lucy has.

We spend the rest of the dance, and part of the next, talking about all the places he's traveled to, Alexander insisting that he can talk enough for both of us when I tell him, too, that I can't dance and chat at the same time. I'm relieved that I get to mostly listen because it's becoming clear that I am . . . fucking exhausted.

This Regency-era-dancing thing is no joke. It's like eighteen TikTok dances and a DJ shouting, "One more time!" after the dozenth "Cha Cha Slide" combined. Complicated *and* tiring.

Alexander tells me about Paris and Rome and his favorite places to go in London, while I wonder how many of those places still exist in 2023. But I find myself more fascinated by the mischief he's managed to get into.

He's slept in a stable in the countryside after getting caught in a torrential thunderstorm, snuck into museums after dark, and watched the sunrise from rooftops. Things I never even considered possible in this world of rules and expectations.

"But, like you, I always prefer staying in cities the most. The pace of it all. Making friends, going out on the town, people-watching."

"So do I," I say. There's no denying that it's beautiful here, with the green grass and the trees and all the open space. But if it weren't for Lucy, it would also be . . . boring.

And not just because my phone doesn't work.

I miss seeing all the different customers who filter into the corner shop, never knowing who or what might be next. Miss my bike rides around the busy streets. Miss feeling the inspiration I pulled from all the people out and about, living their lives.

But have I even really been experiencing it? Not the way he has.

He's reminding me how passive I've been in my own life, like the women here, clustered in groups or quiet on the arm of a gentleman while he makes conversation, society *expecting* them to be passive observers. Planned and regimented and contained. But I actually have a *choice* in that. Talking with Alexander makes me see glimpses of the former Audrey—

ambitious, excited, *inspired*—and for the first time in a long time, it makes me want to get out there, get those parts back.

Maybe this connection with Alexander, him being so eager for travel and adventure, his love of city life, him reminding me of who I used to be, can lead me back home in some way. Can bring us there together. Someone like Alexander would probably be excited by the prospect of traveling to the future. Maybe Lucy was right and there is some kind of loophole.

I hold his gaze as the song comes to a close, willing myself to feel something, to let the logic be enough to start the spark I need.

"I think I'm going to sit the next few out," I say when it isn't. *But maybe it will be.* It's only the second time we've talked after all. I still have fifteen days.

"Already tired?" Alexander teases.

I smirk. "Maybe I'm bored."

He laughs and bows as I curtsy, my legs nearly giving out from under me, my feet *definitely* blistered. I've barely turned away before an older woman swoops in, pulling Alexander into the next set of dances.

I try to glide gracefully instead of limping my way to the punch bowl, but it's damn near impossible. Clawing at the edge of the table for support, I grab a cup and take a huge gulp that . . . sends me into a massive coughing fit.

This shit is *loaded* with rum. Like, two drinks and you'd wake up in bed the next morning wondering how the hell you got there. It tastes like whatever rat poison Charlie used to pour into an old water bottle from his parents' liquor cabinet, which would have the two of us giggling as we sat on the roof of his apartment building in East Liberty, talking about anything and everything.

Already a little warm and dizzy, I shuffle off to the side and try not to collapse against a wall, scanning the crowd for Lucy's golden hair and cream-colored dress. I need to talk to her about my thoughts on Alexander, or . . . I don't know. Maybe I just want to see her, because seeing her always makes me feel better. I kind of wish I was up on a rooftop with *her* right now. Minus the rat poison.

I find her dancing with Mr. Shepherd, her movements smooth and elegant and graceful, so much more perfect and practiced than mine. I watch the way her dress twirls around her, the charming smile she gives him.

What would it be like if she smiled at me like that?

"Audrey," a soft voice says, bringing me back to reality.

Or my current reality, I guess. The one with two hot guys super into me, fighting for my affections, while I am pining for the person I shouldn't be over a cool glass of rubbing alcohol. How very rom-com of me. And how unlike anything I thought it would be.

I turn my head to the side to see Grace, wearing a soft rose dress, face bright and cheerful.

"Grace! Hi." I push off the wall, trying not to appear like

four dances completely and totally did me in for the night. "How's your evening going?"

"Quite well," she says with an excited nod. "I always love a good dance."

We stare at the couples on the floor, and Grace lets out an exaggerated sigh. "It's a shame she has to marry Mr. Caldwell," she says, and both of us screw up our faces at the thought of him. "They would make quite a handsome match, Lucy and Mr. Shepherd, would they not?"

I bite my lip, watching them twirl across the floor for a long moment. Both rich. Both young. Both well mannered and elegant and attractive. Both of this time period.

"They certainly would," I have to agree.

But when my gaze lingers on Lucy, with her golden hair and the soft blush of her cheeks, and I catch the small, charming smile she flashes in his direction, I see it's not quite wide enough for the dimples at the corners of her mouth to appear.

And it tells me that Grace is wrong. Mr. Shepherd is miles better than Mr. Caldwell, but marrying him, she would still be confined in a big, pretty house. Still be stuck behind her carefully crafted polite and perfect facade, in a time where she couldn't just . . . see the world, study at a conservatory, or make her own decisions. Couldn't be the Lucy I've come to know.

I watch as she spins around and around in Mr. Shepherd's arms, but for another tiny, brief moment, her gaze flits past him to meet mine, and the room slows, all the voices and the faces and the music a blurry and distant hum.

Swallowing tears that unexpectedly sting at my eyes, I look away and take a long sip of the punch, thinking about how hopeful I was when I stepped out of the carriage earlier tonight, but now, standing here, all I want to do is forget.

Forget that I have to find someone to fall in love with to get home. Forget that I haven't felt a spark with Mr. Shepherd, or James, or even Alexander, no matter how perfect they seem.

Wanting to forget just how beautiful Lucy looks, dancing with someone who isn't me.

CHAPTER 22

LUCY

June 26, 1812

The day after any dance is spent recovering. From the drinking, the dancing, *and* for some, the socializing. Even being so accustomed to it, I can find it quite exhausting to put on a facade for hours on end, even in a setting far less formal than a ball or a dinner party. Especially after the past nearly two weeks of Audrey's influence on me.

So, there's really no denying how remarkably nice it feels to be spending the afternoon doing absolutely nothing besides playing familiar songs on the piano while Audrey sits in her chair by the window, sketching away. Now that she's started again, she seems hardly able to stop.

I look up every few moments to take in the strands of her chocolate-brown hair falling into her face, and even from all the way over here, all the way across the room, I have a desire to brush them away. To tuck them behind her ear. To feel her eyes holding mine when I do it.

Instead, I force myself to look down at the ivory and black keys, playing all the feelings I can't put into words. Every look. Every hand graze between us. Every stirring of jealousy when I see her with Alexander, or Mr. Shepherd, or James, smiling at them, dancing with them, wanting *them*.

The music has more meaning than it ever had before, and my eyes close tightly as I find a place to put it all.

When the song ends, Audrey's voice rings out from across the drawing room, causing all those feelings to rush back in.

"You danced with Mr. Shepherd for quite a while last night," she says. I open my eyes to see her still looking down at the paper in front of her, pencil scribbling away, eyebrows furrowed in concentration.

"So did you," I say, fingers sliding off the keys in front of me.

"You said you thought he was handsome," she says, pencil lifting as she glances up at me and tucks it behind her ear.

Ah. I thought she found Alexander more interesting. She even mentioned on our way home inviting him to Radcliffe this coming week. But perhaps I was wrong.

She must be jealous.

"He is handsome," I say, like it's a remark on the color of the sky, the green of the grass, or anything as objective and obvious as that. "But I certainly didn't feel a . . . What was it?"

I pretend I'm searching for the word that I have become all too accustomed to feeling these last few days.

"Spark," she says as she tears out one of the pages of the drawing pad and stands, crossing the room to where I sit at the pianoforte.

I look up at her, heart thrumming noisily in my chest, fingers tapping against my thigh as I resist the urge to reach out, to pull her closer so she can see me, understand me, even better than she already does.

"Do you think you could, though?" she asks, completely oblivious to my internal turmoil over her. "Feel a spark for him if you let yourself? Fall in love with him if you wanted to?"

"I'm not sure want has anything to do with it," I say, the past few days certainly teaching me that. "I don't know much on the subject, but like Martha said, I think you either feel it or you don't. It's not something that can be reasoned."

Audrey's brow furrows as she considers this. "Maybe some sparks take time."

"Perhaps," I say, not really knowing what she is searching for here. Assurance, perhaps, if her feelings for him are growing. "Although I very much doubt that is in the realm of possibility with my future husband."

The words are a stinging but necessary reminder of what's to come.

"Right," she says, hesitating, eyes flicking down to the

torn-out page of her drawing pad. "I . . . uh . . ." She holds the page out to me and gives me a wry smile.

"Don't lose it," she says as I look down at a portrait of her, drawn from her reflection in the drawing room window, head bent as she sketches, loose, tumbling strands of hair and all. A smile forms on my face when I notice that the depiction shows her wearing the unusual shoes she had on when she first arrived.

Abruptly, she turns and leaves the drawing room, the door clicking shut before I can even say, "I won't." Perhaps she was not fully convinced of my intentions in regard to Mr. Shepherd.

Sighing, I prop the drawing up on the pianoforte. It is so lifelike, I reach out to finally brush at the loose strands, wishing I were feeling her skin underneath my fingertips instead of paper.

If she saw me now, she would know my intentions couldn't be further from Mr. Shepherd.

That night, as Martha helps unbutton my dress and unlace my corset, I catch her smiling to herself in the mirror.

"What?" I ask as our eyes meet in the reflection, and she shrugs.

"I rather like that Audrey," she says while I step out of my dress. Martha returns it to the ornate wardrobe in the corner and doesn't speak again until she closes the door with a click, hand frozen on the wood. "She makes you . . . happy."

"I suppose so," I say, giving her a small smile. "But I find my mood always greatly improved when Father is away."

"Naturally, but . . ." Her kind eyes crinkle, rosy cheeks lifting. "It's different from that, Lucy. You seem more open. More vibrant. More, well . . . like yourself, before . . ."

Before.

My nails dig into my palms at her unfinished sentence, a part of me despising how true her words are, because like the rest of my freedom, it's temporary. Yes, Audrey's friendship has freed me, but the time when I will have to lock myself back up keeps getting closer and closer as the numbers on Audrey's quarter tick down, and instead of preparing for that, every day I find myself wanting more of . . . something else. Something more than marrying Mr. Caldwell. Something more than what my life is destined to become. I want a life that I have a say in, a voice in, able to do and go and be who I please. A life like Audrey's.

A life with Audrey.

I take a long breath in, smelling the familiarly comforting jasmine scent that Martha has carried through the rooms of this house since I was a baby, and try to stay in the moment. I realize that just like I will lose Audrey, I will lose Martha soon too. And with the realization comes the desire to fill these remaining days with as much as possible, so maybe the memory of them can last me a lifetime.

CHAPTER 23

AUDREY

June 27, 1812

In the late afternoon, after tea, Martha pops her head into the drawing room, grinning from ear to ear like it's Christmas morning.

"Delivery from Miss Burton," she squeals, shifting from foot to foot. "Your dress for the ball, Lucy!"

Why do *I* feel so excited?

I guess without the internet or Steelers games or school, anything besides drawing or practicing my dancing with Lucy somehow feels like opening night for a Marvel movie.

Lucy smiles and closes her book, smoothing her skirt as she stands. "Has it already been brought up to my room?"

Martha nods.

Lucy thanks her, then motions casually to me, saying, "Audrey will help me try it on, won't you?"

"*Me?*" I cough out, nearly dropping the pencil I'm holding

as she languidly fixes her hair, worn half-up, half-down, which has been distracting me for the better part of the day.

"I assume you know how to tie a simple string, right?" Lucy says, raising an eyebrow at me as she floats out of the room. I abandon my sketch of the empty teacup in front of me and skitter off to catch up with her.

"Of course I know how to. I'm just not used to sailor knots tight enough to crush your ribs," I mutter as we head up the steps toward her room. Lucy flashes me an amused smile, which I return with an eye roll as we push inside.

But we're barely past the doorframe when we both skid to a stop.

A beautiful azure ball gown is draped across the bed, with an elegant, wide V neckline, intricate embroidery, and fabric almost like a shimmering waterfall. It looks like it was plucked straight out of the *Pride and Prejudice* Netherfield ball scene, a standout in the sea of gowns surrounding Darcy and Elizabeth as they crackle with disdain and attraction and possibility.

I let out a low whistle.

"Do you like it?" Lucy asks, which, like, must be a rhetorical question.

I reach out and hold up a corner, squinting between the fabric and her face. "It matches your eyes exactly."

She nods, pleased that I noticed.

How could I not?

"I didn't think I would like it, but seeing it here, *now* . . . It's perfect." She motions to the back of her current dress. "Will you help me . . . ?"

I drop the fabric I'm holding and clear my throat. "Right. Yeah. Totally."

She turns, and I slide behind her, taking a deep, unsteady breath. My hand hesitates as I reach up. Then I force my fingers to carefully brush her golden hair away from her neck while my eyes follow the gentle slope of her shoulders. When I undo the top button and the fabric falls away to reveal her soft skin, my heart begins to hammer in my chest, in my head, even in my fingertips lightly pressing against it.

Being this close to her, close enough that I can feel the electricity crackling between us, close enough for her warm lavender smell to completely wash over me, close enough that I could just lean forward and my lips could graze her neck, makes the pull to completely erase the distance between us almost unbearable.

You can't.

I try, instead, to focus on carefully undoing the strings, pulling them loose, until her dress tumbles softly to the ground, landing in a crumpled heap on the floor. Then Lucy turns to face me, and I have nothing to focus on but her. She holds my gaze as she steps slowly out of the dress toward me. Her chest lightly grazes mine, and our hands brush together, the feeling so soft, so light, it's barely more than a whisper.

But *inside*, it feels like the rain before a thunderstorm.

Without looking away, I pull the heavy dress off the bed and help her step into it. Our faces are close enough for me to feel her breath against my cheek, and the temptation alone makes me dizzy. I force myself to pull it up her body, my eyes following as I slide it carefully over her legs, her hips, her chest, until my fingertips dance across her shoulders, dipping into the valley of her collarbone. Then I lower one hand to her waist to turn her slowly toward the full-length mirror.

I take my time tying the back. When my eyes lock with hers in the mirror, the sight is enough to take away whatever breath I still have.

"How do I look?" she asks softly, a blush climbing to her cheeks.

"Beautiful" is all I can say, my voice breathy and strange.

Lucy must find it strange too because she clears her throat and steps away, breaking the electric hum between us, leaving only a tense silence behind.

I internally kick myself. Only *I* would have a full-on bisexual awakening in 1812. For a soon-to-be-married woman.

"Mr. Caldwell won't be able to take his eyes off you," I quickly clarify, not wanting to make things weird between us. "I'm sure he'll propose the minute he sees you."

She nods and drifts over to the mirror, a hand reaching up to tuck a stray hair into place.

"Speaking of. You ready for your dinner tonight?" I say, trying to change the subject and act normal.

"As ready as I'll ever be," she murmurs.

"If you want to leave early, I'd be happy to bust in and cause a scene. I started a food fight in fourth grade. I'm totally willing to throw food across a room."

She cracks a smile at that, and the tension thankfully ratchets down a notch.

There's a light knock on the door, and Martha sticks her head in. "Lucy, dear, your carriage is almost ready to leave. We should start getting you dressed."

"Right, I better . . ." I do an awkward wave and turn to leave the room, my movements feeling almost mechanical as I brush past Martha and out the door.

Really, Audrey? Way to play it cool.

Restless, I pace around the hallways of Radcliffe, past fancy sculptures and four-poster beds, into and out of rooms, seeing the light outside slowly beginning to fade with every step and corridor, until I come across the wall of portraits. I pause and crane my neck to look at the portrait of Lucy's father. His cold eyes peer down at me reproachfully, almost saying, *What do you think you're doing?*

I stare back, wishing I knew. Wishing to just go home instead of figuring it out.

But also not wanting to leave Lucy.

Every moment here with her feels right. Like how it did with Charlie, but also . . . not. The feeling is the same in some ways, but it's like I'm experiencing it differently. Like

I'm discovering a new, unfamiliar but exciting part of myself with it.

It makes me see the cracks in my relationship with Charlie. The critiques that were a little too harsh. Insisting I should leave the portraits I loved doing most in the sketchbook under the cash register, not in my application. Telling me I should drop art altogether when he hit a roadblock of his own.

Lucy makes me want to create again. *Encourages* me to, even when it's hard. Makes me want to seize all the opportunities I can, even though she'll never be able to. We don't have drawing in common, but somehow she understands my art more than Charlie ever did. Understands me more.

When I hear a door close somewhere down the hall, I move to the window and watch Lucy's peach dress disappear into the carriage, my thumbnail digging into the edge of my quarter at the sight of her dressing for his preference. I watch until she disappears entirely in a plume of dust billowing out from behind the wheels and the horses' hooves.

Then I look down at the stupid quarter that brought me here in the first place.

Thirteen days left.

And I think I may be completely falling for the one person I can't have.

CHAPTER 24

LUCY

June 27, 1812

I feel like I can't breathe.

I pull my glove off, pressing the back of my cool hand against my cheek as the carriage heads along the uneven road toward Mr. Caldwell's estate and away from Audrey.

I squeeze my eyes shut, tight enough to see bursts of color, but all the colors form shapes. Her eyes. Her lips. Her nose. The small, barely perceptible scar above her right eyebrow—

No.

My father's face takes her place, stern and expectant.

"*What* has come over me?" I mutter as I set my jaw and pull my glove back on with a flourish. I am on my way to Mr. Caldwell's estate, for heaven's sake. And while I may be enjoying my remaining days of freedom, I have a purpose that must take precedence, just as Audrey has hers with Mr. Shepherd and Alexander and James.

Or, at least, my father has a purpose that must take precedence.

An engagement.

And this dinner, if I perform perfectly, is how I can all but secure it before the ball.

The carriage comes up to an enormous gate, and I peek out the window as we pass through it, really and truly seeing for the first time the life I'm about to have. I watch as we ride alongside a perfectly maintained wall of shrubbery that eventually gives way to a courtyard of vibrant flowers and an estate so looming I have to tilt my head back to take it all in.

The footman opens the carriage door, and I am led up the stone steps, lanterns glowing orange as the door they bathe with light swings open.

"Welcome, Miss Sinclair," the housekeeper says in greeting, giving me a clipped curtsy, no glimmer of Martha's friendliness in her eyes.

I follow her down the hall, knowing Audrey would gawk at the black-and-white harlequin floors, the painting on the ceiling, so beautiful it could pass as a slice of the Sistine Chapel, but instead I find myself wondering what it would be like to look up and see something Audrey created instead, something new and different and entirely out of the ordinary.

When the drawing room doors open, Mr. Caldwell and his younger sister, Anne, stand to greet me from their perches on elegant red velvet furniture with ornate gold trim. They look very much alike, both with skin almost translucent, hair a dull brown, noses thin and pointed. The only thing that strongly differentiates them is their height. Where Mr. Caldwell is tall and spindly, Anne is even shorter than me, though only a year or so younger. She's likely eager to get back to London and away from the countryside, a match of her own potentially awaiting her return. Perhaps that is why she seems so displeased to see me.

Despite all their money, I'm surprised to see Anne wearing a rather simple, almost severe dark dress. The only indication that she shares in the family's wealth is an enormous jeweled necklace around her throat, which looks as if it weighs as much as Moby.

"Mr. Caldwell, Miss Caldwell," I say with a curtsy to each of them as Anne peers at me over her spectacles, her mouth a judgmental line. "Thank you so very much for the invitation. Your estate is quite lovely."

"The house in London is far nicer," Anne says, blue eyes narrowing.

"I don't doubt it," I say, and at least Mr. Caldwell looks rather pleased that I paid him something resembling a compliment.

"I see you wore your peach dress, as I suggested," Mr. Caldwell says with a smug smile as he offers me his arm, leading the three of us into dinner at the toll of a bell. "A *very* wise choice. It suits you so well."

"Yes, I . . . much prefer it to the green," I say. Knowing what is expected of me this dinner, I thought wearing it would help my cause, but the lie comes slower than it usually would.

As I sit down in my chair, my eyes flick quickly around the dining room, trying to take everything in to steady myself. As expected, it is quite large, with paintings lining the wall and a crystal chandelier hanging high above us.

"So," Miss Caldwell says as the first course, a delicious-smelling white soup, is brought out. At least the food seems it will be something of note. "My brother tells me you were in attendance at the *assembly room* dance this past weekend."

I nod and take a polite sip of the wine, trying my very best to ignore the disdain on her face. "I was, Miss Caldwell. My dear cousin Colonel Alexander Finch was in town and insisted we attend."

A stretch, surely, but not entirely unfounded. Alexander loves a good dance, and I never gave a reason for my attendance at Mr. Shepherd's.

"How . . . *charming*. We would never be seen at a country dance like that, would we? I don't know what to think of your cousin if he so likes attending them," she says, and a pretentious look of amusement passes between her and her brother. "It's just so . . ."

"Yes, your brother mentioned such," I say as I take a small taste of the soup from the side of the spoon, the broth warm and delectable, quite unlike this conversation at present. I try to swallow my simmering anger with it, especially at her looking down upon Alexander, as I continue. "I suppose the son of a viscount is allowed to do as he pleases. Even attend a country dance if he deems it worthy of his time."

Her eyebrows rise in surprise either at my thinly veiled insult or the reveal of my cousin's parentage, but Mr. Caldwell draws our attention back toward him. "Do you enjoy dancing, Miss Sinclair? If I recall, you were not particularly fond of it at the Blackmore estate a few months ago."

"To be entirely honest, I much prefer reading or playing the pianoforte," I admit truthfully this time, and both of them give an approving nod.

"You must play for Anne sometime," Mr. Caldwell says, his bony hand gesturing toward the hallway. "We have a rather exquisite Broadwood in our drawing room, which she greatly enjoys. She is *quite* accomplished on the instrument. Perhaps she could give you some pointers."

Anne gives me a challenging smile, while the simmering anger slowly begins to bubble. My teeth grind together as I force my mouth into a smile. "Oh, that would be lovely. I'm sure I could learn *much* from her."

We move on to the second course, an impressive assortment of savory pudding, mutton, beefsteaks, and vegetables. Mr. Caldwell has spared no expense, but all I can think of is that this brings us mercifully one course closer to being done.

I turn my attention toward Mr. Caldwell, who is carefully

and politely serving his sister and me a little bit of everything. "How often do you find yourself in London, Mr. Caldwell? Are you out of town on business quite a lot?"

He hands me my plate. "Yes. We spend a great deal of our time there, save the warmer months."

London. We.

I've been plenty of times, but spending the majority of my time there with people I can hardly stand, away from Grace, away from the town and the place so familiar to me, makes my stomach lurch.

I would travel the world if it was with the right person, but Mr. Caldwell is certainly not that. And I'd rather hoped to stay behind and continue my small pockets of freedom when he is away on business.

"Country air is said to be quite refreshing," Miss Caldwell says, though nothing about either of their expressions would imply that they find this to be the case. "Although the company . . ."

"Is so charming," I say as I take small, polite bites of food, attempting to silence whatever insult she was about to conjure up. I'm finding it increasingly difficult to keep my composure and pass her barely subtle tests. I notice from across the table that she is even making it a point to take smaller bites than I am, the morsels barely fitting on the tines of her fork.

I press my lips together to suppress a laugh, wanting to tell . . .

"Unlike Miss Cameron," Mr. Caldwell says, as if he is reading my mind, startling me. "The girl who was in attendance at Mr. Shepherd's dinner party just last week."

I look up at him, utensils frozen as I wait for him to finish.

"I find myself wondering how exactly *you* are acquainted with such . . ." He looks to his sister, giving her an amused smile. "Uncivilized company?" His usually veiled insults are now clearly thrown out without inhibition when in private.

They both laugh, heads thrown back, while my fingertips turn white around my fork as the steady, rolling boil of my anger bubbles over. "She is a very dear friend of mine, trying her best to exist in a world *very* different from where she grew up," I say, keeping my voice level as I slowly, carefully set my utensils down. "Perhaps you both ought to rethink what uncivilized company means, for sometimes I find myself noticing that, despite a great deal of wealth, such individuals could be dining at this table right this very moment."

I can't believe I've just said that.

I bite the inside of my cheek, panicked, knowing those words have likely ruined any possible marriage prospects between Mr. Caldwell and me. And the prospect of what will happen to me as a result is terrifying.

"Intriguing," Mr. Caldwell says as I tense, waiting to be thrown from the room, and then the house, my father's enraged words already ringing in my ears.

I will be ruined. We both will be.

What have I done?

I brace myself further as he points a fork in my direction and speaks. "You know . . . you may be correct. Even among the upper class, it is becoming harder and harder to find people as accomplished and well bred as we are, is it not?"

Miss Caldwell nods in agreement, both of them apparently far too proud to ever imagine I could be talking about them.

I exhale slowly, a wave of relief crashing down upon me.

Relief. I hate that that is what I feel right now, over not ruining a marriage I don't even want. Not ruining my father's life, when he means to ruin mine.

"A shame what society has come to," she concurs as the table is cleared and dessert is brought out. Every barrier I have put up in my mind since I arrived this evening has been entirely broken down by this conversation, and all I can think about is getting back.

But back to *what* exactly? Audrey? Home? Both will be gone soon, and then *this* will be my home. My future. Sitting at a table all the way in London with Mr. Caldwell pontificating through hundreds of nights just like this one.

I remain quiet and polite for the rest of the meal after that sobering thought, hardly even enjoying the sorbet, though it is an expensive and delicious delicacy.

We retire to the drawing room afterward for tea, and I begin counting the minutes until I can make my exit. However, it seems dinner was just a prelude to what was to come, as I'm soon tested thoroughly on my accomplishments by both Anne and Mr. Caldwell.

And I . . . perform. Just like I always have. Just like I'm expected to.

"Anne speaks four languages," Mr. Caldwell says as she straightens her posture with pride.

"Oh," I say, taking a careful sip of my tea. "Which four?"

"French, Italian, German for singing, and English, naturally."

"As do I," I say, placing my cup carefully onto the matching saucer. "Then I added Latin for good measure."

Mr. Caldwell beams, but Anne scowls. The two cancel each other out, which is mostly how it goes.

They discuss Fordyce's *Sermons*, philosophy, and even arithmetic, asking me an array of questions. I do well but not too well. I flub one on mythology to appease Anne, who proudly swoops in to correct me, and Mr. Caldwell frowns. But a winning answer on the sermons meets with his approval and her disdain. The balance of impressing him and padding her enormous ego is beyond delicate.

The earlier offer to play the pianoforte comes far sooner than expected, and after Anne plays a beautiful but rather simple concerto, I glide across the room and take her place.

This time I don't intentionally fumble any notes. I don't try to somehow avoid the inevitable. My fingers fly quickly across the keys as I play "Les Adieux" by Beethoven, channeling my mess of emotions into the music.

The farewell.

How fitting. I gaze about the room as I play, seeing Mr. Caldwell circling me like a hawk, looking for things to critique or cut down. I try to tuck all the parts of me that have blossomed in the short time since Audrey's arrival back into a neat little box, try to see just how hard it will be to pretend they never existed.

"As accomplished as she is beautiful," Mr. Caldwell says decisively as the last notes are played. His fingers wrap with finality around my shoulders, like I am *claimed*, like I am already his wife. Anne, though bested, knows better than to question her brother and nods her approval, my tests well and truly passed.

I feel sick.

The only relief is that with his decision seemingly made, the night is finally over, and Mr. Caldwell walks me to my carriage. My entire body practically convulses when he leans in close enough for me to see the uneven stubble on his upper lip, and I realize with horror he is trying to kiss me.

I turn my head quickly to the side, my hands forming fists. "Mr. Caldwell. It would be quite improper."

"Waiting for a proposal," he says with a sly smile. I let out a relieved exhale as he leans away, nodding with approval. "All right, then." He holds out his hand and helps me into the carriage. "I very much look forward to accompanying you to the ball, Miss Sinclair," he says, giving me what I assume he thinks is a flirtatious look.

"Likewise, Mr. Caldwell," I lie, my heart hammering as the carriage begins to move, finally pulling me away from here and back to her.

I rip my gloves off, a frustrated sigh escaping my lips as I realize I have just trapped myself in a future far more unpleasant than I even imagined it would be, stamping the expiration date on these final few weeks of *more*.

CHAPTER 25

AUDREY

June 27, 1812

Funny how crash-landing in 1812 didn't make me lose my mind, but *this?*

This is.

She is.

I toss my sketchbook aside, the page, of course, covered in images of Lucy in the beautiful ball gown I helped her try on, because *God forbid* I get a grip.

After pacing around and around, I stop in front of the window, looking out over the fields of Radcliffe. I haven't felt quite like this since that first night.

Trapped.

In this house, in this time, yes. But now more and more trapped in my feelings by the second. I let out a long groan and run my fingers through my hair as I finally leave the drawing room completely. After I push through the front doors and down the steps, my feet guide me across the grass to the stables once again.

The second I step inside, James's blond head pops out from one of the stalls, where he's in the middle of brushing Henry's mane. A wry smile pulls at the corners of his mouth.

He points the brush at me, eyebrows rising. "Come to talk to Moby again?"

I eye the black horse in the corner, who lets out an exaggerated huff as he munches away on some hay, clearly *very* done with me and my ranting. "No. I just needed some air."

"Something troubling you?"

"Nope."

James narrows his eyes at me but doesn't say anything.

"Well, I have to clean out all the stalls *and* go pick up more hay and feed for the horses tomorrow, so that's what's troubling me, if you want to know," he says, returning to brushing Henry's mane.

"That doesn't sound fun."

"It's not," he admits. "Luckily, Mr. Sinclair has two of the horses in London with him now, so it takes a bit of the load off."

"Can I help at all?"

"You? Help in the stables?" He pauses, brush suspended in midair as he looks at me in shock. "America is *quite* different, isn't it?"

"You have no idea," I mutter. I look down at my hands, picking at my thumbnail, teeth gnawing away at my lip.

I wonder how the dinner is going. Is Mr. Caldwell being awful? I mean, probably. To be honest, I don't know whether I'm hoping it goes well or badly. If it goes well, then—

James clears his throat, breaking my spiraling train of thought. "Evidently, nothing is troubling you, but if you *did* want to share," he says with a knowing look, "I'm here."

And, for some reason, that makes me talk.

"I think I've maybe . . . ," I start and then stop, something about saying part of the truth *out loud* kind of terrifying. Like that will make it *real* in a way I'm not sure I can come back from.

I'm not sure I want to come back from it, though.

Yes, *of course* I want to go home, but I spent years ignoring this part of myself even there, quieting it, pretending it didn't exist, not knowing that I was closing off the opportunity to feel this much. And I don't want to push down what I feel anymore.

So I take the leap, my stomach soaring like I'm plummeting down a roller coaster at Cedar Point.

"I think I've maybe started to have feelings for someone."

"Ooh, now, that is *quite* intriguing," James says as he ducks out of the stall, chucking the brush onto a worn table before hopping up on it. He pats the space next to him, and I walk over and take it. "Is it Mr. Shepherd? Or someone you met at the dance?"

"No, it's . . ." I groan and rub my face, not sure what

exactly I should say. "It's someone I never really expected to have feelings for. A friend."

"Is that such a bad thing?" he asks, and I peek out from between my fingers to see his expression growing curious. "Having feelings for a friend?"

"Yes," I say without hesitation, but then I pause. "Or, I guess, in this case."

In this *time*.

"It was just so unexpected. And it's not like they feel the same. I mean . . . they just . . . *couldn't*," I say. Just talking about it makes me feel the weight of the impossibility.

"Why is that?"

"It would be . . . I don't know. Scandalous, I suppose. I'm not sure they would even consider me an option. Since I'm, uh . . ." I hesitate. "From America."

But, secretly, I'm hoping that Lucy *could*. That she does. It's not like queer people didn't exist in the 1800s. I mean, I've read Emily Dickinson's poems.

I cross my arms and lean back against the wall, frowning.

James mimics me, shoulder bumping into mine. We're both quiet for a long moment before he lets out a long sigh, shrugging.

"Listen, I don't know much, Audrey. I mean, I'm not in society, but I can tell you this. My older brother fell in love with the daughter of a duke, and the two ran off together. You want to talk about a scandal? This was an enormous one. It rocked London society for at *least* two seasons."

I turn my head to look at him, smirking. "Is he as good-looking as you?"

He laughs, giving me a wry grin. "*Even better*, if you'll believe it!" Then, shaking his head, he continues. "No one thought they would make it. Even my own parents thought she'd be running back home before a month's end, cursing his name. But three children later, a simple house on the coast, against all odds, I've never seen a couple more happy and in love. Sometimes, I reckon, love—*real love*—doesn't care about what's proper or what other people think. It finds you when you least expect it, where you least expect it," he says.

I freeze, his words making me think of Mr. Montgomery's before this all began.

He told me, *True love might be just around the corner!* before tossing me a coin that sent me around an unexpected corner in time to be here. Now.

And maybe it was.

I think of that moment with Lucy today in her room. Her eyes locked on mine as she stepped closer, our fingertips brushing lightly together, and against all odds I feel that tiny glimmer of hope grow stronger.

Maybe he sent me here because despite everything . . . she *could* feel this way too.

Maybe Lucy has been the answer all along.

CHAPTER 26

LUCY

June 27, 1812

That night, lying in bed next to Audrey, my entire body feels . . . wide awake.

"His sister sounds as awful as he is," she says after I recount my experience to her, her mouth turning down in a grimace. "I would rather let Martha smelling-salt me, then chuck me out of a second-story window, than go to dinner with either of them."

"I'd endure even worse," I admit, a smile pulling at my lips. "But I did tell them, 'Perhaps you both ought to rethink what uncivilized company means, for sometimes I find myself noticing that, despite a great deal of wealth, such individuals could be dining at this table right this very moment.'"

Audrey swings her head over to look at me, beaming, eyes wide. "You didn't."

"I did." I chuckle, then let out a long exhale, still surprised myself. "Though they were obviously far too proud to even consider that I was talking about them."

"Wow," she says, nodding, impressed. "Pretty badass, Lucy Sinclair."

My insides warm at her praise, "badass" a word I only learned the meaning of a few days ago. "Although, admittedly, the food *was* quite good."

Audrey snorts, but then the two of us fall quiet.

"I went for a walk while you were gone," she finally says, eyes focused on the ceiling. "To the stables, to talk to James."

I try to ignore the faint swell of jealousy in the pit of my stomach as she continues.

"He told me about his older brother. The one who ran away with the duke's daughter."

I shake my head wistfully. "My mother *loved* that story. Spent the fall after it happened scooping up every bit of gossip she could. She was *such* a romantic. Always filling my head with talk of love and saying I was destined for a romance just as glorious as theirs. Like the ones she read about but never got."

Audrey is silent for a long moment, eyes narrowing slightly in thought. "What if you were?"

I'm not, I should say, for so many reasons.

But my heart contradicts that.

I hold my breath as I watch the candlelight flickering on the ceiling, my fingers twisting like always into my nightgown to form a fist as I will my mouth to form words. To say something.

"Have you . . . ?" I start, and Audrey turns her head to look at me, hair rustling against the fabric of her pillow. "Have *you* ever been in love?"

"Yes," she admits while I continue staring at the ceiling.

"What was he like?" I say, trying to keep my voice steady. It comes out barely more than a whisper.

She lets out a long sigh and rolls fully onto her side to face me. My heart skips a beat or two or three over how close she is, even though we've spent the last twelve nights like this.

"His name was Charlie. He was a year older than me in school. We were friends, and then, well . . . more."

I loosen my fingers and roll over to look at her, too, studying the unfamiliar sadness in her face, eyes perhaps the tiniest bit glassy, mouth pulling down at the corners.

"He was so cool and . . . *hot*," she says, making me laugh. "He was an artist too, always had a mini-sketchbook stuffed into his back pocket, and the side of his hand was always stained with ink. We really connected over that, from the very first week we met. I think before I got here, I missed that the most. More than him, really. Having someone I connected with so deeply, who really saw and understood me and my art."

I know what that's like.

"But he stopped seeing me. Or, I guess, maybe on some level he never really did. Not the whole me. He started discouraging me from doing portraits and sketches of people, pushing me to change my style away from people. To make it more modern, more abstract, so it could be more distinct and eye-catching on an application. And then, when he didn't get into art school, he told me to give up on art altogether."

"He *what?*"

"Exactly," she says, nodding. "I've started to wonder if it was ever really love if he did that."

Her gaze is steady as she looks at me. Certain.

"Anyway," she says as she blinks, clearing her throat to continue. "He went off to college and dumped me when he came home a few months later."

"Dumped . . . ?" I frown.

"Broke up with me. Ended our . . . courtship," she clarifies, eyes getting a distant look as she stares just over my shoulder, lost somewhere in the past.

Or, I suppose, the future.

"Then I, well, I took the risk anyway and applied to art school. And I was wait-listed. So that's what was behind it when I said I couldn't draw. Both hit me so hard that for *months* I'd just open my sketchbook and stare at it, pen hovering over the blank page in front of me for hours. And nothing I did helped. Not going to art museums or bike rides around Pittsburgh or new pens from Mr. Montgomery." Her eyes move back to meet mine, glowing in the candlelight. "Until I came here, with you. *Because* of you, actually. I feel like I'm more like myself than I've maybe ever been."

I melt into nothing at her words.

Or finally *something*, made up of hoping and longing and wanting.

"Have you . . . ?" I swallow, fighting to collect myself. If I can sit through an evening with Mr. Caldwell and his sister, if I can spend the rest of my life as his wife, maybe I can be brave enough to do something for myself this time. Even if it's just asking a simple question. Even though the answer I secretly desire, my name passing over her lips, couldn't possibly be her response. "Ever had feelings for anyone else?"

She doesn't say anything for a long moment, and I feel an odd sense of fear over having asked, the hairs on the back of my neck prickling with discomfort.

I laugh and add quickly, "Or *have*? With the likes of Alexander and James around, I mean, *surely* you must . . ."

My voice trails off, but Audrey holds my gaze, her face so close and yet so impossibly far in ways greater than just the physical.

"I . . . ," she starts, more cautious, more vulnerable than I've ever seen her. "I think I might have been the *tiniest* bit in love with my childhood best friend, Leah, once, but she moved to North Carolina just before high school started."

She.

I don't think to ask what high school is or how they lost touch or anything else.

My pulse thrums with what that one word could mean.

213

"Feelings for . . . a girl?"

"Yeah. I think I've always had crushes on girls, too, not just guys. For as long as I can remember. My elementary school art teacher, this super cool Pitt student who used to come into the convenience store every day for coffee and cigarettes, even Aubrey Plaza. But I guess I . . . I guess I never really acted on it or took the time to see what all those feelings could lead to." Her eyes dance around my face, studying every feature, like they are searching for something. "I don't know why I didn't. Maybe I was scared, or . . . the timing felt off, or . . . I don't know. I think it almost felt easier to just avoid it completely, or try to. Like it was a risk I wasn't willing to take. And once I fell for Charlie, it felt like I maybe didn't have to on some level."

Scared.

I feel that now, alongside the wanting, the part of myself I find in her words, both beautiful and terrifying. Moments, so many of them, suddenly make sense in a way they never did to me. When I would read romance novels and have small moments of uncertainty as to which character I wanted to be, the suitor or the romantic heroine, thinking it just was about the freedom the male had when it was so clearly *more*. Not feeling anything for men as objectively handsome as Mr. Shepherd or James but being able to really *see* and *feel* the beauty of a woman drifting past in a flowing dress, or dancing at a ball, or holding my gaze in conversation. Feelings I didn't think I should even feel. Feelings I didn't think anyone else could understand.

"Would that be allowed? Is that what you were afraid of?" I ask as I process this.

"Well, in the future, where I'm from, what my parents always taught me is that people can love whoever they want," she says softly, and my stomach flutters, then sinks, soars and crashes. She shakes her head. "But there are still some people who don't feel that way, even in 2023. So, yeah, maybe a little. Without me fully realizing it."

I feel the tiny glimmer of hope that I'd had snuff out.

Even if, by some miraculous chance, she had said she had feelings for me . . . I'm not from the future.

I'm from here. In the present. *My* present. Where a person cannot just love whoever they want, even if that person were a man. Where there are Mr. Caldwells, and rules of conduct, and fathers who must be obeyed, no matter how much I pretend I can escape it all with a few weeks of recklessness.

Where *this*, the terrifying thing I do not, *cannot* put into words simply does not happen because . . .

"Here, in 1812," I say, my voice quiet as I state my problem aloud, spurred on by my bitterness, "that is considered abhorrent."

I can feel Audrey's body stiffen at my words, a door closing quicker than I can throw my arm out to stop it. I hear how they've come out and wish almost instantly that I hadn't been so reactive.

"Yeah, well, you don't have air conditioners or modern plumbing, so maybe you need to rethink what's abhorrent," she says before rolling over, her words reminding me of my own earlier this evening while the Caldwells ranted on about how improper assembly room balls were and the people who attend them.

I've just done the exact same thing. I sounded just as dismissive. As judgmental.

Instinctively, I reach out to touch her shoulder, to tell her *I'm sorry*, that it isn't how I feel, that in fact I know what *she* feels, but I realize it wouldn't change anything. She may be going back to a time where that is far more possible, but I am not. I cannot forget that. Not anymore.

My jaw clenches, and I pull my hand away, fingers curling into my palm as I roll over, knowing all too well it is past time to put an end to whatever it is I am feeling.

CHAPTER 27

AUDREY

June 28–July 2, 1812

Well, that's that.

I brought up my middle school crush on Leah Chapman to see how she would react to it. To see if anything could happen between us, or if I was just being delusional.

And, apparently, I was so far off base, I was out of the damn ballpark.

See, Mr. Montgomery? This is why I don't take risks. It pays to stay in your lane.

I ignore Lucy for most of the next day and the following one, giving her one- or two-word responses and pretending not to see every quizzical look she shoots across the room at me.

"Would you like some more tea? Or coffee, perhaps?" she asks over breakfast to break the prickling silence.

"No."

"I was thinking of going for a walk later today, if you

would like to join me," she says in the drawing room before lunch.

"I wouldn't."

"Do you want to come with me to get a book from the library?" she asks after we finish our meal and return.

"No, thanks," I say, already hunched over my sketchbook, turned slightly away from her.

She even tries playing a few bars of "I Wanna Dance with Somebody" on the piano, but I refuse to stop my scribbling. I know it's probably petty, but I just keep thinking about what she said.

Abhorrent.

I mean, of any word she could have used, she used *that* one?

The music finally cuts out as she lets out a long exhale of air.

"Audrey, listen . . . ," she starts, and my heart jumps in my chest as our eyes meet for the first time all day. But just as they do, there's a knock on the drawing room door, and Martha pops her head inside.

"A Mr. Shepherd is here to see you both," she says, and I could not be more relieved to see a different set of bright blue eyes crossing the threshold.

"Miss Sinclair, Miss Cameron," he says with a wide smile, pulling his hat off as he bows to us.

Lucy instantly straightens, transforming into someone

else so quickly, it's almost disorienting. "Mr. Shepherd, how are you this fine afternoon?"

Fine. I resist the urge to snort.

"Very well, thank you," he says as his gaze shifts to me. He clears his throat nervously. "I was just wondering if Miss Cameron would do me the honor of walking the grounds? I would be most grateful."

"I would *love* to," I say as I toss aside my once-again blank sketchbook, since I've been resisting the urge to draw Lucy for the better part of the day. I'm eager to be out of this drawing room and as far away from her and whatever she was going to say as possible.

I'm halfway out the door when I notice he's not following. "What?"

"We, of course, need a chaperone to accompany us," he says as his eyes flick back into the room to look at Lucy. "If you wouldn't mind, Miss Sinclair?"

Great. *Of course we do.*

I hear Lucy let out a very uncharacteristically impolite sigh and can't help but swing my head back to look at her.

"That is, if it isn't too much trouble," Mr. Shepherd quickly says, and Lucy catches herself, plastering a smile on her face.

"No, no! I was just telling Miss Cameron earlier I wanted to go for a walk, so this is a marvelous coincidence," she says, drifting over to join us. "She declined, but perhaps the offer is *far* more tempting when coming from more desirable company."

Mr. Shepherd beams at that, mistaking my reddening cheeks for flirtatious embarrassment instead of anger. "Well," I say, beaming back at him. "I certainly don't find him *abhorrent.*"

Lucy tenses when he offers me his arm, and I slide my hand through it as the two—well, *three*—of us head out the front doors and down the steps, until we are walking slowly toward the sparkling pond just past the stables.

"Have you been well, Miss Cameron?" he asks, and I nod, you know, like a lie.

"Never better," I say fake cheerily, loud enough for Lucy to hear. "You?"

"I find, in this moment, you are echoing my exact sentiments."

With each step we take, farther and farther from Radcliffe, Lucy's skirts rustling away just behind us, I become more and more frustrated. But also more determined. The original plan is back on. To get home and get the hell out of here.

I have not one, not two, but *three* perfectly charming gentlemen who do not find a possible relationship with me to be repulsive. So I am not going to pine hopelessly after someone who does for the next eleven days.

"How are you liking Whitton Park?" I ask, secretly hoping he's already bored of it and the countryside. Maybe if he is, he would be game for, I don't know, possibly rocketing two hundred years into the future instead.

That is, *if* some kind of loophole does exist, which it better.

"I quite enjoy it," he says, squinting thoughtfully. "My parents passed unexpectedly in a house fire when I was a boy, and I spent a great deal of time away at school or in London with my uncle until I was of age. It feels nice to have a place I can make entirely my own now."

That explains the big-ass house at, like, twenty-one, but missing my home and my parents, I feel for him.

"I'm sorry."

He shrugs. "It was a very long time ago."

We duck under the shade of a big willow tree and gaze out at the water, watching a few ducks float peacefully past. We don't talk much, but it's a comfortable silence, unlike the one I've been in with Lucy all afternoon. I resist the urge for the hundredth time since we left to look back at her, fixing my gaze on Mr. Shepherd instead. I don't know how he's not dying from sweat in that black jacket and cravat thing he always wears.

"Aren't you . . . warm?"

"I suppose so," he says, wiping quickly at his brow.

"You tempted to jump in?" I ask, because I definitely am, and he laughs but shakes his head.

"Certainly, but I could not in the presence of a lady such as yourself. It would be improper."

Ever the upstanding gentleman. I figured he wouldn't set a toe out of line. My eyes move past him toward the stables, where James is leaning against the door, an enormous smirk on his face. He mimes someone talking with his hand, fakes an enormous yawn, and then collapses to the ground, tongue lolling out of his mouth. It's not hard to figure out his charade.

Dying of boredom.

I stifle a laugh and turn back to face the pond, but Mr. Shepherd turns, catching sight of James in the act, and the two lock eyes.

Shit.

I open my mouth to make up some excuse to cover for him, but now Mr. Shepherd is the one with an amused smirk on his face as he turns to look back at me.

"Although," he says as he pulls off his jacket, then sets his long fingers to undoing the scarf around his neck, "I suppose sometimes propriety can be tossed aside."

He casts a sideways glance at James as he chucks both behind him, the look, dare I say, intimidating? And also kind of hot?

I hear Lucy start to say something, but neither of us is listening.

I let out a scream as he scoops me up, running down the bank until we crash into the pond. Both of us surface, laughing, feeling the cool water cascading off us. My fingers clutch at the fabric of his thin white shirt to stop my dress from weighing me down, and I'm surprised to find an impressive layer of muscle underneath, a hint of dark chest hair peeking through the top.

"You surprised me," I say as a mischievous smile I never would have expected appears on his face.

"Well, Miss Cameron," he says as he leans forward, a dark eyebrow rising. "If that's your reaction, hopefully I can surprise you more often."

Perhaps he can.

The second the thought comes, Lucy clears her throat, and both our heads swing over to see her leaning against a tree, arms crossed over her chest. "I would be a rather poor chaperone if I did not intervene to preserve Miss Cameron's reputation."

"Don't worry, Lucy," I say. "My reputation is no concern of yours."

She actually has the audacity to roll her eyes at me! Unbelievable!

I open my mouth to continue, but her jaw locks and Mr. Shepherd sighs. "No, no. She's completely right. I must apologize. I wouldn't want to ruin your reputation in a town I sincerely hope you would wish to stay in," he says as he carries me out of the water this time.

The two of us sit on the bank in the sun to dry off, the air now pleasantly cool. His words give me an opening, though.

"I know you only just moved to Whitton Park, but would you ever leave it? To, I don't know . . . travel?" That's putting it mildly. "Go someplace new?"

He shakes his head. "I don't believe so. I never much liked

going off to boarding school and university and being shipped around Europe. I like a good night of dancing and socializing as much as the next person, but now that I've found a home, I don't much see a need to leave it."

Despite myself, I go to glance back at Lucy, to read on her face what she makes of this, but the spot where she was standing is empty. I guess she's not *too* worried about my reputation, then.

As Mr. Shepherd starts to talk about maybe having people over for a night of cards, I catch sight of her pale pink dress farther down the bank of the pond, back turned, arms crossed over her chest. She's likely just upset that she's stuck with Mr. Caldwell, who would never be caught dead jumping into a pond or having a single moment of fun.

But Mr. Shepherd's answer is a sign that fun or not, he's not the one for me, either.

My plan to throw myself into the actually available dating pool goes better than expected after that.

James whisks me away after dinner later that day, despite Lucy's disapproving gaze, and the two of us spend practically the entire night talking while he does his chores in the barn. He laughs about my jaunt in the pond and Shepherd's tough-guy look, and then I do my best to convince him the feelings I told him about were silly, already passing, as I try to get the flirting energy going again. Still, I'm not sure he buys it.

Then Alexander shows up two days later, asking me to sketch him after we drink tea with Lucy. The afternoon sun is perfectly angled in the window just past his head, outlining his strong cheekbones and curly black hair, and my pencil flies across the page in an attempt to capture it. I'm surprised to find that despite how I've been feeling, my art and my heart aren't so conflated anymore. The lines still come if I just trust myself enough to let them.

I am concentrating hard on the paper in front of me when Lucy stands abruptly, then drifts across the room to play the piano. She's forced to chaperone my bachelorette experience yet again, and she's clearly not too happy about it.

Not that I care, of course.

"Do anything fun since I last saw you?" I ask, kick-starting the conversation.

"Eh, you know. Played some cards at the inn, declined an invitation to a dinner party, a couple of rounds of billiards with a few other officers at an acquaintance's estate, drank a tad bit too much, and woke up fully clothed in my bathtub."

"Well, at least you were fully clothed."

He laughs. "A valid point."

I smile and shake my head. I knew his answer would be interesting. If Mr. Shepherd's a bit proper, Alexander's an adventure in and of himself. On paper that makes him the strongest candidate. I mean, if anyone was going to land the first impression rose, it would certainly be him. There's no denying that his enthusiasm for life makes me excited to live my own.

But I still don't know just yet where he fits into that.

"My dress for Friday's ball arrived today," I say. Abigail helped me try it on, and as expected after having eighty-five measurements taken at the seamstress, it fit perfectly.

Despite myself, I couldn't help but think what a different experience it was from helping Lucy into that shimmering blue dress, the feeling of being so close to her, my hand brushing against her skin.

But I couldn't be put in that situation with her again. Not now.

"Are you looking forward to it?" Alexander asks. "It *is* the social event of the season. I expect half the town will be engaged or otherwise accounted for come Saturday morning."

"I think so. Especially if the company is nice." I reach out, fingertips grazing the stubble on his chin as I turn his head back in the direction it was in. "I already know *you're* looking forward to it, so don't bother telling me. And will *you* ever be engaged or otherwise accounted for, Alexander?"

He laughs, the sound deep and inviting. I can feel the rumble of it in my fingers as they slide along his jaw.

"For the right girl," he says, knowing the perfect thing to say as always.

He's so *charming*.

But in some ways it feels just as practiced as Lucy's and Mr. Shepherd's prim-and-proper politeness, tinged with something false underneath, like Lucy's thin-lipped smiles.

"Perhaps I can steal you away from Mr. Shepherd for a few dances," he says before I can think on it further.

"You know, I went swimming with him the other day," I say, returning to the sketch, pencil scratching as I shade under his eyes, the straight line of his nose. Lucy shifts ever so slightly in my peripheral vision, and I prepare for a lecture about my reputation, but her playing remains as steady as a metronome.

"*Really?*" His eyes widen, his lopsided smirk pulling at the corners of his mouth, making me smile right along with him. "*Shepherd?* Didn't think he had it in him."

"Neither did I," I admit. "Maybe there's more to him than we both thought."

"Well, you know what they say," he says, turning his head to look at me, a teasing glint in his eye. "A man in love can be *greatly* transformed."

I roll my eyes and tear the page out, holding it out to him. "You've clearly used that line before."

"No, I have—" He freezes as he studies the drawing I just did. "Audrey. This is *quite* exceptional."

My cheeks burn at his compliment, pencil tapping on the page in front of me. "You're just saying that."

"Truly I am not! You are *brilliant.*" He grabs ahold of my arm, excited. "Can you paint? I would be honored if you did a complete—"

Lucy lets out a frustrated groan and plays a clash of notes on the piano, sending both our heads swinging to look over at her as she stands and slams the lid shut.

"It is *impossible* to concentrate with this never-ending stream of bachelors interrupting." Her eyes meet mine, and it's the first time I've really looked at her in two days. Her normally perfect hair has a few loose strands, and dark shadows I've never seen before linger underneath her eyes.

"If you'll excuse me," she says, ripping her gaze away from mine as she storms out of the room, fingers curled tightly into fists.

Alexander lets out a low whistle as the door slams shut behind her. "*That* was unusual. I'm not sure I've ever seen her so . . ." His voice trails off as he motions with his hand, the gesture he makes finishing his sentence. *Worked up.*

Me neither.

He bites his lip thoughtfully. "Any idea what might have caused that?"

"No," I say, eyes locked on the door handle.

I want to chase after her, but I swallow the urge.

Unlike Mr. Shepherd, Alexander doesn't seem bothered by the impropriety of us being alone together. He starts to ask about how long I've practiced art, a subject I'd usually love to chat about, but all I can think about is how ever-concerned-about-our-reputations, should-be-chaperoning-me Lucy just *ditched.*

And why exactly she did.

· · ·

The next morning over breakfast, after another night of sleeping with our backs to each other, I feel my heart leap into my throat when Lucy says my name, finally breaking the silence between us.

"Audrey, I can't do this any longer," she says, her hand reaching across the table for mine. I curl my fingers into my palm and move mine away, resisting the urge to reach out and take it.

Her eyes jump to my face, the expression in them like she's been waiting for this moment for days, but when she opens her mouth to say something, the door to the dining room bangs open before she has a chance. An old man with piercing blue eyes towers in the doorway, despite his rather small stature, and his head swings from me to Lucy, whose face grows pale as she pulls her hand away and quickly stands to walk toward him.

"Father, welcome home. I—"

"Silence," he snarls, stopping her in her tracks. He points an ornate walking stick at me. "Who is *this*?"

"May I present Audrey Cameron, all the way from America. She's a *dear* friend of a new gentleman in town, who is just setting up his estate at Whitton Park, so he is presently unable to entertain any guests," Lucy says as she steps in front of the walking stick, hands twisting nervously together. "He has quite a handsome income and *many* impressive acquaintances.

I thought it would only be polite and expected to allow her to stay here with us, and I'm sure many of those acquaintances would agree."

He lowers his hand slowly, eyes narrowing as he takes in her words. "Impressive?"

"Very impressive. In fact, Mr. Caldwell is among them," she says, and his gaze flicks right to her face at the mention of that asshole's name. "He was present at the gentleman's dinner party, which we attended."

He lets out a long, slow exhale as he processes all this information, and my heart hammers nervously. This dude is scarier than I imagined. Something about his demeanor, his *presence*, is worse than Lucy made it seem. Worse than that portrait in the upstairs hallway.

"Fine," he says, and I can practically feel her start to breathe again.

"We have some last-minute preparations for the ball we must make, if you'll excuse us."

Before he has time to say anything else or rebrandish the walking stick, Lucy turns, fingertips sliding down my arm and into my palm, pulling me from the room and down the hallway.

And for maybe the first time, I see.

I see why she hasn't even tried to stop her engagement to Mr. Caldwell. I see why she parrots what's "proper" and does everything she can to appear so *perfect*. So polite. So tucked into a neat little box of her own. It's more than just 1812 societal expectations.

She's afraid of him.

And, worst of all, she can't escape him. Unless she marries, she'd have no place to go, no home, if she doesn't do exactly as he says.

"Lucy . . ."

She whirls around in the middle of the hall, hands reaching up to grab ahold of my face. All the air gets knocked out of me at the feeling of her thumbs pressing anxiously into my cheeks, her body up against mine.

"Are you all right?" she asks, blue eyes searching.

All I can do is nod.

Slowly, her hands slide down my neck, and she steps back, one step, two, until she is pressed against the opposite wall. "I'm sorry," she says, her voice barely more than a whisper, her apology for more than just this moment. "What I said that night, Audrey, was inexcusable. I need you to know that I . . . I don't think that. I don't believe that."

Her apology lowers the walls again, and just like that, I'm right back to where I was. Wishing I could close that distance but knowing now, more than ever, that I can't.

It's not her fault she's from 1812. It's not her fault she doesn't . . .

She doesn't want me the way I want her.

Even if she somehow did, she, out of anyone in this time, couldn't. To even allow herself to *think* about it . . . The risk would be too high. And I know a thing or two about avoiding risks.

I shouldn't let that ruin our friendship. She needs me to get through this engagement, and I need her to get through these last days.

I just have to not think about the fact that this moment with her feels more romantic than the moment in the lake with Mr. Shepherd, Alexander's laugh rumbling underneath the press of my fingertips, and James lifting me off a horse combined.

CHAPTER 28

LUCY

July 3, 1812

My fingers tap anxiously on the arms of my chair as Martha pins up my hair. The night of the ball is finally upon us. I look into the mirror, tilting my jaw upward as I inspect my face. Eyelashes darkened with elderberries, cheeks dusted with a deep rouge, lips covered in a vermilion pomade.

Despite myself, I cannot help but wonder what Audrey will think when she sees me.

"Nervous, Lucy?" Martha asks, eyebrows raised as if she's been trying to capture my attention.

Yes. For all the wrong reasons.

"No, I . . . Just excited, I suppose," I lie.

"Mmm." She gives me a curious look before frowning with concentration as she inserts one final pin, then steps back and beams at her handiwork. "Lovely. Just lovely. And I'm sure Audrey will look just as beautiful as you do!"

I startle at her words before she flashes me a smile and adds, "All the young ladies will, will they not? In this season's best?"

"Yes, of course," I say, clearing my throat. "Especially since Miss Burton's arrival."

"And about the . . ." She hesitates. "About the engagement. To Mr. Caldwell. I know you don't—"

"I'm fine," I say curtly, softening once I see her face in the reflection. "It's fine, Martha. Really."

Her eyes grow glassy, and I bite the inside of my cheek to keep my face convincingly resolute. "Lucy, I just want you to know . . . your mother would be so *proud* of the young woman you've become. Whatever happens tonight, don't forget that."

"Thank you, Martha," I say, giving her hand a quick squeeze, but I feel entirely undeserving of that statement. I can't think of anything my mother would be less proud of than me marrying someone I despise.

Standing slowly, I regard my reflection one final time. The azure dress I picked out a month ago at Miss Burton's is finally on. The day I've dreaded, the day my father has dreamed of, is finally here. Mr. Caldwell is waiting to whisk me off to the ball.

My time has run out.

Tears sting at my eyes as I think about the past weeks with Audrey. Finding her in the field. Listening to music from the future in the drawing room. Sprinting on horseback after her. The spark in the carriage. Our talks late at night. And now the last few days before my father's arrival, wasted because I bit my tongue instead of apologizing, because I was too scared to . . . Well, it doesn't matter now.

"It was enough," I whisper before pulling my gloves on, grabbing my reticule, and exiting the room.

I pause in the hallway, hearing laughter coming from the guest room, where Audrey is readying herself with the help of Abigail, and I twist my hands together nervously as I drift toward the door.

Shall I knock? My hand rises.

Shall I wait downstairs? My hand lowers.

I squeeze my eyes shut and turn before I can change my mind again, heading down the staircase to the entryway. I peek outside to see my father standing with Mr. Caldwell beside the carriages in the drive, one gnarled hand rising to adjust his collar, the other wrapped tightly around his cane.

Mr. Caldwell, despite your best efforts and his warranted hesitation, has invited you to accompany him, and I sincerely hope you use this opportunity to secure his proposal once and for all. His words from almost a month ago echo loudly in my head as I prepare to make them come true.

I am distracted from the thought by a door opening upstairs, voices and footsteps following. When I turn my head toward the sound, I swear I forget how to breathe, how to *move*, perhaps even my own name.

All I can see is Audrey, floating down the staircase in a cream-colored gown, the silk fabric flowing behind her as her gloved fingertips glide along the railing. Her hair is pinned away from her face in loose ringlets, her lips a warm, tempting red, and her painted eyes lock on mine.

She comes to a stop in front of me, and I open my mouth to say something sensible and coherent. To tell her it is time to go. That my father is waiting for us just outside. That I'm glad the dress from Miss Burton fits without alteration.

But all that comes out is one word.

"Beautiful."

I'm not sure if it is the rouge Abigail applied or my secret, fervent hope, but I swear her cheeks grow red in color. I am acutely aware how much I want to reach out and touch them. To touch her.

Instead, I clear my throat and regain my voice, casting a glance at the door. "We should . . ."

"You'll be fine," she says, unexpectedly, and my head swings back to look at her. "He'll propose and you'll . . . you'll be fine."

"You think so?" I ask, my voice barely more than a whisper.

"I know so," she says, almost making me believe it. "I mean, *look at you.*"

This time it's my cheeks that warm at her words. "And you. Mr. Shepherd, or Alexander, or James even . . . Whoever you pick, I'm sure it will all work out exactly as it was supposed to. It will be fine."

Fine. The word seems to echo for both of us.

But then Audrey nods and moves past me, her shoulder

brushing lightly against mine. My skin prickles in her wake, and I squeeze my eyes shut, collecting myself before turning. Mr. Thompson opens the door for us, and we descend the stairs to the carriage, toward Mr. Caldwell, who awaits us with a wry smile on his thin lips.

I hold my breath, waiting for my father's criticism, some comment on my hair, or the dress, or my general demeanor, but thankfully, shockingly, he gives me an approving nod.

"Miss Sinclair," Mr. Caldwell says, ducking his head in a bow as he holds open the carriage door. "You look beautiful this evening."

I thank him, then without thinking, I grab ahold of Audrey's arm. "Ride with us," I whisper, grip tightening. I am not ready to be alone with him. Not ready for the question to come yet.

All she does is nod, and we ignore Mr. Caldwell opening his mouth to object as she glides past him inside.

I don't dare look at my father; that glimmering moment of approval is certainly gone.

I take Mr. Caldwell's hand, murmuring my thanks as he helps me into the carriage as well, and I slide onto the seat next to Audrey.

My heart should be hammering over the possibility of what she might say to offend or befuddle Mr. Caldwell or over what I just did, but I know it's at her closeness and the warm smell of orange blossoms I've come to associate with her, and the way her hair lightly tickles my collarbone when she turns her head.

The ride to the Hawkins estate is silent, Mr. Caldwell glowering out the window while Audrey's pinkie brushes against mine on the seat between us, hidden underneath the fabric of our skirts.

I hold my breath and stare straight ahead as I carefully, cautiously, slide my hand over hers, my fingertips lightly grazing the grooves between each knuckle, desperate to feel the skin underneath the glove with each second the ball ticks closer.

When the carriage jolts to a stop, I quickly pull my hand away, reaching up to pat at my hair while I peer out the window at the line of people leading up to the Hawkins estate.

Remember yourself, Lucy.

That's what I tell myself, over and over again, as we crawl to the front and eventually climb out of the carriage, my father following just behind us. By the time we finally make our way through the queue of guests up the steps and into the ballroom, confronting the sea of colors and glowing candles and familiar, smiling faces, I feel resolved again.

This is what I know. *This* is the world I am from.

I let out a long exhale of air, then push a smile onto my lips.

As long as I remember that, I shall be perfectly—

My heart stills, calling my bluff, as Mr. Shepherd approaches us, gliding through the crowd of people to get to Audrey, as if she is the only one here. He bows, then makes polite conversation with Mr. Caldwell and my father, inquiring about his time in London while my father asks him about his arrival in Whitton Park, but he keeps his blue eyes on Audrey practically the entire time.

After a just polite enough pause, he finally asks, "Miss Cameron, may I interest you in a dance?"

"Absolutely, Mr. Shepherd," she says, and all I can do is stand there as jealousy, deep and unforgiving, entrenches itself worse than ever in my stomach. I watch her hand slide into the crook of his arm, and she disappears with him into the crowd.

My feet move almost instinctively after them, but my father's hand wraps tightly around my arm as he hisses in my ear, "Lucy. You are not here to gallivant about with your new acquaintance. Remember, you have far more important matters to attend to."

At that moment my gaze darts across the room to meet Grace's, where she stands with one arm looped through Simon's, and I see her expression darken as she watches my father turn me back into the eager and waiting arms of Mr. Caldwell. It takes everything in me to plaster a smile onto my face.

"I look forward to dancing with you this evening, Mr. Caldwell," I say in an attempt to repair some of the damage from the carriage ride.

"Indeed," he says, the wry smile from earlier slowly, *thankfully* returning to his face. "This is going to be quite a special night, Miss Sinclair."

He offers me his arm, and just like that, he confirms that all my father's dreams are about to come true.

CHAPTER 29

AUDREY

July 3, 1812

Focus, Audrey.

I'm definitely not a good enough dancer to be this distracted.

I try to zero in on Mr. Shepherd's face in front of me, his blue eyes shining, mouth opening to ask me about the weather or the ball or who knows what, but my gaze moves for the thousandth time past his head to Mr. Caldwell's hand on Lucy's waist and the fingertips that grazed mine in the carriage resting on his shoulder.

She glances quickly in my direction, and our eyes lock for a fraction of a second, which is apparently long enough to make me trip over my own two feet.

"Are you all right?" he asks kindly, and that makes me feel even more awful for literally fantasizing about someone else while I'm dancing with him. "Are you feeling faint? Do you need me to fetch you a drink? Something to eat?"

"No, no," I say, twirling around him, careful this time not to fall flat on my face. "Just a bit nervous, I think." I lean in, lowering my voice to a whisper. "This is my first ball."

His eyebrows jump up in surprise. "Really? Your first ball *ever?*"

"Don't rub it in," I say with a teasing glare, my hand sliding into his. "What's your favorite part? About going to a ball."

"I like the excitement of it all. Everyone in their best attire, the weeks leading up to it, the night finally being here. Being able to be this close to you again," he says, pulling me into a tighter embrace, a trace of that warm, mischievous grin from the pond appearing.

There's no denying it's super romantic, a line out of a love story.

"And, when I was a boy, watching drunk people make a spectacle of themselves." He pauses, eyebrows furrowing. "Actually, that *still* may be my favorite part."

Now, *that's* right up my alley.

"*Same.* Okay, so at prom two years ago . . ." I hesitate. "A . . . local dance where I'm from . . . a couple of boys decided to dance on a table, and the entire thing collapsed out from underneath them. Harry Wilson bruised his butt so bad, he couldn't drive his car—" I stop when I realize what I've said, and naturally Mr. Shepherd looks confused. "Uh, *carriage* for an entire week."

"Once, I went to a ball in London with my uncle Alfred,

where the host ran through the ballroom completely nude, straight out the front door, and was found in the park the next morning, fast asleep on a bench. Top hat covering his . . ." He motions discreetly downward on a turn, and the two of us dissolve into laughter.

"You're kidding!"

The song ends, and he bows while I curtsy, our conversation briefly put on hold as we bite our lips to stop from giggling.

"I'm not! I swear it," he says once I take his arm again, and he guides me off the floor to get drinks. "It was the talk of the season. I think it even made the papers. I'm sure Miss Sinclair has heard the story."

Lucy.

I glance over my shoulder, searching the crowd of people for the blue of her dress, the gold of her hair, her general aura of practiced grace and perfection, but I can't find her. I swallow, trying to ignore the pang of disappointment.

"Drink?" Mr. Shepherd says as he holds a glass out to me.

I turn back to take it from him as a familiar voice calls out his name, and our heads swing around to find the source.

"Shepherd," Grace's husband, Simon, calls again, worming his way through the crowd. His brown eyes are squinting with excitement as he slings an arm over Mr. Shepherd's shoulder. "Do you remember Thomas Wilkes? Father owned that shipping business?"

Mr. Shepherd nods.

"He's here with his new wife. And *she* snuck in some absinthe from France, if you two are looking to make this night a little more interesting."

Mr. Shepherd glances back at me, and while I would usually be game to give it a go, I want to keep my wits about me tonight. I need to solve this puzzle and get home. And since the punch at the assembly room nearly took me out, I honestly can't even imagine what nineteenth-century absinthe is like.

I wave him on, eager for a minute alone to get myself together and figure out a plan of action. "Go ahead. I need to, uh . . . go to the water closet."

I watch them go before slipping quietly out a side door. The voices fade to a buzz in the dim hallways of the house, where far fewer people mill about, giggling couples trying to find a minute alone, friends gossiping in close circles.

Funny how some things never change.

It's like the Oakland house parties Charlie and I would sometimes sneak into, just without the phones, pumping bass, and Pittsburgh skyline.

I don't miss Charlie anymore, I really don't, but fuck, I miss home.

I slow to a stop, studying yet another painting of a regal-looking old guy, sitting on a horse *almost* as majestic as Moby, when a voice catches my attention.

"Again, Mr. Caldwell, my sincere apologies for how she behaved earlier."

I glance to the side to see Lucy's father and Mr. Caldwell hidden in the shadows, talking, and my hand clutching my glass goes completely numb.

Mr. Caldwell sniffs, nodding. "Clearly she has had some"—he pauses, mouth turning down—"questionable influences as of late."

Me.

"To be dealt with, I assure you," Mr. Sinclair says, turning my blood cold. "You will still be proposing, I hope?"

"Yes, shortly. She redeemed herself a bit. She seemed to think I planned to do it here and said she wants something a little more . . . *intimate*. More private. Obviously that is more proper. As if *I* would do it tonight, among the riffraff." He snorts. "She asked if I would do it a week from tomorrow."

A week from tomorrow.

The day after I'm supposed to be leaving.

"But I think it would be best to have the matter settled sooner," he continues, dismissing her request.

"Couldn't agree more," Mr. Sinclair says.

"I'll call tomorrow morning. Just after breakfast." He leans forward, a wormy grin on his very punchable face. "That is, if I have your permission, of course."

They both dissolve into laughter, like it's all some big joke. Like Lucy's life is dispensable to them. I turn, walking briskly back down the hallway, trying not to lose my shit.

Propose.

I knew it was coming, *tonight* even, but now I'm actually going to have to sit there and *watch him* propose. To Lucy.

Tomorrow.

And she's going to say yes. I know she is. She has to.

I let out a frustrated groan as I turn a corner and run smack into—

"Alexander," I gasp out, and his hands wrap around my shoulders, stopping me from spilling my drink on both of us.

"Audrey," he says, eyebrows furrowing as he studies my face. "Are you all right? You look rather upset."

I shake my head, biting my cheek to stop from crying. "I'm fine. I just . . ."

Without another word, he takes my hand and pulls me down a long corridor, outside onto a candlelit balcony, where the cool breeze helps me collect myself.

He leans against the ledge while I wrap my fingers around it, squeezing my eyes shut tightly.

"Is Mr. Shepherd that horrendous of a dancer?" he asks, and I laugh, shaking my head.

"If anything, *I'm* the horrendous dancer. I still can barely dance and talk at the same time. I think I almost stepped on his foot about thirty times."

I glance up at him, and he gives me that lopsided smile of his, warm and safe and familiar. "Well, Audrey"—he tilts his head closer to mine—"I would be *honored* to have you step on my foot during a cotillion."

I roll my eyes, pushing his chest, the fabric of his uniform rough under my fingertips, but before I can let go, his hand catches mine, holding it there. I can feel his heart thrumming unevenly as his gaze lowers to my lips.

For the briefest moment, I think about how *easy* it would be. To lean forward. To kiss him.

To pretend my heart didn't belong to someone else.

The part of me that wants to be home so badly tells me I should. But I pull my hand slowly out of his and look away, letting out a long exhale of air.

We stand shoulder to shoulder for a long moment, looking out at the rolling fields, which are gently lit by the moonlight.

"Mr. Shepherd?" he asks, his voice low and soft.

I shake my head. "Worse."

And, like the friend he's much better suited to be, without saying a word, he takes my hand once more, loosens his cravat, and says, "Let's go."

"Where?" I ask as he pulls me back inside.

He doesn't answer, but instead leads me down the hallway, swerving smoothly around people, the muffled sounds of music and voices guiding our feet. He skids to a stop in front of a grand staircase, looking both ways suspiciously.

"Alexander, what are we—"

"I completely agree, such a lovely event we have here tonight!" he says loudly as two girls in pastel dresses pass by. Then he lowers his head and voice to hiss, "Just trust me."

As soon as they're gone, he drags me quickly up the steps, pressing a finger to his lips as we tiptoe along the corridor. At the very end, he grabs a candlestick and peeks his head into a door, checking that the coast is clear before we slide through it.

I let out a faint gasp as he raises the candlestick to reveal what might actually be the library from *Beauty and the Beast*. Rows and rows of tall bookshelves line the walls, complete with a rolling ladder and a golden fireplace.

"Holy shit," I say, and Alexander laughs. He hands me the candlestick as I poke around the room, looking at the different books, so many shapes and sizes and colors.

"That's not all."

He goes over to a bookcase, carefully pushing on it until it gives way to reveal a secret door leading to a narrow set of stairs.

"How do you know about this?"

"I was friendly with the eldest Hawkins daughter growing up."

I raise a questioning eyebrow and lift the candlestick to illuminate his face. "'Friendly'?"

He shakes his head sadly and grabs the candlestick back from me. "Let's just say she was promised to an aristocrat instead of the youngest son of an aristocrat."

Ah.

I follow him through the doorway, the winding steps leading to a hidden room with low, angled ceilings, a desk, and a dusty-looking fireplace. At the very end is a large window overlooking the roof.

Alexander, of course, goes right over to it, pulls it open with a grunt, and ducks out onto the roof. After a few moments, he pokes his hand back inside for me to take.

"You're kidding."

I've been on many a roof, but not in an incredibly heavy dress and not one that used smooth slate instead of grippy shingles. I mean, I have no idea what 1812 building standards were, but one wrong move and I'm sure I'll be finding out.

"Audrey Cameron, raising the white flag?"

Naturally, as he knows it will, that makes me grab ahold of his hand, and Alexander guides me through the window and out onto the roof. I peer out at the waiting carriages, some people already leaving, some arriving incredibly late.

We sit, slowly, carefully, and he blows out the candle.

"Watch."

Above us, the stars come to life, so many of them and so bright that I'm shocked this world is the same one I live in.

Pittsburgh isn't exactly the star-watching capital of the world. But this . . .

"Wow," I breathe out, and the two of us lie back to take it all in.

"Being up here makes everything seem simpler. Doesn't it?"

I nod, feeling so small underneath all these constellations and universes, the moon bigger and brighter than I've ever seen it. And it makes the sting hurt a little less. The confusion and the fear and the worry about getting home feel a little smaller too. More manageable.

"The Hawkins girl . . . ," I start. "What did you do when you found out she was going to get married?"

"Just . . . tried to enjoy our final moments together," he says with a shrug. "We wanted to make it count while we still could."

Make it count. I want to.

"You remind me of her in a lot of ways," Alexander says. "Beautiful. Fun. Adventurous. Unusual."

"*Unusual?*"

He laughs and turns his head to look at me. "In a good way."

CHAPTER 30

LUCY

July 3, 1812

It is rather late by the time we get back to Radcliffe. My father surprises me by actually saying good night before he marches off to bed. I watch him go, my stomach turning with each tap of his walking stick, the pleasantry a reminder that though the proposal did not come tonight, I have . . . succeeded.

A week from tomorrow I will be Mr. Caldwell's fiancée.

But not tonight, I tell myself. *Not until she's gone.*

Dizzy from the punch and the exertion of dancing, Audrey and I walk languidly up the steps before collapsing onto the bed, heads spinning in a pile of silk and tulle.

She starts to hum the tune of the waltz we both danced to this evening, a new one that is burning its way across the country. I smile slightly, turning my head to look at her hazel eyes, warm in the glow of the candlestick Martha handed me when we came through the door.

"My feet are aching," I say with a grimace, shaking my head. "I think Mr. Caldwell spent more time stepping on my feet than actually performing any of the dance moves."

She stops humming, studying my face as she falls silent.

I don't know how to tell her that he didn't propose yet but that he will.

"He's proposing tomorrow," she says, beating me to it, but my eyebrows furrow in confusion at the last word. "I heard him tell your father."

"Tomorrow?" is all I can whisper back. "But I told him . . ."

"A week from tomorrow," she says, shaking her head. "I know. But they didn't listen."

I swallow and pull my eyes away from her face. I thought I'd bought myself more final bittersweet stolen moments here, with her.

And now they're going to be cut even shorter. My nails dig into my palms.

"Things didn't work out with Mr. Shepherd. Or Alexander," she continues.

I freeze at her words, fighting to form my own. "Well, there's always James."

"Mmm," she says, but it isn't convincing. Or perhaps that's just what I want to hear. Finally, she lets out a groan as she stands and grabs ahold of my hands. "Well, come on, then."

I frown up at her, confused. "Why? Where are we going?"

"We're going to dance," she says. "One more time. While we still can."

"We can't . . . ," I start, but she pulls me to my feet and starts to hum again, ignoring my objections, and the two of us fall almost instantly into the movements, slow and careful.

We pulled off our gloves in the carriage, so I am acutely aware of the feeling of her skin beneath my fingertips every time our hands collide, every time they glide gently up her arm before brushing over fabric. Tiny sparks of desire seem to crackle through me every time she pulls me closer, growing larger and larger, until I'm completely ablaze with a desperate longing, so deep it almost consumes me.

This same dance done with Mr. Caldwell only hours ago is entirely transformed. I never knew dancing could be romantic like this, outside of the novels I've read in secret. *Intimate* like this.

And I will never experience it again.

Our eyes stay locked on each other, and her face is so close, so *beautiful*, I don't even realize we've stopped moving until her humming gives way to a gasp as my fingertips graze against her collarbones, then slide up her neck until my thumbs find the skin of her cheeks.

My gaze lifts to her full lips, slightly parted, the red faded over the course of the night. They drift closer, *closer*, until her nose is brushing lightly against mine, and then . . .

She pulls away. My hands clutch at open air as she turns

her face to the side, out of the flickering candlelight, eyebrows furrowing.

"We should get to bed," she says, moving to do so.

All I can do is nod, head reeling as we get undressed, this act feeling so much more *charged* than it has on previous nights. I glance back to see her dress sliding down to reveal her shoulders, the dip of her lower back, but I look away until we have to unlace our corsets, my fingers fumbling with the ties, hers steady and sure and leaving me wanting. When we get under the covers, I can feel my heart ricocheting off the walls of my chest. The light of the candle flickers out, and her breathing slows while I lie completely still, staring at the dark ceiling.

After a long moment I roll over to look at her, fast asleep next to me, and try to put aside these last few moments and think instead of how I will remember her. The girl who, for a short time, completely upended my world. The one who saw me, who understood me, who wanted more for me.

I try to memorize it all. Long eyelashes, smooth skin over high cheekbones, the small scar just above her right eyebrow, brown hair framing her face, even the familiar ache I've battled against for weeks now, grown to the point that it never completely goes away.

Finally, surrounded by total darkness, I allow myself to give it a name.

Love.

CHAPTER 31

AUDREY

July 4, 1812

We almost kissed.

I stare at my cup of tea, still swirling from mixing my sugar in, and my untouched breakfast.

I can't even bring myself to eat.

All I want to do is to look over at her, to try to figure out what the heck she's thinking, what that *meant* to her, but I can't do that, either.

Everything feels . . . super precarious. Like when my dad tried to carry six teetering boxes of old-fashioned root beer in one trip and ended up coating the shop floor in glass, sticky soda, and soggy brown cardboard when his feet got tangled in the bunched-up welcome mat.

I don't want to figure out what my version of the bunched-up welcome mat is, but if I had to guess, it would be

Lucy's jerk of a dad, humming happily to himself all morning, bright eyed and bushy tailed.

As if on cue, he clears his throat, and we both turn our heads to look at him as he dabs at his mouth with the cloth napkin. "Mr. Caldwell will be stopping by in an hour or so, Lucy."

There we go.

"So soon?" she whispers, head swinging over to look at me, her expression stricken.

"He thought it would be best to get things squared away sooner rather than later. He has some business to attend to this evening," Mr. Sinclair says as she turns back to face him. "And I obviously gave him my blessing, so as a formality, he will be asking you for your hand in marriage."

I swallow and look away, ears ringing too loudly to make out their voices, too loudly to even realize he's gone until I hear Lucy say my name.

"Audrey." Her eyes are rounder than the stupid quarter that brought me here, her face pale. "I don't . . . know," she starts.

When I don't say anything, her brow furrows and she continues, her voice barely more than a whisper. "I don't know what to do."

And I don't know what to tell her. I don't know what I can possibly say that would do any good. I take a slow, mechanical sip of my tea, barely registering the taste, or the temperature, or the smooth porcelain. I put the cup down slowly, staring at the tiny pink and blue flowers, wanting to tell her to say no, to be with me instead of him, to *love me.*

But what can I offer her besides the slim, completely untested possibility that I can get both of us out of here together?

I mean, for all I know, she could be left here with the consequences, or we could *both* be stuck here, in a time when what I feel for her is . . .

Abhorrent.

I hear her voice saying it, making it that much worse. I can't put her in that position or stay in a time that feels that way about me.

And I can't risk raising either of our hopes.

So all I say is, "This is exactly what you've been working for, isn't it? Unless . . . you see another way?"

She inhales sharply and looks away but doesn't deny it, which is answer enough.

After breakfast, we go to the drawing room like everything is perfectly fine and normal. The grandfather clock ticks loudly in the corner. She plays the piano while I draw. Or, at least I try to.

None of the lines seem right. Every time I try to sketch her face, her eyes, even her outline, it comes out wrong. Off, somehow.

A pang of fear echoes through me, like this entire damn trip will turn out to have been totally useless after all. Just more heartbreak on top of heartbreak.

I quickly draw the sofa, the fireplace, even the piano she is sitting at, all of them fine, *great*, even, thankfully. But the moment I try to draw the person actually sitting at the piano, I just . . . can't.

So, instead, I sketch out all the scenarios that could stop this from happening, my eyes flicking up only to check the grandfather clock in the corner ticking our time away.

At the fifteen, I sketch us leaping out the drawing room window and running across the fields as far as we can. At the thirty, us kissing and instantly zapping back to Pittsburgh, like the end of a Disney movie. At the forty-five, Mr. Caldwell choking on his breakfast and never making it here to propose.

None of them will come to pass, though. And all I can do is wince when the clock finally rings out and her eyes fly up to meet mine. A knock echoes punctually from somewhere down the hallway, followed by a commotion, muffled voices, then approaching footsteps.

I notice her chest rising and falling, fast enough for me to be able to see the motion all the way across the room. As we stare at each other, no more time and nothing left to say, a wave of impending doom crashes down on me, like a Port Authority bus screeching down a Lawrenceville hill with a broken hand brake.

My thumb presses into the side of the pencil until it snaps completely just as the door swings open. We jump to our feet as Martha enters with Mr. Caldwell and Lucy's father.

I know I should stay, be her moral support, but I just . . . I can't watch this. I can't.

Before anyone says anything, I blurt out loudly, "Excuse me," and brush past them out of the room with my sketchbook. I look back, but only Martha is still watching me over her shoulder with a worried expression.

I run up the steps, tears stinging at my eyes as I push into Lucy's room, grabbing all traces that I had been in there: the reticule she lent me, the altered dresses, my blanket from the first night. I fight to hold all of them in my arms as I stumble down the hall to the guest room I should have just stayed in all along.

Maybe if I had, maybe if I'd kept my distance, I wouldn't feel like *this*. Again. But somehow so much worse.

Locking the door behind me, I slide down onto the floor and pull my phone out of my bag for the first time in weeks, desperately holding the power button and hoping it will turn on for even a fraction of a second, long enough to see Cooper's face, some small glimpse of my real life.

I squeeze my eyes shut and tilt my head back against the door and just wait for elated voices to ring out from downstairs.

When they do, it's like the Steelers made it to the Super Bowl or the Pirates finally had a winning season, and a tear slips out of my eye and down my cheek. I wipe it away angrily as I hear congratulations, well-wishes from all the staff, and all I can do is wonder, like I did on that very first day, *why* I am even here in the first place.

If it was to find true love, why did I fall for the one person I couldn't have?

These thoughts cycle for hours, paused only briefly by Abigail coming to call me down to dinner, but I refuse. The afternoon fades into evening, and evening fades into night, until the room grows dark around me.

Eventually, I pull the quarter out, feeling more lost than ever.

Was the point just to show me I *could* love again? Maybe that was all this ever was. Maybe it was never about finding true love at all but just realizing I had the capacity to feel something real for someone other than Charlie. That I can love again after heartbreak.

But if that's the case, the message, which sucks by the way, has clearly been received. So *why* am I still here? What is the quarter counting down to still? I let out a frustrated groan as the back of my head falls against the door with a thud.

A faint knock on the door sounds, almost like a response, and I hold my breath, waiting, hoping it isn't Abigail this time.

Finally, I hear her voice, so quiet and soft, whispering my name. *"Audrey."*

I stand, fingertips sliding along the grooves of the wood until my palm is completely flat. I don't say anything. I just . . . stay there. Feeling her, on the other side, hearing her breathing, the rustle of her dress. I have so many things to say to her, I can feel the pressure of them pounding against my skull, thick on my tongue.

But none of them will help, so I stay silent.

We both do.

Finally, her footsteps pad away, back to her room. Away from me.

Letting out a long sigh, I look down at the six on the quarter in my hand.

Six days.

And then what?

Will I be stuck here, trapped centuries in the past, so far away from Pittsburgh and my family and everything I know, unable to one day finish my portfolio or ever go to art school, because I couldn't figure this out? I mean, *where will I even go?* What will I do? Mr. Sinclair is sure to boot me out the second he gets the chance.

Or will I just . . . go home and never see Lucy again? Leave her all alone here, with no one who really sees her. No one who really cares about her and her thoughts and her feelings and her wants. Trapped.

And what will *I* do without *her*?

Either way I lose.

CHAPTER 32

LUCY

July 5, 1812

I can't sleep.

I toss and turn for most of the night, listening to the sound of a heavy rain against my window, the roll of thunder shaking the glass.

I'm engaged to Mr. Caldwell.

In the books I read, the heroines would always be so *happy* during moments like this. Set to ride off into the sunset with their husband-to-be.

For me, it couldn't feel more different.

Finally, I give up trying to sleep and throw my legs over the side of the bed, wrapping myself in a shawl as I stand. I grind my teeth together as I begin to pace around and around the room, but I end up feeling more trapped.

The sky is just barely lightening amid the storm when I slip out of my room and down the staircase, across the entryway, until I'm pushing through the front doors. The rain soaks me almost instantly, but my feet crunch forward along the gravel drive anyway, faster and faster until I start to run. Across the grass, along the pond, past the stables.

I run until I can't run anymore, until my gown is heavy and soaked, my breathing ragged. I'm so exhausted for a full minute, I almost don't even see her.

But then, all at once, there she is. Sitting in the exact spot where I first found her.

Audrey.

She looks over at me, and I turn right around, stumbling a few paces back toward the house. It's too dangerous for me to see her when I am this raw.

But something stops me, holding me in place, so I squeeze my eyes shut as my fingertips dig into the bark of the tree beside me, my face lifted toward the sky.

"Will you ever be happy?" her voice calls out. "Marrying him?"

I open my eyes and whirl around to see her walking toward me, her face illuminated for a breath as the sky above us flashes with lightning. She's wearing the pants she first arrived in, her nightgown stuffed hurriedly into them, as rain falls in sheets between us.

"No," I call back to her, the air catching in my chest. "But it's not like I have much of a choice either way, do I?"

I'm stuck like this. Hardly recognizing the person I've

become. Audrey has brought me alive in ways I never thought possible. She has made me *feel* in ways I never thought I had the capacity to feel. But all it has done is remind me that I will never feel those things again.

"No. I suppose not," she says, as if she already knows this to be true.

"But it will be perfectly fine," I say, tears and rain stinging at my eyes, my hand reaching up to wipe them away angrily. "My mother was wrong. I don't need love. It will be an adequate marriage. I will be comfortable. And you'll go back home, possibly drag James on some great adventure, and keep living like nothing happened. One day we'll forget *all* of this happened."

Audrey looks stricken, her mouth clamping shut, hands curling into fists. "Why did you come out here, then? Just for us to go back around in circles?"

"I don't know" is all I can say. And it's not enough. I know it isn't.

"You don't know?" she says, shaking her head. "Of course not. You don't know what you think, what you *feel*, because you just let your father, or Mr. Caldwell, or society do it for you. You refuse to leave that safe little box and actually deal with anything, so you just pretend to feel nothing at all."

"What about you, Audrey? Going after Alexander, and Mr. Shepherd, and James but not making a choice? Turning away from me yesterday? *Leah* and how you couldn't even tell her?

Holding back your application so you won't have to face a rejection? I'm not the only one who goes to such great lengths to avoid leaving a safe little box, no matter what shape your box may take."

She turns away from me, heading back toward the house.

"Where are you going?" I call out, my voice cracking on the last syllable, betraying me completely.

She stops, looking down at her feet. "I'm leaving. I'll stay at the inn in town until my time is up."

"Don't—" I take a step closer, but she whirls around, her face contorted.

"You don't understand, Lucy. You don't know what it's like for me to know you would nod and agree if they said I'm . . . I'm . . . What was the word? *Abhorrent.*" Her mouth curls around it. "That I'm wrong and perverse when what I feel for you, when all that I am is in . . ." Her voice trails off, jaw locking as she bites back tears, stopping herself from saying the words that, despite her criticism, we're *both* too afraid to say.

"I wouldn't."

"But you *would*, Lucy. They aren't even here right now and you're still—"

"Audrey . . ."

"Censoring yourself! *Refusing* to just *be honest* with me even if—"

"*Listen to me*," I say, as another crack of lightning bursts across the sky. "I am not from your time. I am from *here*." I motion around us, to the estate my sons will inherit before me. To the world I know, where falling in love with another girl and telling everyone so we could *exist* together would leave us both with no prospects, no life at all. I have racked my brain for any way to make it a *possibility*, and I cannot find one. And for all she says, she can't either.

"I am stuck, Audrey. In a time and in a place where I cannot tell you . . ."

My voice breaks, trailing off too.

We stare at each other for a long moment, and all the air is squeezed out of my lungs as I look into the eyes I will miss every day for the rest of my life. At the face that blurs the words on every page I try to read. At the person who makes my piano playing actually *mean* something. But, finally, she turns to leave me forever, and I feel my world crumbling around me, the trees and the field where we met and Radcliffe all turning to dust.

I can't bear the thought of marrying Mr. Caldwell when all I will think about, all I will *want*, for the rest of my life is her. I can't bear the thought of *this* being the last time we see each other.

We might not have a future, but we do still have the present. And in the present I don't want to focus on what makes this, *us*, impossible.

I want to embrace it while we have the chance.

"Kiss me," I call out to her.

I say the words before I have any time to think and suppress yet again what I have wanted to say so badly it makes my skin ache.

"What?" She turns around, the sky thundering above us.

"Kiss. Me," I repeat, firmer.

"Lucy, I—"

I take two steps forward, and my hands grab the smooth skin of her face, pulling her closer myself, *needing* her closer. And, suddenly, as our lips press together, I am found. I am *saved*.

We stumble our way back to Radcliffe, the rain still drenching us, but the feeling of Audrey's hands touching my waist, her fingers curling into my sides, the desperate answer to these weeks of longing, makes it barely register.

I pull her through a side door. The house is still quiet, no one yet awake to worry about, though I don't think I would even care at this moment. Her body presses up against mine, and she is still kissing me as we climb the stairs to my room. My palm rests over her heart as it pounds unsteadily through the thin, wet fabric of her nightgown.

I pull her inside, lock the door behind us, and let my shawl drop slowly to the ground. For the first time, we pause to stare at each other, lightning still flashing on the other side of the window. This time Audrey is the one who carefully, cautiously, reaches out, her fingertips tangling in the fabric of my nightgown as she pulls me closer, her eyes dark and wanting, the look in them making my whole body warm.

I melt into her when our lips collide, my breath catching as her hands dip below my nightgown, grazing along the skin of my leg, up my hip, finding the soft dip just below my rib cage.

"I've never . . . ," I whisper against her mouth. Never kissed anyone. Never been touched like this. Never *felt* like this before.

She pulls back, but I draw her back in, thumb stroking at last over the small scar above her eyebrow, pushing the loose strands of hair behind her ear.

"Neither have I. Not with a girl, I mean," she says, lips gently touching mine. "We can stop. We don't have to—"

"I don't want to stop." If we stop, we will never have another chance.

And I want her. More, perhaps, than I've ever wanted anything.

Every part of me burns with the feeling as our eyes lock. Then Audrey slowly, gently pulls my nightgown off, like that day she helped me try on my ball gown but so much better. My legs go weak as her eyes travel down, taking me in. I reach out and take her hands, guiding them onto my body, and a gasp escapes my lips at her touch.

"I don't want to stop either," she says, silencing my gasp with a kiss as we go tumbling back onto the bed.

"What would you say?" she whispers against my neck. "If you lived in my time instead of yours?"

My fingers tangle in her hair, every ounce of want and desire and love I have for this girl from the future filling me as I consider her question. I think of every smile from across the drawing room, every conversation that has made me long for *more*, and every stab of jealousy that has made me wish I were Alexander or Mr. Shepherd or James, when all I needed to be was myself. Every single moment of the last few weeks.

I pull her face up, her parted lips hovering against mine.

"That you've consumed me completely," I whisper into her mouth.

Her eyelids flutter closed, and finally, *finally*, I say it.

"That I love you."

CHAPTER 33

AUDREY

July 5, 1812

It can't be much past eight a.m. when the rain finally stops on the other side of the window. My arm is numb underneath Lucy, but I don't mind. I burrow my face in her golden hair and squeeze my eyes shut tightly, the smell of lavender filling my nose.

I can't get to sleep. The sound of the grandfather clock in the corner ticking away reminds me that in five short days my time will be up, no matter how much I wish I could freeze this moment. So I might as well make the most of each second and at least move my stuff back into her room.

Smiling to myself, I carefully slide my arm out from underneath her, trying not to groan as it drops like a lead weight, pins and needles radiating all the way to my shoulder. I pull on my damp nightgown and grab my pants, then tiptoe out the door and down the hall to my old room, where I shove my sketchbook, reticule, cell phone, real clothes, and a couple of odds and ends into a bag I find at the bottom of the closet.

And, of course, as I slip back out of the room, I run smack into the last person I want to.

"Mr. Sinclair," I say, quickly trying to smooth my hair and cover up my nightgown . . . and my ripped jeans, hanging over my arm . . . and my bag of stuff. Really, a brown paper bag over my entire body would be incredible right now.

His lip curls as he looks at me, his piercing gaze inspecting my general disheveled mess of a person.

"I question every day what you're doing in my house, Miss Cameron."

You're telling me.

"And I can't thank you enough for such kindness and hospitality," I say, trying to keep things light. Casual. Chill.

"I hope you know your mere presence here is endangering her reputation," he says.

"She doesn't seem to mind," I say, the words slipping out before I can stop them.

"Mr. Caldwell does. He had doubts about a proposal because of it."

I think about the night at Mr. Shepherd's, how he made it pretty clear he wasn't a fan of me. His look of disgust when he invited Lucy to dinner without me before we left. The night of the ball, when I was called a "questionable influence."

"I know from what I've heard, and observed, that it makes

perfect sense he would question your upbringing. And exactly what your connection to Mr. Shepherd is, especially when you were seen disappearing with my unscrupulous nephew, Colonel Finch, for a great deal of the evening."

I am shocked but don't say anything as he takes a step closer to me, mouth twisting into a cruel smile. "Do you know what happens, Miss Cameron, if Lucy is associated with someone who behaves *so* improperly? If her reputation is tarnished? If Mr. Caldwell changes his mind about the offer he has made?"

When he doesn't continue, I stare him down, daring him to speak.

"She'll be ruined. No one else will pursue her, and she will become a spinster with no possible upward mobility. Which means I'll have no use for her. And when I die, she will get *nothing*. Have *nothing*. Although, with such little value, she would certainly no longer have a place here at Radcliffe long before that," he says, and my entire body goes numb at his words.

I didn't think . . .

I didn't think he would just *throw her out*.

"Mr. Caldwell wants you gone by the end of the day. *I* want you gone now."

He takes another step closer, his face now inches from mine.

"You being here, Miss Cameron," he whispers, "is going

to destroy her entire life. So I hope you will take your much overdue leave by the time I return from town this afternoon."

His words are like a slap to the face. A bucket of ice water being dumped straight over my head.

He brushes past me, leaving me standing in the hallway, clutching my bag to my chest as my ears ring loudly.

I'll destroy her life.

Getting her out isn't a certainty, and here I could give her nothing. It isn't 2023, where I could just find a job at a cool indie bookstore, or make lattes at a Starbucks, and we'd find a way to make it work. And if I am zapped back to Pittsburgh and she *stays*, she'll be dealing with the consequences all alone.

Any hope that secretly bloomed after last night is ripped out of me.

That's too big of a risk, despite what Mr. Montgomery might say. Lucy was right, no matter how much I didn't want her to be. Her father is right, no matter how much I *really* don't want him to be. Admitting our feelings for each other isn't enough to change the world around us. And she has too much to lose.

I let out a long exhale of air, my chest aching at just the thought of us being separated by centuries and continents, seeing her only in my memories, her every feature etched into my mind. Especially knowing what I know now. Knowing what we could be and what her life could become.

Which is why . . . I have to go. Now.

Before I make things even worse.

I pull my sketchbook out of my bag, the pages fanning out in front of me, and realize I can't take it with me.

I can't face her picture again, let alone *her*. And I know if I open the door, I'll see her still fast asleep, golden hair scattered across her pillow, lips slightly parted, more beautiful than any drawing I've ever done or will ever do, and I'll never go. So I scrawl a note on a blank page and leave it on top.

I'm sorry.

That's all I can say.

I'm sorry I can't save her from any of this. I'm sorry that falling through time and space and landing smack into her life has only made things worse. I'm sorry I can't be with her the way I so desperately want to. I'm sorry I have to hurt her to save her.

Then I slide the entire sketchbook under the door and walk down the steps and through the front door, putting Radcliffe behind me for good. One thing is for certain: if I ever get back to 2023, I'm going to kill Mr. Montgomery. His days of free coffee and newspapers are *long* gone.

It's only as I walk through the same fields she found me in, and where we found each other again, that I realize the thing I might be sorriest for: I never told her I loved her.

CHAPTER 34

LUCY

July 5–8, 1812

I despise her.

I throw the sketchbook across the room, pages flying out and slowly raining down in front of me. A sharp feeling of betrayal lances straight through me as my fingers curl around her note.

I'm sorry.

That was all she could say to me, after . . .

After.

Tears blur my vision as I stare at all the papers lining the floor, Audrey's short time here brought to life, yet so easily left behind. I sink slowly to my knees and reach for one.

A drawing of me at the piano.

I reach for another.

Me, riding through the small glade of trees.

I keep reaching.

Me, laughing at the dining table.

Me, fast asleep, hair strewn across my pillow.

Another and another and another, until my arms fill with the papers. All of them, drawings, sketches, of me. Evidence of Audrey seeing a version of me that I had always wanted seen. Had always wanted *known*.

A version that will no longer exist.

I retreat under my covers, curling into a ball, pages crinkling as I squeeze them to my chest. Morning fades into afternoon, and afternoon fades into evening. I leave Martha's knocks on the door unanswered and let trays of food go cold outside while I fight to close the gaping wound Audrey left behind.

Once the sky has gone completely black, Martha finally manages to break her way in with a key from Mr. Thompson's overflowing ring. Her tea tray clatters onto my bedside table as she presses the back of her hand against my forehead and cheeks, checking for a nonexistent fever.

"Lucy, *Lucy*," she coos. "Are you feeling unwell? A cold? A fever?"

"No, I . . ." I shake my head as tears spring into my eyes.

Her gaze moves from my face to the pile of sketchbook pages clutched in my arms, and my stomach twists as understanding slowly settles into her features.

Yet she makes no comment. No questions or remarks. All she does is scoop me up into her arms as my body is racked with sobs, ribs aching underneath her reassuring hands.

"Oh, Lucy. Oh, my dear," she whispers, soothing me, staying with me until I finally drift off into a fitful sleep.

It takes me three whole days to rise from my bed, though my body still feels fragile enough to be blown over by a strong wind. Martha helps me get ready while I stare at myself in the mirror, eyes red and puffy, cheeks gaunt, hair a disheveled mess she is gently, carefully trying to comb through.

"She's gone?" she finally asks as our eyes meet in the mirror. "Audrey?"

I wince at the sound of her name but force myself to answer. "Yes."

"Where did she go?"

"I don't want to talk about it."

My voice cracks, the wound unavoidably splitting back open. I squeeze my eyes shut, fighting for and finding my resolve.

Martha puts her warm hand on my shoulder, giving it a soft squeeze. "Lucy, I . . ."

I shake my head, and she stops midsentence, not pushing any further. I was right from the beginning. There is no "more" out there for me.

With a little powder, some blush, and a fine dress, I begin to look almost human again. Or, at least, a rather believable illusion. Steeling myself, I leave the room and head down to breakfast, Martha trailing just behind me. I think of what I am going to say the entire way so when I arrive the determined words tumble from my lips before I am even fully seated.

"I wish to speed up my upcoming nuptials to Mr. Caldwell."

We hadn't set a date yet, though it was assumed the affair was likely to be held at the end of summer, but what does it matter now? Might as well get it over with so I can leave this place behind, just like Audrey did.

My father glances up at me, bushy eyebrows rising in surprise. I see Martha still just over his shoulder, a cup rattling in her usually so sturdy hands.

Resolute, I continue. "The day after tomorrow, I think. A small affair, at the church in town." I pour myself some tea, stirring in some sugar.

"The day after—"

"You said Mr. Caldwell was eager for us to be wed," I say as I take a sip from the cup. "As am I. As are *you*. I know you have no interest in me staying here any longer, so let's skip the pretenses. If we are all in agreement, I don't particularly see the point in waiting any longer."

He nods, looking rather pleased, the expression entirely unfamiliar to me. "I will send word to him straightaway."

My vision blurs as I calmly eat my breakfast. My father calls in Mr. Thompson, the message is sent off, and plans begin to be hurriedly strung together for a dress and flowers and invitations to a careful selection of guests. And I just sit there as it all fades to a dull hum.

When my father stands to leave, for the first time since I was a small child, he places a hand on my shoulder and gives me some semblance of a smile as he passes.

What a gift to him it seems to soon be rid of me.

I ignore Martha's stares, her questioning looks, not wanting a single expression from her to threaten my newfound resolve.

When I finally rise from the table, I head along the upstairs corridors to the library, teeth grinding together as I start a roaring fire and pull up the floorboard, throwing book after book into it until the space is empty, until there's nothing left.

I cross my arms over my chest as I stare at my mother's portrait, fingers digging into my sides, burrowing deep into the gaps of my rib cage.

"You were wrong," I say, tears stinging at my eyes. All this time, all these years, I always *wanted* to fall in love, even when it seemed impossible. *Because of her.* What she had said.

And now I wish that I never had. I wish that I never knew I could feel so deeply, so I might have been fine feeling so little.

CHAPTER 35

AUDREY

July 9–10, 1812

My feet still ache from my marathon walk running away toward town four days ago.

I was intercepted halfway there by none other than Mr. Shepherd. Well, *Matthew*. The two of us are on a first-name basis finally, after he found me crying on my way to the inn during his afternoon walk and snuck me in to crash in one of his guest rooms. I've been moping around and wailing there ever since, wrapped in a shawl, like a Victorian ghost.

Luckily, his house isn't fully staffed yet, so I won't ruin his *and* Lucy's reputation all in one month.

My goal is to just stay in my room and wait out the last few days until the quarter decides to teleport me back (or not), but a little after noon on my second day there, I hear voices and laughter in the entryway downstairs, and my curiosity gets the better of me. Grumbling like an angry old man with kids on his front lawn, I roll out of bed, throw on a dress without the million layers underneath, and tiptoe down the hallway. When I peek over the railing, I see two expectant faces gazing up at me.

Matthew, obviously. But beside him is none other than Colonel Alexander Finch.

He gives me a small wave, and I let out a long groan.

"And it is a *pleasure* to see you, too!" he says with an exaggerated bow while I suppress a small smile, putting my elbows on the banister, my chin in my hand.

"What are you doing here?"

"Shepherd here thought it might do you some good to see a friendly face."

"Well," I say, glaring at Matthew, who gives me a sheepish grin, "Shepherd would be *wrong*."

"That's a shame," Alexander says with a shrug, holding up a cloth-wrapped box and shooting me a side-eye. "To think, I brought sugar cookies, fresh from the bakery, but I suppose . . ."

The words are barely out of his mouth before I'm down the stairs, swiping them from his grip.

"All right," I say, patting him on the shoulder. "You can stay."

We go into the drawing room for tea, and I take the couch, while Matthew and Alexander plop onto the chairs. I try to nibble the edges of my sugar cookie and ignore the two of them staring at me expectantly, but eventually it becomes impossible to avoid, like when Cooper would beg for food at the dinner table.

I let out a long sigh. *"What?"*

"It's just . . . you seem . . . ," Matthew starts, but Alexander puts a hand on his arm.

"What if I said something so absurd, it may be the truth?" he asks, and I sigh, settling back into the couch.

"Better idea. How about I go first?"

He nods, motioning for me to talk.

"I'm from two hundred years in the future."

They both stare at me, unspeaking, for fifteen, maybe twenty seconds. Then, finally, they burst into laughter, Matthew doubling over as Alexander wipes tears from his eyes.

"Well, I see you have not lost your sense of humor!" Alexander says, but I hold up a single finger to silence him before running out of the room and up the stairs to grab my reticule from beside my bed, returning to two very confused faces.

"Look."

I overturn it on the table in front of them, my cell phone and my wallet tumbling out. The two of them are quiet as they lean forward to study the unusual screen and camera lenses, the crumpled five-dollar bill, my photo ID, and my library card. I watch as they hold the money up, scratch at the picture on the ID, and poke at the glass.

Finally, Alexander looks at Matthew, dark eyebrows raised. "Well, that would explain the dancing."

Wait—*what?*

"I was thinking the same thing," Matthew says, tapping

my phone against his palm. The pair of them settle back in their chairs, gossiping away like I'm not even here. "Also, she occasionally says things that—"

"Make absolutely no sense?"

"*Yes!* At first I thought society must be extraordinarily different in America. But just yesterday morning—"

"All right, all right!" I say, jumping up and grabbing my possessions back from them, not in the mood to get roasted after the week—no, *weeks*—I've just had. "I get it. I wasn't a master at blending in!"

They both laugh, but then Matthew frowns and takes a long, slow sip from his cup of tea as if thinking something over. "If you don't mind me asking, how did you get here?"

"An old guy who comes to my parents' shop spouted some crap about me hiding from love and, well . . . life tossed me a coin, and *POOF*." I wiggle my fingers. "I landed in the middle of Lucy's field."

My jaw clenches, reflexively, at her name.

I need another cookie.

"Interesting," Alexander says, biting his lip thoughtfully as I reach for the box.

I point my cookie at him. "Pretty sure whatever absurd thing you were going to tell me, it can't top that."

He shakes his head. "I suppose you're right, but . . . Matthew says you've been crying, lying about, gazing forlornly out windows. . . ."

Jeez. Really painting a great picture of me here. I can hear my mom saying something similar back when Charlie dumped me. I motion for him to continue.

"I think . . ." He stops and clears his throat, shifting nervously in his seat. "I think you're heartbroken."

My enormous bite lodges square in my windpipe. Coughing, I take a big gulp of tea, narrowing my watering eyes at him once I can actually feel oxygen making its way to my lungs again.

"Yeah, *totally*." I snort. "Your dancing was so bad at the ball, I just—"

"Not over me."

I cross my arms over my chest, my stomach fluttering nervously.

"You think Shepherd, ditching me to go drink absinthe—"

"Not over Matthew."

My eyes flick quickly over to the guy next to him, who gives me a wistful yet shit-happens shrug, midsip.

"All right, then." I lean forward and raise an eyebrow. "Who am I heartbroken over?"

He leans forward too, mirroring me. "Lucy."

Where's Martha with her smelling salts when you need them?

"Lucy? Me? That's . . ." I let out a loud laugh, trying to cover my ass by acting like that's the funniest thing I've heard in my entire life, but from their expressions, it's pretty clear they aren't buying it.

Dropping the act, I let out a long exhale of air. "And if I did have feelings for her, you wouldn't think it's . . . abhorrent?"

Matthew snorts. "Hardly. I went to an all-boys school."

I look at Alexander, who smirks. "I am *extremely* well traveled."

"Yeah, well, clearly not everyone got the memo on that one. In fact, according to Lucy, that's pretty far from the general consensus." I clasp my hands in my lap as both of them nod, conceding the point.

"Did she reject your feelings for her?" Alexander asks.

"Well, not exactly." I squeeze my eyes shut, images from that last night flashing across the back of my eyelids, there every time I close my eyes, every time I let my mind wander, no matter how hard I try not to think of her. Lucy's face illuminated in a crack of lightning, her skin under my fingertips, the shape of her body under the sheets.

I guess, if anything, I rejected *her* by leaving. But . . . I had to.

"Her father told me I had to leave. That Mr. Caldwell insisted on it. That my mere presence, by association, was going to completely obliterate her life. And, anyway, it just wouldn't work. It was stupid to think it ever could." My voice rises, the frustration I've felt for weeks now pouring out of me. "I mean, *here? Now?* What life could we possibly have? And who would I be to ask that of her?"

Matthew looks down at his hands, brow furrowing. "Do you not think that's Lucy's decision to make?"

I freeze, his words taking me by surprise.

Because he's right. I *did* make the decision for her.

Just like Mr. Sinclair and Mr. Caldwell.

"But I don't even know if I'm going to be here that much longer," I counter. "When my time runs out, I could be sent right back to 2023 without her. And all that is completely ignoring the fact that she's *engaged*. In a few months she'll be *married*."

"Tomorrow," Alexander says.

"What?"

"She's getting married to Mr. Caldwell. Tomorrow at noon. At the chapel in town."

My ears start to ring as I struggle to process what he's telling me.

No, I mean . . . he can't be right. *Tomorrow?* She's getting married *tomorrow?*

I stumble to my feet, and they jump up too, faces lined with concern. Alexander reaches for me as Matthew starts, "Audrey—" but I shake my head, and his mouth clamps shut as Alexander's hand freezes in midair.

"I'm sorry, I just need to . . ."

Mechanically, my legs carry me out of the room. I can't look back at them. Can't stand to see the pity on their faces.

With each step I take, I feel a deep, pressing anger bubbling up inside me. A suffocating frustration over the fact that I can't do *anything*.

I can't make any of this better. I can't stop the marriage and save both of us. I can't tell her how much I love her. Not anymore.

And, worst of all, I was so afraid of the risk, I took away her last chance to take one, to choose something for herself.

Letting out a desperate cry, I rifle through my sheets until I find the quarter that sent me here, fingers curling around the cool metal. I hold it up, watching as it reflects the afternoon light. The number one shining in the center.

Tomorrow is my last day.

Tomorrow is Lucy's last day.

And all I *can* do is wait for our time to run out.

I toss and turn the entire night, head shoved under my pillow as I think about Lucy standing at the altar in just a few hours, across from Mr. Caldwell. Not just because of him or her father.

Now also because of me.

Groaning, I finally chuck my pillow aside and climb out of bed, rubbing my eyes as I slowly get dressed. The sun is still low on the horizon, but I wonder how long it will take for something to happen, when the quarter's time will run out.

I trudge down the stairs to the drawing room and find Matthew just inside, talking to an older gentleman who is tending to the fire, his back facing me.

"Ah, Audrey," Matthew says, standing. He motions to the man. "Allow me to introduce to you my new butler, a Mr. Montgo—"

CHAPTER 36

LUCY

July 10, 1812

I am getting married today.

One would think those words would come with a wave of joy. Nervous jitters. Excitement.

I know I once dreamed they would, but all that thought evokes is dread, so deep in my bones they start to ache. Even though the timing at least was my choice.

I gaze out the window of my carriage, biting my cheek to fight the unwelcome tears that sting at my eyes. Just as I think I have pulled myself together, though, Martha reaches out from the opposing seat to take my hand, pushing me dangerously close to being a blubbering mess.

"Lucy, I can tell something is troubling you," she whispers, stating the obvious. Like we are not presently on our way to Miss Burton's for some exceedingly last-minute alterations to the wedding dress I will wear in less than four hours' time as I am standing at an altar next to Mr. Caldwell.

As if my entire person, my chest, my legs, my *fingertips*, don't ache when I think of her.

"I'm fine, Martha. Truly," I say instead, with all the brightness I can muster. I squeeze her hand and force a smile to my face as we enter town, the streets far busier in the morning than in the heat the afternoon brings.

"I . . . ," she starts. "Mr. Caldwell. This marriage. I *know* this isn't what you want, and I'm . . . *I'm sorry*. Your mother wouldn't want to see you like this. Wouldn't want you to be doing the same as she did. I wish I could—"

"My mother is not here, is she? And what business is it of yours?" I snap as I rip my hand out of hers, feeling instantly guilty as her gaze drops from mine, her hand curling slowly into her lap. This woman has cared for me my entire life, been there for me after my mother died, stayed when I wouldn't have. She was by my mother's side on her wedding day, and now here she is, watching her daughter follow in her footsteps and trying to protect me, even though she can't.

I am no better than my father.

"I'm sorry, Martha. I . . ." My voice cracks, finally betraying me. She only nods, reaching out to pat my leg, understanding.

A few minutes later I find myself in a daze as I stand in front of the mirror while Miss Burton pokes and prods at what was previously my mother's wedding dress, my skin prickling underneath the off-white French evening gown. Her assistants take copious notes beside her, to hem the sleeves and the bottom, to take in the hips and waist.

My father, whose shorter stature has evidently rubbed off on me, must be paying a small fortune to have so much work done on such short notice.

She taps my extended arms, and I lower them until my fingers graze the cursed fabric that is soon to usher in its second unhappy marriage.

"To think," Miss Burton says as I cover myself with a wrap while the dress is whisked away for work to begin immediately, "just a month ago I was helping you pick a gown to catch Mr. Caldwell's eye, and now a *wedding*. I'd say you more than caught his eye, Miss Sinclair!"

I give her a small, polite smile as her eyes widen with excitement, but all I can think is how much has changed in that month. How much *I've* changed in that month.

"Oh, I just remembered! That gown you ordered," she says, motioning to one of her assistants, who scutters from the room to retrieve it. "I was going to send it to Radcliffe this week, but I suppose it should actually be sent to Mr. Caldwell's estate now."

The second I see it, silk and lilac and absolute flowing perfection, I burst out laughing. This ridiculous dress, which I thought could be a small act of rebellion, a reminder of one small thing I chose for myself. How foolish. Now it's sure to just waste away in my new closet. I don't want to be reminded of that at all.

Miss Burton frowns in confusion, so I shake my head, wiping away a tear. "I'm so sorry," I say, fighting to collect myself. "I don't know what came over me. Thank you, Miss Burton. It's lovely, truly."

And it is.

Lovely and pointless and pathetic.

Martha motions for them to leave the dress, and the two of us are left alone to await the finished alterations.

"I know," Martha says finally, pulling a small emerald-green bag from her reticule, "that you will try to stop me from saying any of this, Lucy, but I care about you—I care about *your mother*—too much not to."

I am silent, nodding for her to continue.

"When I fell in love with my Samuel, the whole world became brighter. Because I was completely taken with him but also because, being around him, being loved by him, I felt like I understood myself better than I had in years. And seeing the person I had become and who I could become was . . . exciting."

She gives me a small smile, rosy cheeks lifting.

"I have looked after you for your entire life, Lucy. Watched you grow and become the beautiful young woman you are today. But I have also seen your light dim and change. Seen you become a ghost of the vibrant, happy, *opinionated* girl you once were. Do you remember that time your father was having a business dinner with the textiles company? You couldn't have been more than six." She chuckles, shaking her head. "He had that dress made for you of their fabrics, and you went missing late that afternoon. We looked for you for hours only for you to return just after the dinner bell rang, *covered* in mud, dress torn to shreds."

"He was furious," I say, picturing my father's face, nostrils flaring, eyes ablaze. I don't think I've ever seen him so mad to this day.

"And yet you sat right down and picked up your fork, saying you 'thought it was best to test out the product before any business agreement was made.' The room just *erupted* with laughter. Not your father, granted, but everyone else. Your mother and I whisked you away to get cleaned up, giggling the whole way, but *that*, Lucy. That's what I'm talking about."

"I wasn't allowed outside for a whole month after that," I say. The deal was still made that day, but I suffered the consequences anyway. That's what I remember now from almost every choice I've made—the consequences.

"It's been so hard over the years to see that girl be forced to disappear. And then, well, *she* came, and with every day that passed, I saw parts of you, slowly, come back and also new parts of you I had never seen before."

I clasp my hands together tightly at the truth in her words, but I cannot let it in.

"Well, she's not here anymore," I say, quickly reaching up to wipe away the unwelcome tear rolling down my cheek.

When Martha responds, her voice is barely more than a whisper. "But you are, aren't you? You are still here, Lucy."

She opens the small emerald-green bag in her hands, slowly pulling out a necklace.

My breathing stills.

It's not just any necklace.

A thin gold chain with a single teardrop pearl.

My mother's. From her portrait.

Carefully, she brushes my hair aside, the chain cool as she clips it around my neck. My hand reaches up, and my finger-tips find the pearl at last.

"Don't quiet all those parts of you. Be the person you were when your mother was here. When Audrey was here. Even if they no longer are. Even if you must be wed. Because, Lucy, *that* is who you are."

And her words make me wish.

I wish it were enough for me to grab that lilac dress and run from this dress shop, to say no to Mr. Caldwell, to never see my father again.

But I don't even know what I would be running to. A note slid underneath my door, saying *I'm sorry*? A girl who might already be back two hundred years in the future? Feeling, hop-ing, wanting once more only for it to crumble into nothing and leave me worse off than ever?

Before I can even consider it further, Miss Burton comes back in with the altered gown, presenting it to me like the answer to my unspoken question.

"Ready?" she asks.

I nod and fix a smile on my face.

Despite how much Martha's advice touches me, it's useless in the end. All I can do is stand there in my mother's wedding dress, now *my* wedding dress, and pretend I haven't changed at all.

CHAPTER 37

AUDREY

July 10, 1812

Mr. Montgomery.

The old man turns, and I'm met with familiar green eyes. Eyes that would wink at me when he came to collect his morning coffee and paper, or squint at the pages of my sketchbook to take in every tiny detail, or widen when I'd tell him stories.

His name isn't even out of Matthew's mouth before I'm flying across the room, unsure if I'm going to tackle or hug him.

Before I can decide, Matthew steps between us, grabbing ahold of me while I flail like a cartoon character, arms and legs and fists swinging at a million miles an hour.

My words are a jumble of "I can't *believe* you sent me to *1812*," and "You are the absolute *worst*," and *"How did you even do it?"*

"Audrey," Matthew says once I've simmered down a bit, but my eyes keep bouncing from Mr. Montgomery's face to his. He puts his hands on both my shoulders. *"What* exactly is going on?"

I point past him. "That's the guy who sent me here!"

His eyes narrow, and he turns his head to look at Mr. Montgomery, who raises his bushy eyebrows and gives a small, sheepish wave.

Matthew lifts his hands, releasing me. He turns his body to let me pass and motions for me to continue. "After you."

But I just . . . stand there. Frozen. Facing the tiny old man who tossed me a quarter and sent me two hundred years into the past to get my heart broken again. This time without even my family or my dog to help me.

"Why . . . ?" I start, my voice trailing off. "Why did you even send me here?"

He lets out a long sigh, his eyebrows furrowing as he puts the fireplace tongs down. "I don't decide exactly where you land, Audrey. That's up to the universe."

"The *universe*?" I snort, outraged.

"I mean, sure, I might be inspired by something. A sign, I like to call it. Like . . . a picture, or a country, for instance. But the specifics, where you are needed most, where you need to be most, that's out of my hands."

"Well, if the universe is wrong and I didn't find love . . . what happens when the time runs out?" My stomach leaps, and I lower my voice to a whisper, leaning forward. "Am I going to implode or something?"

He belly laughs at that, which is a good sign. Not imploding is always preferred.

"Of course not," he says as he settles down on the sofa, patting the empty spot beside him. "You'll just go back home."

I'll just go back home. It's as simple as that. I squash the urge to say I might not have overcomplicated it so much if he had just *told me that* in favor of another question. A more important question. "But, then, what was the point?"

"What do *you* think it was?" he asks.

I let out a long exhale and look around the room, realizing Matthew is gone, probably not wanting to be an accomplice in case this conversation goes south. Slowly, I sink down onto the sofa next to Mr. Montgomery, watching the flames crackle in the fireplace. I think of our last conversation and how much else has happened in these few short weeks.

I filled up a sketchbook for the first time in months. I found inspiration again. I left the safety of the corner shop, and even though I missed it and everyone, I found things, people I loved here too. I came to terms with my sexuality. All in all, if it weren't for the heartbreak, I went on a pretty wild adventure.

And, all at once, it makes sense.

There's just as much heartbreak in not putting yourself out there, because it guarantees you're going to miss out. And I'm not just talking about love.

It was *more* than just finding love or art. I found myself. I learned that my art was never dependent on a crush or a heartbreak but on *me.* Believing in myself enough to put a pencil to the blank page even if a drawing wouldn't turn out

296

perfect. I took risks on and off the page, knowing that pain could and *would* probably follow, but . . . I enjoyed the good and I faced the consequences, too.

Except for, well, the biggest risk of all . . .

Lucy.

And at this moment it's so clear, so *obvious*, what the answer to my question is.

Where you are needed.

The universe sent me to Lucy. Because she needed me as much as I needed her.

"And what if I *did* fall in love?" I ask, looking over at him. "Will I be stuck here forever with them?"

He smiles, the corners of his eyes crinkling as he leans forward. "It doesn't *have* to be that way. Not if you both want something different. Not if you're brave enough to ask the universe for more."

Holy shit.

That means . . . if Lucy wants it too, we could *both* go back to the present. There *is* a loophole.

She doesn't have to marry Mr. Caldwell.

She can write music, and go to college, and do whatever the hell she wants.

She can . . . *be with me.*

If I'm brave enough.

And now I am. After these past few weeks, after this truly unbelievable journey, I *am* brave enough to ask her for that. To take the risk and hope that she chooses me. But, more importantly, that she chooses *herself*, too. I think she's brave enough to do that. And I should never have doubted her.

"You know, Audrey, one heartbreak doesn't mean you're more likely to experience it again. If anything, you have to meet the wrong person to truly know who the right one is," he says, giving me the same look that got me blasted through time and space in the first place. "But even true love doesn't come without pain, without risk. And that doesn't make it something to run from or leave behind. It can be scary, and unexpected, but when you have it . . . don't let anything—not even your fear or time itself—keep you from it. Like with all things, all you can do is take the leap and trust and hope that they catch you on the other side, just as you are, and that you're strong enough to survive if they don't. But if they're the right person, they will."

That's all I needed to hear.

That and the fact that I won't implode.

I bolt upstairs, Mr. Montgomery laughing as he calls, "I'll see you back at home," after me.

I put on my Converse and the clothes I got here in, hopeful that it'll be some kind of sign to the universe that I *am* going home, with Lucy right beside me. I tuck my cell phone and wallet in my pocket, and my fingers curl around the quarter as I run down the steps to the front door. Matthew is there, lounging against it, that mischievous grin on his face.

"I've already called the carriage."

He holds out a brown leather bag and gives me a sheepish shrug. "Take the rest of the cookies." I peer inside to see them wrapped in a blue cravat resting at the bottom. "For you to remember us by."

Tears sting at my eyes as I pull him into a hug, grateful for this prim-and-proper guy who showed me that Prince Charming could have a bit of a wild side. And can turn out to be a really great friend if you change the story just the teensiest bit.

But after today I will never see him again.

"Can't wait to look you up in the future and see which lucky lady gets to marry you," I mumble into his shoulder. "I'm going to miss you."

"Likewise," he says, squeezing me tighter and chuckling.

And then, with one final look, I'm off. The carriage flies toward Radcliffe, my face pressed up against the glass as we breeze along the countryside, past the road to town where I met Alexander, past the fields Lucy found me in, past the stables where I befriended James and became frenemies with Moby, past the pond I swam in with Matthew.

We've barely come to a stop before I'm out and bursting through the front door of the house, calling her name. I run up the staircase and down the hallway to her room, Mr. Thompson waddling after me, telling me to stop.

"Lucy, I'm sorry—" I say as I push inside, freezing when I see that the bed is neatly made, the vanity empty.

My fingertips trail along the quilt on the bed, and I stop

when I see the pages of my sketchbook on her bedside table, a few of them crumpled and folded. I pick them up but nearly drop them again as the door flies open behind me.

I whirl around to see Lucy's father, nostrils literally flaring, blue eyes ablaze, Mr. Thompson just behind him.

"What in God's name are you doing back here?" he asks as I tuck the pictures into my bag.

"What am *I* doing here?" I say, crossing my arms defiantly over my chest. "I'm here to save Lucy. From you and from this shitshow of a wedding."

His eyes narrow, and a smirk curls across his lips. "From the moment I saw you, I knew you would be trouble. Mr. Caldwell only confirmed my suspicions. And now *this*."

"From the moment *I* saw *you*, I knew you were completely undeserving of having someone like Lucy as a daughter. And it's so pitiful that you have no idea *who* she is because you've spent so many years forcing her to hide all the remarkable parts of herself. The kind and the caring and the adventurous and the *fun* parts. She deserves so much better than you. So much better than *all* of this."

I move to push past him, calling out her name, hoping she'll hear me. "Lucy!"

"She's not here," he says, wrapping a hand around my arm.

"Then I'll go to the church," I say, ripping out of his grip. "I'll do whatever—"

I skid to a stop in the hallway, seeing that Mr. Thompson

has brought company. Two burly men grab ahold of my arms, and Mr. Sinclair chuckles as his cane echoes off the wooden floor behind me.

"Do you honestly think I'd let you compromise this wedding? Lucy's *future*?"

"Don't pretend you care about her future," I spit back at him.

"All right," he says with a laugh. "*My* future. The status to be gained. The business ventures to come when the Sinclairs and the Caldwells become one." He looks over my shoulder at the two men, nodding down the hallway. "Tie her up in the library."

As I'm dragged away, wriggling desperately to try to get away from them, I see him straighten his jacket, smiling to himself. He checks his pocket watch, then clicks it closed. "Now, if you'll excuse me, Miss Cameron, my daughter is about to marry the richest man in the county."

I let out a frustrated scream as the men pull me around the corner and along the corridor of portraits to the library. I try fruitlessly to dig my heels in, to wrench myself free. They throw me into a chair by the window, and I try to stand so I can run past them to the open door, but one of them presses me back down while the other ties my hands behind my back and my ankles to the chair legs.

"Come on," I say, trying to plead my case. "I know you two probably don't like him either. Can't you just—"

One of the men, a gruff-looking guy with thick brown hair and stubble, just glowers at me, pulling the holds even tighter before he and his friend clomp out of the room.

Guess not.

"Help!" I scream as they lock the door behind them. I thrash against the ropes restraining me, my arms rubbing raw.

Is this even real life? Suddenly my little *Bridgerton* romance is turning into a straight-up Regency-era *Dateline* episode.

I glance out the window, wondering if I could survive a second-story drop and roll my way to the church.

Doubtful.

Sweat starts to bead on my forehead, and I can almost *feel* my time running out. With each beat of my heart, the clock ticks slowly closer and closer to the end.

Soon she'll be married.

Soon I'll be gone.

I let out another frustrated groan, straining against the ropes once more. The chair rocks underneath me, and the whole thing crashes to the side so I land *hard* on the floorboard Lucy's books are tucked under. I'm slightly relieved that I don't go straight through the floor, but my head knocks against it and my forehead radiates with so much pain, I have to bite my lip to stop from crying. Still I don't give up. My gaze travels up the wall, searching for something, anything to help, but I find only a portrait.

Wait.

My eyes widen in shock when I see a woman with golden hair and warm brown eyes wearing a delicate necklace with a gold chain and a sage-green dress.

I've seen her before. Seen this portrait. And not just a passing glance that first day in here with Lucy.

It was the day Mr. Montgomery sent me here. One of the paintings I swiped through looking for inspiration.

And lying here, studying her familiar features, the same golden hair, the same delicate nose and curving lips, it all makes sense.

Lucy's mom.

Magic, science, the universe at work, whatever the hell Mr. Montgomery called on, it was no accident.

She brought me here.

For Lucy.

She always wanted her daughter to experience love, *real* love, and here I am.

So I have to trust that she and the universe are still on my side.

I fight against the ropes with renewed strength, swearing I can hear church bells tolling in the distance but hoping I can still get to Lucy before it's too late.

For both of us.

CHAPTER 38

LUCY

July 10, 1812

Standing in the back corner of the church, I stare up at the ornate ceiling as guests filter inside.

I don't want to lower my head and see Mr. Caldwell waiting at the end of the aisle. Or my father, happier than I have seen him in years, exchanging pleasantries with our arriving guests.

Maybe if I keep staring at the intricate columns, the gold trim, the circular pattern, it will all just disappear.

"Lucy," a familiar voice says, sounding almost surprised to see me, even though it's my wedding. I lower my chin reluctantly to see Alexander, Mr. Shepherd just beside him, and my hand slides into my cousin's. Both their gazes are wandering around the room like they are searching for something.

"Did Audrey not . . . ?" Mr. Shepherd starts, eyes snapping to my face.

My heart jumps into my throat at her name. "Did Audrey not what?"

"She left Matthew's earlier to . . ." Alexander's brows furrow as his voice trails off. "I only assumed you felt the same."

"Lucy," my father's voice says impatiently from just behind me. My ears are ringing as my head swings around to look at him. "It is time."

Sure enough, the processional music is starting. My hand slides automatically out of Alexander's as my father grabs my arm, my entire body numb as he begins to lead me down the aisle.

I only assumed you felt the same.

She . . . she came looking for me. Or they thought she came looking for me.

So that means . . .

Before I can finish my thought, before I even realize it, I'm propped up across from Mr. Caldwell. I look from his face to my father's to Martha's in the second row to Alexander and Matthew still frozen at the end of the aisle.

"We are gathered here today," the minister starts, but his voice fades to a buzz.

I realize, all at once, that I have a choice to make.

For so long I have been resigned to this unhappy fate. And when I wasn't, all it brought was pain. I think of waking up to the sketchbook slid under the door, Audrey nowhere to be found. The past few days, feeling like my entire body was being ripped apart because of her.

But then I think of Martha's words at Miss Burton's. Audrey's own words that night, sheets of rain pouring down all around us.

What do *I* want? What do *I* feel? Could I live with myself if I didn't take even the slimmest shot at *more*, even if it's perhaps the greatest risk of my entire life?

"Should anyone present know of any reason that this couple should not be joined in holy matrimony, speak now or forever hold your peace," I hear the minister say, and my eyes snap to his face.

The time to choose is now.

And the words come almost instantly.

"I object."

Instantly, the room goes quiet.

"I'm sorry," Mr. Caldwell says, face twisting. "Did you just . . . ?"

My father is there in an instant, letting out a bark of a laugh. "She doesn't know what she's doing. She—"

My hand reaches up, fingers gliding over my mother's necklace, and it gives me strength. "I know exactly what I'm doing," I say as our eyes lock. "I'm choosing myself."

I give him a small smile. A final farewell he doesn't deserve. "Don't worry. You'll never see me again."

I move to run back down the aisle, to find Audrey before

it's too late and she's gone, but his hand wraps around my arm, jerking me back. I watch as Alexander takes two steps forward, but Martha gets there quicker. She shoves her tin of smelling salts under his nose, startling him enough for me to yank my arm out of his grasp.

"Run, Lucy!" someone calls. Grace. My eyes meet hers and then Martha's, and I try to send a silent goodbye to them both. Two of the only people who made my life here bearable, and then . . . I do. I make a break for it, an unexpected laugh bubbling out of me as I push through the doors of the church with Alexander and Mr. Shepherd on my heels.

The three of us run down the steps, and Matthew whistles.

"Take my horse!" he says, a jet-black stallion *far* larger than Henry suddenly at the ready. "She must still be at Radcliffe."

He helps me climb onto it, and I swing my leg over instead of sitting sidesaddle. My dress rips, but I couldn't care less as I scoop up the reins, ready to go. Then the two of them surprise me by clambering onto Alexander's horse, my cousin giving me a big smile.

"Let's go get her," he says, while Matthew grabs ahold of his waist in a sight I just know Audrey would find spectacularly amusing. I just hope I'm in time to tell her. We dig our heels into the horses' sides and take off through town at a gallop. People jump out of the way, a few shrieking, but a path clears. Shocked faces turn up to gape at the woman astride in a wedding dress whizzing past them scandalously.

As we fly along the winding road to Radcliffe, the horse's powerful legs churning underneath me, wind whipping at my unbonneted hair, for the first time I feel truly *free*. I have made my own *choice*, wherever it might lead.

Hopefully to a happily ever after if I can get to Audrey before her time runs out.

I grit my teeth, snapping at the reins as Radcliffe comes swinging into view. We weave through the fields, the grass finally giving way to the gravel drive, hooves crunching noisily as we zip down it.

The horse has barely stopped before I'm sliding off the saddle and running up the steps, bursting through the front door, Matthew and Alexander just behind me.

"Audrey!" I call out to the empty house. I wait, listening for a reply, but none comes.

"Audrey," I try again.

"Miss Sinclair?" a voice finally calls out. Surprisingly, James appears from down the hall, wielding a pitchfork from the stables.

"Good Lord," Alexander says. James quickly lowers the pitchfork as Matthew sweeps an arm out, moving me behind them both.

"I saw Mr. Shepherd's carriage arrive here earlier," he explains before Matthew can attempt a right hook. "I got suspicious when Audrey got out but never left."

"Do you know where she is?" I ask, and he shakes his head.

My eyes flick to the second floor, and I grab ahold of the

railing, pulse pounding wildly as I wind my way up the steps, Matthew, Alexander, and James following after me. "Audrey! Are you here?"

Fear prickles its way across my chest. Am I too late? Is she already gone?

"Aud—"

I stop when I hear it. *Her voice.* Saying my name.

"Lucy!"

I run down the hall and around the corner, the sound growing louder with each step.

"Audrey?"

"I'm in here!" she calls, the sound muffled through the library door.

I try the handle, but it's locked.

"I'm tied up. I can't—"

"Is there a key?" Alexander asks as James pushes against it, trying to get it open.

"Mr. Thompson might have one. I can go look for him."

"Perhaps the pitchfork?" Matthew suggests.

Oh, enough of this. With a running start, I throw myself against the door, once, twice, until I finally bust through it. Matthew lets out a squeak of surprise as the wood splinters around me.

Audrey's eyes widen in shock from where she lies on the floor, tied to a chair, a gash on her forehead. "Did you just . . . ? Did you just break a *door* down?"

My hand glides across the desk to pick up a letter opener. "Yes," I say as I kneel in front of her, cutting through the rope.

"My hero," she says with that warm smile of hers as I help her sit up until the two of us are staring at each other. And I feel like it. I feel like *I*, Lucy Sinclair, am the hero of my own romance story. At last.

I hear Alexander sniff behind us and look back to see Matthew pulling out a handkerchief for him, while James motions hastily for them all to leave us alone. Soon their footsteps disappear down the hallway.

"You left," I say as I slowly reach out to touch her forehead. My words come out like a question, and she grabs my hand, holding it in place like an answer.

"I'm sorry," she says, eyes shining. "Your father demanded I go and said I was threatening your reputation by staying, and I . . . I was so worried I was going to destroy your life, but I never let you choose what *you* wanted, Lucy, what you were willing to risk. And I didn't give you all the information to even make that choice. So, I need to say this."

Audrey takes a deep breath, grip tightening on my hand. *"I love you."*

My heart soars at the words I've waited to hear, spoken aloud for the first time.

"I don't have however much ten thousand a year is in 2023 or a big-ass house with a pond and a library and a butler to wait on you hand and foot. I'm still in high school, and

I live in a two-bedroom apartment in Pittsburgh with my parents and work for a morning coffee and a bag of chips at our struggling convenience store," she says with a laugh. "But we all support and love each other. And I know they'd support and love you, too."

Her other hand unfurls to reveal the quarter, and both our eyes travel down to look at it.

"I'm not saying we'll be together forever, even though I hope we are, but," she says, looking back up at me with a small smile, "I am saying that I love you, more than anything, and I will *always* be there for you, whether we're together or not. And that, if you choose me, if you choose *yourself*, we don't have to stay here. I believe if we are brave enough to try, we could leave . . . together."

The air catches in my lungs.

I can leave Radcliffe. And my father. And Mr. Caldwell. I can make a life for myself, one where I can play the piano and dance to something called "Whitney Houston," travel where I please in something that shoots through the sky, and ride a horse as fast as I want.

And I can be with Audrey. Really be with her.

I reach out, hands sliding up to hold her face. The girl who came and completely upended my world as I knew it. "Maybe in another life, if I had never met you, I could have married Mr. Caldwell and pretended it was perfectly fine," I whisper, shaking my head, eyebrows pulling together. "But that was before you, Audrey. That was before I knew what love, real love, is. Before you changed *everything*. I don't ever want to go back."

She pulls me in, and it feels like time stops as our lips touch lightly. It's all my mother ever said it would be and so much more. It's all the romances I've ever read combined. They may be burned to nothing, but my own has taken their place. We melt into each other until I don't know where she ends and I begin.

Everything else fades away until I hear the sound of a coin hitting the ground, and suddenly, without warning . . .

Everything goes black.

CHAPTER 39

AUDREY

April 22, 2023

I feel a light tapping on my leg. Once, twice.

Slowly, I open my eyes, squinting against the bright sun to see none other than Mr. Montgomery poking at my thigh. He stops when he sees I've come to, his green eyes mischievous beneath bushy white eyebrows.

"Looks like you stuck the landing," he says, chuckling to himself as he holds up a quarter, the metal glinting in the sun.

"Barely," I groan, head pounding, made worse by the fact that someone is blasting their horn, like, *right* in my—

Wait.

My eyes widen as I sit bolt upright, memories overwhelming me.

The library.

The quarter.

The kiss.

Everything going dark.

And now a horn must mean . . . I'm actually here. Finally *home*.

The familiar sights, the familiar streets, the familiar smells all wash over me. But what about Lucy? My stomach jumps into my throat, and I swing my head around wildly.

I see the edge of her ornate wedding dress first, but it's enough to confirm she's here, actually *here*, right beside me. Her eyes are wide as she sits up, taking in 2023 and my little corner of Pittsburgh. The brightly colored cars whizzing past, the tall buildings and street signs, all the *noise*, so much louder and busier than Radcliffe or Whitton Park or the town we walked around.

I reach out carefully until my fingertips slide into her palm and lace between her fingers, squeezing gently.

Only then does she look over at me, those blue eyes locking on mine, just like they did that day in the field when she found me.

Before she went on to find me in so many more ways than that.

"Welcome to the future," I croak out, voice still hoarse from screeching for help two hundred years ago, in a toppled-over chair in her family's library. But instead of asking any of the millions of questions she must have, she pulls me in for a kiss, fingers curling into my shirt. Heat radiates through my entire body the moment our lips touch, and I—

"All right, all right, there'll be plenty of time for that," Mr. Montgomery says, poking me in the shoulder with his cane.

I glare up at him, but it inevitably softens as realization overwhelms me. "I'm . . . shocked I'm saying this, but . . . thank you."

"Eh." He waves his hand. "Count it as your graduation present."

"My graduation present?" I snort, rubbing at my once-again-bruised forehead. "I have a feeling after missing *all* my final exams and the last month of school, I'll need to wait a bit before seeing *that* diploma."

"Or," the old man says as he pulls out a rolled-up newspaper from where it was tucked underneath his arm and tosses it in our direction, "maybe time passed a bit differently in the present."

My eyes widen as Lucy leans forward to read the date underneath the heading.

"April 22, 2023," she says. My jaw falls open.

I *sold* him this newspaper.

"Wait. No time has passed? That means . . ."

"You still have time to finish your portfolio, if you wish," he says with a shrug, using his cane to pick up the leather bag next to us. In it are the sugar cookies wrapped in Matthew's cravat and . . . pages and pages of my drawings.

Drawings that show how much I have changed. That tell a story and have *me* in it, my style, my vision, instead of what someone else tells me that vision should be. My feelings for Lucy. Hers for me. My physical self in some. All exactly the type of art *I* want to be doing and feel passionate about.

I reach out and grab the bag, smiling to myself.

I know now that if I get in, I can go to art school. I can leave Pittsburgh without leaving my parents and everything behind. I *can* take risks, if I trust myself. No matter the outcome, if I trust that . . . it'll all work out, even if not in the way I expected. Maybe even *better*. Like this one did.

"That is, unless you two want to take a trip down the Oregon Trail. Maybe medieval Europe?" he suggests.

"No, no, think we're cool with not getting the plague," I say as I stand and brush myself off. "Think we'll see what 2023 has to offer us."

I turn around and hold out my hands to Lucy, pulling her to her feet. As we walk down the street, Lucy clutching at my arm, I watch as she takes in our surroundings, *definitely* having the culture shock of her life.

I can relate.

A few people give her attire a questioning glance, which she returns with equal question. Short skirts, nose piercings, ripped trousers, visible undergarments, *pink hair*. It's all so different from what she knows.

Finally, we slow to a stop outside the familiar storefront, and I feel tears well in my eyes. I can't wait to see my parents again, but I turn to look at Lucy first, studying her face.

"You good?" I ask, worried it's too much, worried she thinks she just made the biggest mistake of her life. But she just smiles.

"Never better," she says, reaching out to tuck a strand of hair behind my ear.

I point above my head to the faded sign that reads CAMERON'S CORNER SHOP in thick red letters.

"Home" is all I can say. A word I'd missed and longed for. A word I was afraid I'd never have or see again.

I pull open the door to the familiar jingle of bells, and the two of us walk, hand in hand, into the future. Well . . . the present now.

But our future.

Lucy's life, my life, from this day forward will be whatever we decide to make of it.

We're barely through the entryway before my mom lets out a scream, practically bowling me over in a hug.

"Oh, my baby! *Where were you?* I thought you were kidnapped! The cash register unmanned, the whole store empty. And you hit your head *again?*" She squeezes my face between her hands. "*What am I going to do with you?* You're going to end up with fewer brain cells than your father—"

"*Mom,*" I groan, wrenching my face out of her hands. But I'm already crying. "I missed you."

"You were just gone for a few . . ." I watch as her gaze moves to look at our interlocked hands, then Lucy's wedding gown, before climbing to Lucy's face.

Lucy's fingers tighten their grip around mine as I say, "This is Lucy."

She's nervous.

I swing our hands up. "She's my, uh, girlfriend."

I'm nervous. I mean . . . I've never introduced either of my parents to a girlfriend before. Never even really thought I would. I didn't think I'd ever let that part of myself see the light of day.

And now, here I am, gone for just a few hours of her time and back dating a girl who probably looks like I just broke her out of a doomsday cult.

"She's from 1812," I say with a small shrug, figuring she probably won't believe me, but I'll tell her later it's not actually a joke. Graduation present or not, Mr. Montgomery owes me. He can help explain.

Oddly, Mom doesn't even bat an eye, doesn't even giggle. She just beams at us. Lucy freezes, likely debating whether she should curtsy or not, before she quickly holds her hand out, like she's just remembered our first tea at Grace's. "It's a pleasure to make your acquaintance."

The words are barely out of her mouth before my mom is bypassing her outstretched hand and scooping her up in a hug. "Lucy, dear! Oh my goodness, it is so nice to meet—"

"Look who's back from lunch," a voice says from the opposite end of the store. My dad comes around the corner with Coop, who is somehow even cuter than I remembered. He runs over to dance happy, excited circles around both our feet, Dad following just behind him.

I pull Dad into a tight hug, and he pats me on the back before leaning against the counter, looking confused. His gaze swoops over Lucy's attire, but then a look almost like recognition dawns in his eyes. *How is everyone being so chill?* "Well," he says, grinning warmly. "Where'd you come from?"

"She's from 1812," my mom says as she leans on the counter next to him. I assume she thinks she's just continuing the joke, but when the door jingles open and Mr. Montgomery toddles inside, she immediately says, "I'm glad she got out of town, but *1812*, Mr. Montgomery?" She points at my bruised forehead. "*And* you returned her in damaged condition!"

"Just a scrape," he says with a smile.

Wait.

My head swings back and forth between the two of them. "You know Mr. Montgomery can . . . ?"

"Sure," Dad says. "He sent us to early 1900s Paris back when you were in elementary school because we were having a stupid argument over one of your mom's family recipes."

"The boeuf bourguignon?"

He nods. "It had been passed down through so many generations, one of the lines was smudged and hard to read. Twenty-five days of bliss tracking it down helped us figure out we weren't really there to nail down that recipe at all. We were there to figure out what we wanted out of life. What

319

to do with the store. *And* each other." My dad laughs, while my mom swats at his shoulder, but she can't contain a wistful grin either. "Even met this one's great-grandparents, if you'll believe it. They owned a grocery store on a small side street."

"It's how I knew joining your dad in the store, helping build our community, was in my blood too. It made me brave enough to take the leap away from nursing. And to think, Lou, we just brought back the clothes on our back and a couple of small souvenirs," she says, nodding to Lucy. "This one brought back a whole girlfriend."

"Yeah, but at least he *told* you you'd be coming back after twenty-five days," I say, motioning to Mr. Montgomery. "I thought I was going to implode or something."

Everyone doubles over with laughter. Even Lucy lets out a giggle.

"*Implode?* You thought you were going to—" My dad shakes his head and wipes at his eyes before making eye contact with Mom, sending the two of them erupting into another fit of laughter.

I cross my arms over my chest, but a smile breaks through when I see Lucy reach down to pat Cooper's head as her eyes roam around the store to take in the shelves and the electric lights and the humming wall of freezers, filled with brightly colored drinks.

"Okay, but how can you . . . ?" My voice trails off as I turn back to face Mr. Montgomery.

"Side effect of being trapped in the Maple Creek coal mine when I was a boy with nothing but a quarter and a lunch pail. Wished I was anywhere but there and somehow woke up in the middle of a jousting tournament in the 1300s for twenty-five days, where I met my best friend, Nicholas. He came back with me." He gets a wistful look on his face. "Nice guy. Majored in history at CMU. Lives in Braddock now. Liked being a squire about as much as I liked mining."

He shrugs, shaking off the memory. "Anyway, it took a few years to figure things out and a few more after that to see how it was always connected to helping people, like I was helped with my wish that day in the mine. Find true love, figure themselves out, get through their rough patches. It's not always smooth, mind you. My brother lost an arm to a saber-toothed tiger, but he found his first wife, so . . . you win some, you lose some."

"Lost an arm to *what?*" Lucy says.

"Going to grab a bit more coffee before I head out. Pirates are playing later today," Mr. Montgomery says, shuffling behind the counter to help himself like he didn't just drop a bombshell.

We all look around at one another until finally my dad shrugs and grabs the leather bag from my shoulder.

"Lucy's, um, going to have to stay with us," I say as he reaches past me to turn the shop sign from open to closed.

"Of course she can!" Mom says, giving Lucy's arm a reassuring squeeze.

"No sleeping in the same bed, though! Couch. Or, uh, sleeping bag," my dad adds as we wave goodbye to Mr. Montgomery and head toward the narrow staircase to our apartment. "I think there's one in the closet for you to sleep on, Audrey. I'd say this one deserves some modern conveniences."

Lucy giggles, and a knowing look passes between us, so I know she's also thinking about all the nights we spent in the same bed the entire time I was at Radcliffe.

As I look once more into the blue eyes that locked on mine in the middle of a field two hundred years ago, I feel suddenly so grateful for everything that happened and so *excited* for everything to come. Whether that's art school, or traveling, or helping Lucy find her place here like she helped me in her time. It all feels possible now.

She squeezes my hand, and I know the best part will be getting to do it all with her right beside me.

LUCY

One Month Later

"Mom," Audrey groans from the steps outside the apartment.

"*No!* Go annoy your father downstairs. She's not ready yet!"

I see a flash of Audrey's brown hair just over Mrs. Cameron's shoulder when I peek quickly out of the kitchen, where Mrs. Lowry is curling my hair with a device called a *curling iron*, which is far faster than the curling papers Martha used back at Radcliffe.

Martha.

I feel a pang deep in my chest at the thought of her, my mind briefly traveling back to one of the only things I miss about 1812 while Mrs. Cameron coos about how beautiful Audrey looks on her prom night before shutting the door in her face until I'm ready too.

Though, I must say, curling irons are a mere fraction of the interesting things 2023 has to offer.

So far, I like jeans and Barnes & Noble and *Stranger Things*. I like riding a bike even better than a horse and watching movies late at night. I like McDonald's Big Macs but *not* their crisp Sprites. The shock I got from that was worse than Martha's smelling salts.

Most importantly, I like all the things I never even knew were possible. Things I could never have *dreamed* about. Like working the register with Audrey on weekend mornings and stealing kisses when the bells jingle as someone leaves and the store is empty. Or playing a "gig" at a bar down the street. I'm still learning this century's music, but Mr. Cameron handed out flyers that Mrs. Cameron made to every person that came through the shop, inviting them to come.

Best of all is being able to say how I feel and being able to *do* so much. Being supported. Being *loved*.

"Done!" Mrs. Lowry says, and I close the GED book I'm supposed to be reading, sliding it over Audrey's RISD acceptance letter.

The drawings she brought back tipped the scales in her favor, but she won't be going this fall. She's going to take a gap year so we can explore the modern world and help me catch up to it. She'll be there for me to tug lightly on her shirt when I don't understand something or need reassurance, like she did to me at tea or dances or dinner parties, and I'll be there for her when she starts to miss home.

And when we make it to England, we can look up a few of

our old friends in the history books and see what adventures they got themselves into.

"Oh, Lucy!" Mrs. Cameron gasps as I stand up, and the two of them zip me into my new lilac gown, the same color as the one from Miss Burton's shop but so different.

It's long and flowing like hers, but this one is sparkling, with thin straps and a deep V-neck, showing far more skin than my father would have ever deemed appropriate.

And I could not love it more.

I catch a glimpse of myself in the hall mirror, and I look how I feel, like *myself.* Not the shell of a person I saw so many times in the mirrors at Radcliffe.

"Let's go take some pictures!" Mrs. Cameron says, giggling as I tread carefully down the wood steps in a pair of exceedingly unpleasant high heels, two hundred years doing little to improve their design, but I'm excited to see Audrey.

I turn the corner and . . . there she is.

She looks so beautiful, I forget how to breathe. It takes me back to the night of the ball. A night I thought would be the end of my life but turned out to be the beginning.

My cheeks burn as I reach out to touch a strand of her lightly wavy brown hair, styled half-up and half-down, before my eyes dip down to take in her off-the-shoulder black dress.

"You look hot," I say, and the two of us exchange a knowing grin.

"So do you. I got you, uh . . ." She holds up a corsage, a

white rose surrounded by lilac delphiniums the same shade as my dress. She only just manages to slip it on my wrist before Mrs. Cameron herds us outside for sunset pictures.

That is one thing about the future I am still not used to. I feel so *awkward* taking pictures. Standing there, smiling, posing this way and that. Unlike a portrait, you can have *many* bad snapshots before a good one. And I never feel like I look like myself in them. Call me old-fashioned, but I still much prefer Audrey's drawings.

Luckily, Audrey pulls me in for a quick kiss that makes me forget myself enough to take a good one at last, smiling when she makes it the background on her phone while Mr. Cameron drives us to her school.

I grab at her hand nervously as we walk up the steps and inside the door labeled GYMNASIUM.

"Bit different than a ball at Mr. Hawkins's estate," she says, echoing my thoughts as I squint against the flashing lights to take in the dancing students, the twisting white streamers (which look suspiciously like toilet paper?), and the cloth-covered round tables. "But it's a bit the same, too."

As we find one to place our Kate Spade reticules on, she points out a gossiping group of friends in their finest attire, shy and nervous duos eager to be here alongside their crush, the more confident pairings who are much more . . . intimately involved with one another as they sneak into the corridor.

And she's right; in so many ways it is the same.

But it's also so *loud*, the music shaking the glossy wooden floor underneath us.

It seems like *everything* here is loud.

I feel a light nudge, and Audrey holds up a box labeled EARPLUGS. She opens it and squashes two orange ovals into my ears, dulling the sound instantly but not making it disappear completely. I give her a grateful smile as her hand lingers against my cheek.

She leans in close to ask, "You want to dance?"

I look past her at the swaying figures, each of their moves so . . . unique. "This time I'm the one who doesn't know the steps."

She laughs and kisses me, right here in public. No one pays us any mind, and her familiar smell washes over me like it did that rainy morning at Radcliffe and in the library when I rescued her, her mouth tasting like the Trident bubble gum I've since learned how to chew without swallowing. The feeling of my face in her hands is familiar now but still so thrilling, so filled with open-ended possibility.

When I pull away, our noses brush lightly against each other, and a smile dances onto Audrey's lips as she says, "We'll figure it out together."

And we do.

ACKNOWLEDGMENTS

Book five! Honestly a bit surreal to be typing those words, and I can certainly say I wouldn't be here without the help and support and hard work of so many people.

First and foremost, a huge thanks to my incredible editor, Alexa Pastor. To work on FIVE of these together has been such a privilege. Here's to many more to come.

To Justin Chanda and the amazing team at Simon & Schuster, who have shown my books so much care through the years.

To my agent, Emily van Beek, who is truly the absolute best. I feel super grateful every day that my stories are in your hands.

Thank you to Sydney Meve and the rest of the team at Folio Jr.

To my friends and family, Mom, Ed, Judy, Mike, Luke, and Aimee. May we one day plan a vacation that somehow miraculously doesn't align with a round of edits. Here's to many board games, lake trips, and a pole barn impossibly big enough to hold all of Mike's aspirations for it.

To BookTok for supporting two late-twenty-something moms. Your perspectives and love of books have made a real impact on me, and I'm grateful for the community we've found on there.

And, finally, to Alyson and Poppy. Everything I do is for you. I love you.